I0598488

Warrior Lover

by

Karilyn Bentley

Draconia Tales, Book Two

Warrior Lover

Cover Art by *Tamra Westberry*

The Wild Rose Press, Inc.
PO Box 708
Adams Basin, NY 14410-0708
Visit us at www.thewildrosepress.com

Publishing History
First Faery Rose Edition, 2013
Print ISBN 978-1-61217-690-1
Digital ISBN 978-1-61217-691-8

Draconia Tales, Book Two
Published in the United States of America

"You don't mind leaving?"
All brawn, no brain obviously.
Hadn't she just said that downstairs?

"That's right. I want to leave. You want to take me. It works out well for both of us. Now, how much can I take?"

"You do not feel a need to take your entire shop, do you?" A small wrinkle appeared between his brows.

"As you noticed earlier, there's not much to take. I have clothes and personal items. A couple of bags, maybe."

"One bag. Thoren travels light. Insists we do the same." He glanced to the bed and back to her, grinning. "Besides, the less time you take packing, the more time we'll have for pleasure."

Lily's whole body stiffened, as blood pounded in her ears. Oh, Goddess, not now. She hadn't left the town. Now she'd never leave. He'd crush her before she could be free.

He took a swaggering step toward her, cupping her face in his hand. "Don't be frightened. I won't hurt you."

Sure you won't, look at the size of you.

Bending forward, he placed his lips against hers, pressing gently. And just like that, her nervousness vanished.

Dedication

To my wonderful husband:
Thank you for all your support on my writing journey.
I love you!

Chapter 1

"How much?" Lily pushed two paintings across the wooden countertop and tried to slow the tripping thumps her heart passed off as beats. Why hadn't she moved the learn-how-to-bargain-successfully entry on her to-do list up to the top? After all the time she spent in this store, haggling with Old Tom the shopkeeper, she should have learned the skill.

Not that it would have done her much good. Tom had her between a stone wall and a rabid bear and enjoyed taking advantage of the situation.

Raising his gaze from her artwork, he smirked. "I'll give you two silvers for the paintings."

"What?" Lily's head pounded, no doubt due to the way the muscle between her brows puckered. *Don't look so surprised, don't look so surprised, don't look so surprised.* With an effort, she calmed her muscles into something less like a snarl and more like serene acceptance.

She hoped.

"I know for a fact other paintings like these sold for two golds each. These should be at least worth five silvers apiece."

One bushy slash of gray hair rose to meet his hairline. The meet-and-greet attempt failed miserably as his hair had slunk back to form a ring around his neck, leaving the top bald. The brow continued to creep upward while his brown eyes focused on her. The skin of her cheeks heated.

What choice did she have? Old Tom might cheat her out of her fair share, but he was the only one in town who would even deal with her. She had to eat somehow.

"Fine. Three silvers."

Tom's other brow joined its mate at her words. "I said two silvers."

"You know you can pay three." *You miserly old coot.*

"Two. It's final. If you think you can get more, go someplace else."

Sure she could. No one else in this town gave her the time of day. All because her skin, hair and eyes were the wrong color. Ridiculous, superstitious fools.

Her fingers stroked the wooden box she held in her hands. Her parents gave it to her years ago, back when they lived, back when they protected her from fanatical townsfolk. She'd hoped not to have to offer it, hoped Old Tom would give her a fair price. If hopes were gold, she wouldn't be bargaining.

Lily slid the box onto the counter, her fingers fastened to the edges. "A silver for these?" She forced her fingers to open the lid, to show the greedy bastard what lay inside.

His eyes widened as he picked up one of the paintbrushes. Twirling it from side to side, he gave her a glance. "Where'd you get these?"

"A silver for them or not?"

"No more paintings without these." He shook the brush at her face.

No more paints left to use them with. "A silver?"

He placed the brush back into the box and shut the lid. Reaching into a money pouch on his belt, he pulled out three silver coins and slapped them down on the counter. "Go on with you. Get." One hand waved toward the door.

Lily grabbed the coins, slid them into her pouch, yanked the hood of her cloak over her head and darted out the door. The tinkling of the bell hanging over the door cast the only noise in the street. How odd. Usually in the mornings the shop streets echoed with cries of townsfolk.

Her rapier bounced against her leg as she walked, its soft slapping a reminder she had absolutely no idea how to use the thing. It belonged to her father, its thin steel blade a false security sheathed on her belt.

Illusions were everything.

If only her parents still lived she wouldn't be selling her paintings for food. Or her brushes. She shuddered. What would she do without her brushes?

Faint cheers sounded from the town square, rousing her out of her thoughts. Maybe a crowd gathered, which would explain the lack of people in the streets. If that was the case, then she needed to get inside fast.

Crowds loved her.

Probably because she tended to be the focus of their wrath.

She'd be safer inside her store than out here in the middle of the street, fair game for slurs, stones and— her favorite—spit. Her feet picked up the pace as she darted the last half block to her shop, her home.

Only to come to a stop, her breath frozen in her chest. With a gasp, her lungs sucked in air, bringing with it a healthy dose of this-can't-be-happening. Her fists clenched as her head started another round of pounding fury self-talk refused to calm.

Lily cursed. Bloody vandals had thrown rocks through her store windows, shattering the glass, but the iron bars crossing the windows and door held and it didn't look like anyone entered. With shaky hands she pulled her key from her cloak pocket and stuck it in the door. It took two tries, but that's what happened when one's hands flapped like moth's wings. A turn and a push later and she crunched over glass shards, her teeth locked together, her pulse pounding.

She shut the door and locked it, the wood a thin veneer of protection against vandals. Thieves didn't bother her, as not even they touched her store. Her shop sat empty, the shelves which once held goods from all over the land, dusty. When her parents died last winter, the store's patrons dried up like a stream in the desert, leaving her penniless.

If it hadn't been for the dry goods sitting abandoned on their shelves, she would have starved months ago. What she couldn't eat, she sold for less than the items' worth to the greedy old bastard known as Tom Shopkeeper.

A dismal air sat about the empty store, like a drizzling rain on a cold winter day. It sank into her bones and for a minute the cold crept into her soul. *Why bother? Why not just let the mob catch and hang you? It would be much faster than starving to death.*

Snap out of it, Lily!

She wasn't the only person the townspeople hated and shunned. Her best friend Keara was in the same predicament for the same reason. Both women possessed the wrong coloring. While Lily was pale of skin, hair and eyes, Keara had flaming red hair and bright green eyes. No one bought from Keara's apothecary shop either. When Keara's grandmother died several months ago, the slurs against both women escalated and recently crowds gathered in the square to preach about the evils of differences.

And now it looked like the slurs came attached to rocks and her windows their targets.

Lily kicked the glass shards, watching as sunlight threw dancing prisms of light across the walls. Why had she stayed so long in this town? Why did she insist upon remaining here? Why not go someplace else? She and Keara could leave and set up shop in some other town that didn't have superstitious rules.

What if the other town didn't like her? What if they rejected her too?

Well, she'd never know if she didn't try, now would she?

Turning on her heel, she ignored the glass mess and marched to the back door. Today, she would find Keara and convince her friend they needed to leave. Today she would take charge of her life. Today would be a new beginning.

Lily tripped and fell with a thud against the back door. *Ouch.* That hurt. Her hands stung from where they slapped against the wooden panels, breaking her fall. *Could she be any clumsier?*

After locking the back door, she cut through the gate leading to the alleys. Sounds wafted from the town square, wild voices carrying on the wind. She heard Keara's name shouted and Lily's determined stride hitched. What now?

Due to some oddity with the wind or the way the curving streets funneled the voices, she heard Lord Simon's voice stand out above the roar of the crowd.

"I will tame the witch, Keara, by marrying her and driving out her evil! Help me to help you!"

Had he lost his mind? Wait, was she really going to answer that rather obvious question?

Judging by the mob's reaction to the aristocrat's words, they didn't believe him crazy. Of course, they were just as insane. Even the priests were vicious.

Lily forced her jaw to unlock. If her nails dug any deeper into her palms, they'd leave bloody lines. She needed to warn Keara of the danger. Without being caught herself.

The alley led to a dead end, but she should be able to cut across a back garden.

Or not.

The mob cut into the alley, stopping her movement, forcing her forward into the center of the mass, into its heart. The crowd's hatred flowed around her, pushing against her. Why had it taken her this long to realize she needed to leave?

These people were crazy. The whole lot of them.

Sweaty bodies pressed against her, chanting Keara's name. Every time she tried to turn, to sneak through an opening under an arm, the bodies would press together, forcing her forward. Herding her.

Lily felt her heart pound in her chest, her breath catch. What if they noticed it was her under the cloak? Would they do the same to her they did to Keara?

Maybe if she went along with the crowd, if she moved forward, an opening would appear and she could take it.

Or not.

She stood at the front of the crowd surrounding the town square, close to Lord Simon, too exposed to run. Her gaze darted around the square, looking for an opening, an escape. Nothing. The crowd squeezed together tighter than a crate of eels and just as slithering.

The crowd continued to chant Keara's name, parting as several people shoved Keara into the square. Lily swore her heart stopped beating, resuming its pace with a thud and a staccato beat. Her body heated, sweat running between her breasts. Her friend. Her only friend was about to die.

Or worse, be forced to marry Lord Simon.

A small hand touched her fingers and Lily jumped a foot in the air, the hood of her cloak slipping to hang down her back. No one noticed but the boy who stood beside her, whose palm pressed against hers. Jamie, Keara's apprentice.

"They're not going to hurt her. And they're not going to hurt you either. I'll see to it."

Lily blinked at the ten-year-old boy who practically gave her a heart attack a minute ago. Was that steam coming out his ears? Must be a trick of the light. His jaw twitched as he started for Keara, his voice loud enough to hear above the roar of the crowd.

"She said, let her go!"

"Step back, Jamie. Now!" Keara waved a hand at Jamie and Lily grabbed his arm, yanking him back. As soon as she touched him, he turned, snarling at her. As if letting the boy die was an option, which would surely happen if she released him.

"We'll help her later."

Jamie raised an eyebrow as she spoke, his steel gray eyes holding not a trace of fear. How did Keara's normally shy apprentice turn into a fearless boy? If she ever got out of this mess, she'd give it some thought. All that mattered now was her friend. How was she going to get Keara free from Lord Simon's clutches?

Lily's gaze darted around the square, looking for an escape route, landing instead on what had to be a walking mountain. Her breath caught, her mouth fell open. And despite the surrounding danger, she continued to gawk like a child at a candy shop.

Tall. Sweet Goddess, was he tall, with blond hair tied at his nape, wearing a black shirt and leathers and was that a sword strapped to his back? With an effort, Lily closed her mouth. The man, mountain, whatever, exuded power and strength and held her fascinated, longing for something she hadn't felt before, a wanting that froze her in place.

And then a man stepped away from the crowd, another tall man, this one with black hair, and he claimed Keara for his wife. How much worse could the day get? Her poor friend. The man saved Keara from Lord Simon, but the raven-haired man was a stranger. What would he do to her friend? How would she save Keara now?

As Keara's new husband exchanged verbal spars with Lord Simon, Lily's gaze caught the Mountain Man's and locked in place. The crowd seemed to fall away, the noise of the mob fading into the background, nothing mattering but his gaze and the tightening in her lower abdomen it evoked.

He belongs to me.

Jamie grabbed her hand, jostling her back to

reality. The roar of the crowd hit her like a pitched flour bag and she jumped as she looked at Jamie. What just happened? How could she get so lost in someone's gaze she completely blacked out on everything else? A quick glance showed the Mountain Man had vanished, swallowed by the mob.

"Lily?" Jamie tugged on her hand. "Come on! We've got to get back to the shop before those men leave town with Keara."

They might have already left. A probable fact she refused to worry Jamie with. "How do you know they're going to her shop?"

"Where else would they go?" His steel-gray eyes met hers and narrowed. "They aren't going to hurt her. Don't worry." He pulled her in the direction of Keara's store, his steps the determined stride of a child who knows what he wants and how to get it.

"How do you know that? They could have already left with her!" Did her voice really sound that high-pitched?

Jamie stopped and rolled his eyes. "I know. Now come on. You have to go with me."

As if going back to her shop or standing in the square with a crazed mob was an actual option. She turned and jogged after Jamie.

****

Son of a goat. Enar raised his foot, looking at the sole. Smelly brown globs covered the bottom of his expensive leather boot. Not that a Watcher should care about such trivialities as a boot, but he found his appearance went a long way toward promoting fear in everyone he met. And he needed expensive leather boots to help create that fearsome look. *Right.* And

Draconi males could leave their mates.

Wiping his boot on the only clean stone he found in the filthy alley, he looked up, only to see Thoren and his female Keara—not that Thoren would admit the red-headed apothecary was his female, stubborn dragon—at the end of the alley, about to turn down another odiferous path.

If he'd recognized Keara as a Halfling Draconi the day before when she treated his headache, it would have saved them the rescue Thoren pulled off moments ago in the town square. He felt his cheeks heat and slammed down the embarrassment before it started doing something crazy like turn his face a nice shade of tomato. Oh, wait. A bit too late for that.

"What are you doing back there?" Thoren turned, his brows a quizzical slash of black.

Keara shot Enar a half smile, but remained quiet. Like Thoren, Enar's best friend, Keara belonged to a race of sorcerers whose males were shape-shifting dragons. When the Council, the assembly of Watchers and Draconi males who assured the safety of the Draconi, sent Enar and Thoren after a Halfling boy, they should have mentioned a Halfling female lived in this Goddess forsaken town of River's Run in Cautasia.

Clearly a lapse in intelligence gathering.

"Nothing." Enar jogged to catch up with Thoren and Keara, diligently avoiding all puddles and brown globs, until he reached his best friend.

A sharp stab of longing surged through him as he watched Thoren walk beside Keara. He wanted what Thoren had. Not a Draconi or a Halfling, but a woman who would be with him forever. Like the pale-skinned woman from the square. The one he had locked gazes with until everything else fell away, the roar of the crowd, Thoren's rescue of Keara, the stink of the town.

Instead of being thirty feet apart, it seemed like they stood inches from each other, lost in their own world. No other woman had ever caught his attention to the exclusion of everything else and he wanted nothing more than to go on his own personal seek-and-find mission. To find his woman. To claim her. To begin the journey down the road of forever.

Clearly the foul stench of this town had rotted his brain.

He was a Watcher, a guardian of the Draconi. Watchers did not form bonds with women, they claimed them as their child-bearers, as an outlet for their lust.

His friendship with Thoren and the time they spent together meant his thoughts formed a line behind Thoren's Draconi beliefs—females were to be cherished, cared for, loved.

He wanted the unattainable.

Pulled out of his thinking by a stop at a gate, Enar stared at his surroundings, wondering where they were. Looked like a back alley behind a row of shops. He glanced at his boots. Whew. Clean. Praise the Goddess he missed stepping in other globs of excrement.

Keara darted through the gate, a cry of "Jamie!" on her lips.

Thoren exploded like lit liquor, slamming the gate against the fence in his dash through it. His friend had it bad for the Halfling. Should be interesting to watch how long it took Thoren to realize his mate had red hair.

By the time Enar stormed through the gate, Keara

held a boy in her arms, pressed tightly against her chest. The lad poked his head around her arm, glaring at them. Shoving out of her arms, he marched in front of her, hands on hips.

"Don't you hurt her."

Point for the boy. It took a lot of nerve to stand before them and speak those words. Bravery, especially in one so defenseless, was admirable.

"Jamie! What has gotten into you? He's our master now." Keara pushed Jamie behind her. "I'm sorry, he's not normally like that."

"He's brave. Who is he?" Thoren asked.

"This is Jamie. I found him, took him to the town square and claimed him as mine and since no one refuted the claim, he's now my apprentice." She took a deep breath, looked at the sky and then at Thoren. "He's part of my bride price."

Judging by her glance upward and her held breath, she obviously lied. Not that it mattered to Thoren. His best friend seemed bent on giving the female anything she wanted. Although in this instance even Enar would give in and take the boy. One didn't find bravery like his every day.

The whole bride price thing confused him. Keara tried to explain it to them on their walk to her shop, but it seemed to him the fathers in this town wanted to give away their daughters and had to pay off the hapless groom. But what would he know about marriage? The only examples he'd seen were the Draconi bonded pairs, although Draconi didn't call matings marriage. Closer to home, there was no such thing as marriage or bonding. Watchers claimed women. They definitely didn't bond with them.

So why did he want his own woman so badly?

He looked past Keara to the door of her shop and his brain forgot the question.

The exquisite woman he saw earlier in the square, the one whose gaze had locked on his, the one he had been thinking about just moments ago, stood frozen in place, eyes wide with fright or wonder. *Mine*, whispered through his head, as he tried to stop the impending erection from forming. No such luck.

The brown tunic, black pants and black cloak she wore made her pale skin glow, highlighting the white hair that streamed down her back. Piercing blue eyes, the same color as his, gazed back at him from an elfin face. Besides those blue eyes, the only color in her face was in her lips. Lush red lips, parted slightly, as if she didn't know whether to scream or not. Lush red lips that would fit well around his staff as she suckled him.

He had known many women, lusted after more than that, and yet none of them made him feel the way this one did. What was different about her? Her coloring? That had to be it. All Watchers wanted a woman with pale skin, their ideal beauty, although none of them had gotten so lucky. None but him.

His woman. His for the taking.

Thoren's words snapped Enar back to the present. No surprise his friend had just agreed to Keara's request to take Jamie with them.

"Is that one part of your bride price, too?" Enar pointed to the pale-skinned woman.

Asking was the polite thing to do. Not that the answer mattered, the woman was his, but if she was included in this ridiculous bride price, it might make things easier on all involved.

He had it on good authority that claiming a woman had a tendency to frighten her.

"What?" Keara glared at Enar, who paid her no heed as he remained staring at his soon-to-be woman. "No, she's my friend, Lily."

"I see." Goddess's teeth. That made it harder.

And Thoren's glare wasn't helping any, either.

"What in the Goddess's name do you think you're doing?" Thoren threw his hand out, smacking Enar's chest. "We're on a mission, fool. You can't lay claim to her."

"She's mine. I claim her. You don't have the right to tell me who I can and cannot claim. And she's mine. Look at her. Exquisite."

Thoren's eyes narrowed, one finger pointing at Enar's chest. "What are you going to do with her? We still have to find the Halfling boy and we already have a female and a boy. This is becoming a traveling circus, not a reconnaissance mission. We. Do. Not. Need. Another female!"

"Forget you. She's mine." Enar turned his attention to Lily, who still stood hand on the door, only now Keara stood beside her. "Woman of the exquisite coloring."

Both females jumped, what little color present in his woman's face bleeding out. He strode across the yard until he stood in front of them. Grabbing Lily's arm, he pulled the claiming necklace from a pouch hanging off his belt.

"Lily of the exquisite coloring, I claim you for my woman." With a quick flick of his wrist, the strand of beads fell around her neck, the ends snapping closed.

Magic streamed through the beads, holding the

necklace in place until his death, which he had no plans of meeting anytime soon. The magic also kept the woman from running off like she often wanted to do after being claimed by a Watcher. Once he returned Lily to his village, she would remain there, since the magic in the necklace kept her from walking past the village gates. He didn't know how far she could wander from him before then so he needed to keep her close.

Gathering her stiff and wide-eyed body into his arms, he gazed into her eyes and felt something shift inside him.

His.

He couldn't stop the smile from spreading across his face.

Chapter 2

Lily stared into blue eyes the color of her own and felt the same tie holding her immobile in the square bind her to the walking mountain. Goddess help her, but she liked the feel of his arms around her, liked feeling his hardened muscles press against her. Liked how his arms encircled her, trapped her, claimed her as his.

She was clearly losing her mind.

He was her captor. Her potential torturer. A man who could do anything to her and get away with it.

So why did being in his arms make her feel so at peace?

Next up on her to-do list: find her lost mind.

"Leave her alone!" Keara screeched, breaking Lily from her trance, as she pulled with no effect on the giant's arm.

"What? You do what with me?" Lily shivered, the warmth from his arms leaving her trembling.

"Claim you. Like Keara did with the lad."

"But...but you can't do that anyplace but the town square," Lily said. Not that it mattered. She was his no matter where they were.

"No, I just did it. With this necklace. You belong to me. It cannot be removed. It cannot be broken until I die. And I don't plan to do that anytime soon. Therefore, you are mine. But do not fear. I won't be a hard master to please. I will even allow you to bring some of your things with you." His mouth curved into a grin.

Good thing he held her. Her knees went all wobbly at the sight of his smile. Or maybe the knee-wobbles were due to the sudden stinging in her neck.

"Ouch. What—" Lily scratched at her neck. What was that sharp pain? Spots appeared at the edge of her vision, blurring her sight, panicking her. She felt Mountain Man's arms tighten, supporting her, and the panic receded, giving way to blackness.

Someplace in the darkness voices spoke, faded as if from behind a veil of fog. Lily focused on the sounds, listening to the cadence of male voices, the rise and fall of words that didn't make sense.

Magic and Halflings. As if those things existed. As she concentrated on the voices, she felt arms clasping her against warmth and hardness. Where was she?

And then it came back. The last moments of her life. The moments before the Mountain Man had charged in and taken her for his own. He must be the one who held her, who stroked her arm, played with her hair. Played with her hair?

Lily's eyes flew open, only to look into eyes the same color as the town's rivers after the snows melted. Her brain noted she was in Mountain Man's lap, his arms around her, sitting at Keara's kitchen table, Keara's new husband sitting across from them. The invisible tie that bound the two of them together tensed and the kitchen faded, leaving only her giant captor in her awareness. His eyes flared, crinkling at the corners as he smiled.

"You're awake."

****

Her eyes fixed on his and for a moment Enar forgot where he sat. Didn't even know what words he spoke. Hopefully they made more sense to her ears than they did to his.

"Who are you?" The pitch of her voice remained high, reminding him of a trapped animal.

It meant she remained scared. Of him. She wasn't the first person to feel that way, but for once he didn't like it. She belonged to him and it was his duty to ensure she never feared anything again.

What in the name of the gods was he thinking? Since when did a Watcher care if his woman feared him? Most Watchers induced fear in their women. What was wrong with him?

Her gaze remained locked on his, waiting for his response. What had she asked? Oh, yes. Name.

"I'm Enar." He nodded in Thoren's direction. "He's Thoren. You're Lily, right?"

She swallowed. "Yes." The low tone of her voice resonated in his blood, which of course pooled lower.

He shifted, to no avail.

Thoren cleared his throat. "Since Keara's upstairs packing, why don't you take Lily to gather her things? And while you're at it, stop by the inn and retrieve our bags and horses."

Enar nodded. Unlike Thoren's last suggestion— don't claim the woman—this one Enar agreed with. There was something odd about the man in the square who tried to take Keara. Something Enar didn't like, but couldn't identify, and it had nothing to do with the man treating a Draconi female the way he had. Some strange look in his eye, as if his store was open but someone else manned it. As a Watcher, there wasn't much that scared him, but he had to admit the quicker they left this town, the better.

And Thoren's suggestion gave him some much needed alone time with his woman.

Enar stood, placing Lily's feet onto the floor, grabbing her around the waist when she swayed. Claiming necklaces left the woman unsteady for a couple of hours until her body adapted to it. The magic woven into its stones prevented the woman from leaving the Watcher who claimed her, outside of his death. And it would be a dark day in Draconia before he willingly gave up this woman.

His hands pressed against a sword belt as he held her steady. A sword belt? Hanging at the wrong angle, might he add.

"Give me the rapier." What was his woman doing carrying around a sword? Especially since she clearly didn't know how to use it.

Her eyes widened. "Why?"

"Woman, surely you don't expect to draw the sword with it hanging at that angle?"

She glanced down at the sheath where it hung against her thigh. Grasping the handle, she tried to draw the rapier out, but he caught her hand before she hurt herself.

"Unbuckle it and hand it over. I'll protect you."

She narrowed her eyes, took a deep breath and did as he asked. Slapping the sheathed sword against his outstretched palm, she turned and marched out the door. He watched the sway of her hips as he buckled the belt around his waist.

"Where is your home, woman?" he asked once

they stood outside the shop in the alley.

"My name's Lily, not woman." She crossed her arms over a chest that wasn't as ample as he was used to and glared at him.

Were claimed women supposed to glare? Shouldn't they be cringing? Whenever his mother had stood up to his father the crazy old bastard had hit her. Should he do the same? He couldn't imagine putting his hand to this exquisite woman though, she'd snap in two. And hate him.

For some strange reason he wanted her to like him.

As if that would happen. *Since when did claimed women like their Watchers?*

"Fine. Lily-not-woman. Where is your home?"

Her eyes narrowed, her little tongue licking over her lips. He thought of a dozen places that tongue could lick on him before she spoke.

"My quarters are above my shop. Not too far from here."

"Lead the way then." Enar gestured toward the alley entrance.

She started off down the alley, pulling the hood of her cloak up, covering her hair. Why would she cover such wonderful hair? He almost pulled the hood back, but became fixated on the sway of her hips beneath her trousers. Oh yes, she'd feel good beneath him. It had been awhile since he'd tumbled a woman and this one was taking him to her home. Where there was bound to be a bed. He smiled.

Lily chose that moment to turn around. As if checking to make sure he hadn't left her. Maybe she felt all the lust pouring off him because her eyebrows shot up while a nice rose color suffused her face.

He winked and then smiled so wide his cheeks hurt.

Her mouth opened and closed as she drew in a breath through her nose. He thought she might run, but instead she stood her ground.

"Why did you come to River's Run and why did you give me this necklace?"

Was he really going to answer? And it appeared like the answer was a resounding yes. As if operating on their own volition, his lips started moving, attempting a clarification of his actions.

"Thoren and I were sent here to find Halflings."

"Halflings?"

"Half Draconi, half human."

"Draconi?"

Maybe his woman was a bit dense, seeing how she repeated everything back to him.

"Draconi are sorcerers. Lately the males have been mating with humans and the resulting offspring are Halflings. Our job is to track down the Halflings and return them to Draconia."

Technically his job was a reconnaissance specialist, one who went into the lands surrounding Draconia to discover threats to the Draconi. Lately, though, those fact-finding missions had turned into find-the-Halfling adventures. The word, adventures, being used liberally in this case.

Boring.

He'd rather have a good fight than be a nanny, but as Thoren's guardian, the one Watcher assigned to him, he went where his friend did and Thoren liked serving the Council.

For whatever reason.

"Do their fathers hire you to return them?"

"No. The Council requires we return them. The fathers don't realize they've fathered children." Which is why he'd always used protection. The last thing he wanted was to discover he had an unknown child. He refused to abandon a child to a life of not knowing their father.

"How can they not realize they have a child?"

He stared at her. Was she truly so innocent she didn't know the answer? "Woman, we need to get moving. Where's your store?"

"This way. So why don't the men know they have a child?"

"Sometimes it just happens. How far to your store?"

Her brows snapped down over her eyes, a look of this-isn't-over-yet crossing her face. With a humph she turned and hurried through the streets like a mouse with a cat on its tail, avoiding the crowds that surged around her.

Ah, his exquisite woman possessed a bit of a temper. A fact he needed to remember since his gut told him her questions had only just begun.

In the blink of an eye, some idiot jumped out of the crowd and pushed his woman against the stone wall lining the street.

"Look, here's the other witch! Let's—"

One minute the man held Lily against the wall, and the next thing Enar knew, his dirk pressed against the man's throat. It happened so fast, he couldn't remember moving, but the lack of the memory didn't bother him nearly as much as the idiot's hand on Lily.

"She. Belongs. To me. Understand?"

The man squeaked as the tip of the dirk pressed deeper into his neck, causing a drop of blood to spill. Through his shirt, Enar felt the vibrations of his broadsword, Blood Seeker, as it became aware of the scent of blood. What a shame the streets were too narrow for him to pull the sword. It was thirsty and he was itching for a fight.

Unfortunately, the man he held wasn't a worthy opponent. Too much trembling. And if Enar's nose smelled right, the bastard had soiled his trousers.

Lily shook, crossing her arms over her chest as if to hold back the tremors that cascaded through her body. A crowd gathered around, and despite his wanting to spill more of the man's blood, Enar decided to settle with the man's trousers-soiling routine as enough punishment.

Besides, a fight meant less time to spend with his woman once they arrived at her house.

"Anyone touches her and he has me to deal with. Disperse." The crowd stood transfixed, eyes wide. "Now!" he bellowed, watching with satisfaction as the mass scattered. The man he held turned the color of snow and fell over. It was always nice to know one's bellow was fierce enough to be sleep-inducing.

Enar grabbed Lily's arm, swinging her to face him.

"Did he hurt you?" His gaze glanced over her slight form that still shook, although not as violently as before.

"N...n...no. Thank you." Her eyes stared at his feet as she drew in a breath. "Do you still want me? Should I give you back the necklace?"

Was she daft? "What are you talking about, woman?"

"If you think me a witch like everyone else, I'll give you back this necklace."

Enar snorted. As if she could get the thing off. "As I said when I claimed you, the necklace can't be removed unless I die. And before you go thinking that sounds like a good idea, it takes a lot to kill me. And frankly, you don't have it in you."

Her eyes widened, her gaze fixating on his face as one hand grabbed the stones of the necklace. "It can't be removed?"

He shook his head. It did seem as if his woman was dense. Brains didn't matter, she had all the necessary parts, but it would be nice if he didn't have to constantly repeat himself.

"So I'm yours? Forever?"

"I'm not that bad." He hoped.

"And you want me knowing I'm a witch?"

Ah, the real problem. As if he'd believe a word the bastard said.

"Are you?"

She made an unladylike noise. "They say I am. I'm different. My coloring. It's not like everyone else's."

"And that's a problem?"

"They say it is."

"Do you believe everything you hear?"

"Only when it's followed through by a mob threatening my life."

Something roared inside him at her words. "Who?"

"It's nothing. You're taking me away, right? So it doesn't matter."

"It matters. You belong to me now. I'll protect you."

Throwing an arm around her shoulders, he escorted

her down the street, glaring at all who dared glance their way. How dare these blithering, superstitious people not like his woman. She didn't have to worry about them anymore. He was here. And he would ensure she remained safe.

Chapter 3

"You never did say why you gave me this necklace." Although one look at his face and Lily knew part of the reason. Something in his eyes, a spark when he looked at her face, a tingling on the back of her neck when he stared at her body. She might not have up close and personal experience with what a man looked like aroused, but she wasn't a complete idiot.

His brows slammed together. "It seemed obvious." Did that mean he found her attractive?

Men did not find her attractive. At all. But Enar had snapped a string of beads around her neck and claimed her.

Maybe he was crazy?

Maybe. But she liked his protective streak. And the fact he didn't mind her coloring. During the short interval between Keara dashing through the gate and Enar claiming her, Keara had mentioned her husband didn't mind what the townsfolk thought of her either. How odd. But comforting to know Enar saw past the pale wrapping of her skin. Until her brain weighed in on what being his forever meant.

"So if I can't take this necklace off, does that mean we're married?"

Goddess, she hoped not. Marriage had never been on her to-do list. Her parents' constant bickering, fighting and general disinterest in each other had dissuaded her from being one of those girls who pined for a man. Not having a man pay her a whit of romantic attention helped cement the matter. And while Enar seemed to be helping with the top goal on her to-do list—leaving town—she didn't want him to be the object of her heart's desire. She didn't want to form an attachment at all.

It would be easier that way when he started fighting with her and sneaking out to spend time with other women. If she didn't care, then his actions wouldn't bother her.

"The necklace means I claimed you. That's not marriage."

Whew. She touched the stone beads of the necklace resting against her neck. "Wait a minute. What does being claimed mean?"

"Do you always ask so many questions?"

"Only when I don't get the answers."

His focus on her face sent prickles down her spine, lodging in her lower belly. Her body protested her mind's earlier self-talk to remain aloof.

Treacherous feelings.

Judging from the way her neck and other parts of her tingled, she didn't need the answer. She knew one thing he expected and it wasn't his dinner on the table at the end of the day.

He would crush her when she became his horizontal servant. After all this time, the Goddess had seen fit to send her a way out of the town, and that way would kill her before she saw freedom. Although being crushed by Enar seemed a more pleasant way to die than being burned at the stake.

His face had been merciless, eyes cold as glass,

when he held his dirk against the priest's neck. She should have been scared, petrified, when he looked at her then. Instead, she felt a warmth glowing through her at the knowledge he would kill to protect her.

No one had ever cared like that before.

"This is your home?" Enar's hand dropped to her shoulder as Lily twisted the key in the lock on the back door.

"It's my store. I live above it." She pulled away from his hand, his heat, walking forward as she slid back the hood of her cloak.

Enar shut the door behind him and walked through the kitchen into the store, brows pulled together as he strode to the damaged door. "Someone broke in and cleaned you out." He walked around the small space as if looking for the perpetrator.

"It happened this morning. When I was out."

"Someone threw rocks into your store?" He picked one up, tossing it up and down in his palm.

"You heard them. They think I'm a witch and witches should be killed."

She watched surprise turning to anger flit across his face as he white-knuckled the rock.

"Kill you? Those bastards. I'll kill them all. Do you want their heads?"

Yuck. He couldn't be serious. One look told her he was. Lily shook her head.

"They don't matter anymore. Unless you plan on leaving me here?"

"Of course not! What part of 'you belong to me' do you not understand, woman?" His eyes hardened as he looked at her.

His glare dared a man not to tremble in fear. She

imagined most men quaked when faced with Enar's wrath. But not her. She knew he wouldn't harm her, knew it like she knew the color of her hair.

"I'm glad. Because I really want to leave this town."

He jerked like he stepped on a snake. And then his long strides ate up the distance between them. Right before he got to her, he slammed the rock down on an empty shelf, his fingers brushing against the wood. His eyes blinked, once, twice, as he stared at his dusty fingers. A quizzical look turned her way.

Despite the heat blooming in her cheeks, she met his gaze. "No one shops here anymore." She headed toward the stairs, refusing to look at the pity shining in his eyes.

"I would offer to clean it up, but we're leaving, so it doesn't matter."

And with that one sentence, he summed up her life in River's Run. It didn't matter, now did it? Hopefully, where she was going would be better than what she had here.

It couldn't get worse.

She hoped.

He caught up to her as she mounted the stairs, following behind like a dog on a rabbit trail, apparently unwilling to let her out of his sight. And if that didn't put her in her happy place, she didn't know what would.

Pushing through the door into her room, she wished she'd made the bed. How was she supposed to know someone would be following her home? Seeing the way she lived? *Aloof, Lily, act aloof.*

She turned to her wardrobe, pulling out a satchel

and shaking it.

"How much can I take?" Not that she had a lot to bring. A few clothes. Nothing else. Stuffed to the brink with memories, her room held little else. Eating took priority over decorating.

When he didn't answer, she glanced over her shoulder, shaking her bag. "How much? One bag, two?"

"You don't mind leaving?"

All brawn, no brain obviously. Hadn't she just said that downstairs?

"That's right. I want to leave. You want to take me. It works out well for both of us. Now, how much can I take?"

"You do not feel a need to take your entire shop do you?" A small wrinkle appeared between his brows.

"As you noticed earlier, there's not much to take. I have clothes and personal items. A couple of bags, maybe."

"One bag. Thoren travels light. Insists we do the same." He glanced to the bed and back to her, grinning. "Besides, the less time you take packing, the more time we'll have for pleasure."

Lily's whole body stiffened, as blood pounded in her ears. Oh, Goddess, not now. She hadn't left the town. Now she'd never leave. He'd crush her before she could be free.

He took a swaggering step toward her, cupping her face in his hand. "Don't be frightened. I won't hurt you."

Sure you won't, look at the size of you.

Bending forward, he placed his lips against hers, pressing gently. And just like that, her nervousness vanished.

Firm lips moved against hers, his tongue licking the seam of her mouth. She parted her lips for him and moaned as he thrust his tongue inside. Tentatively, she tangled her tongue with his, surprised when he thrust deeper, tightening his arms around her waist.

She felt his arousal press against her stomach, which had the odd effect of causing an unfamiliar ache between her legs. She moved, wanting to assuage it, wanting...something. What was it about this man that brought out all these strange sensations? All her thoughts swirled away in the fog swimming through her mind, allowing her body to thrum from the gentle assault on her senses.

Enar's hands rubbed up and down her sides, barely grazing her breasts before slowly crawling down to her hips, only to do it over again and again, each swipe driving her deeper into the sensual fog. Up to brush his thumbs against the outsides of her breasts, down to stroke closer to the growing ache between her legs, until she feared she'd go crazy if he didn't do something right now. Then he picked her up, pressing her against the wall, drawing her legs around his waist and ah, the thick ridge of his arousal pressed right where she needed it.

If she moved, just a bit, right there, oh, that felt good. Oh yes, a woman could learn to like this. She pushed faster, stroking him, grinding herself against him as the pressure built inside her lower belly.

More. Did she actually moan that? Apparently so, if his erotic deep chuckle meant anything.

Enar's hands drifted beneath her tunic, his thumbs rubbing against the sides of her breasts, skin on skin, slowly moving toward her nipples. She twisted slightly, forcing his finger to cross her tightened nipple, moaning at the pleasure of his rough pad over her sensitive nub. She felt as if she hurtled toward a precipice, toward pleasure beyond her wildest dreams.

And then the bang of the front door hitting the wall echoed through the room, breaking the fog of desire. Enar broke his embrace, lowering her legs to the ground before drawing the huge sword that hung down his back, looking completely unaffected by what just transpired between them. She glanced down. Well, maybe not completely.

He motioned for her to stay put—as if she could move—and started down the stairs with amazing quietness for a man his size. Lily pressed against the wall, trying to breathe. A deep gulp in, an exhale out. Repeat. Her heart thumped hard enough for her to see the movement through her tunic. She hadn't wanted him to stop, completely forgetting her earlier fear of him crushing her. Tingles shot from a spot between her legs she hadn't realized existed. She pressed her legs together until the ache diminished enough for her to walk.

Perhaps being claimed by him wouldn't be as bad as she feared.

She stuck her head out the door, watching as Enar disappeared into her shop. The fact he wanted to defend her was surprising. The men she knew wouldn't bother.

She tiptoed down the steps, her tread soft on the wooden stairs. Poking her head around the corner, she saw Enar, the tip of his broadsword pressed against the throat of one of the priests.

****

The brown-robed idiot dared enter his woman's store. If that wasn't bad enough, he had done it right when Enar was about to get a taste of his woman's sweet core. For that alone the man deserved to die. Two strikes already against the stranger, but the interloper hadn't stopped there. The bastard brought others with him. Those others stood against the door, pressed together like a mass of worms, suspended between wanting to protect their man and escape the wrath of an angry, sexually frustrated Watcher. Escape won for several of them and they scurried down the street.

What a shame. Blood Seeker wanted to drink and Enar felt like feeding it.

Although how much nourishment it could get off these weak-willed, sniveling creatures was another matter.

"Why are you here?" Enar pressed the tip deeper, causing a trickle of blood to form.

The man tried to take a step back and ran into his friends. White eyes rolled as he swallowed. "The witch ran in here. If you've seen her, we'll take her from you."

"In case you haven't noticed, she belongs to me now. You won't be taking her anywhere. Now get yourselves gone before I feel obliged to remove your heads."

The mass of worms popped out the door, leaving the one at the edge of his sword remaining.

"So, what do you plan on doing with her, if you don't mind my asking?"

"None of your business. And since you're still standing here, I assume you don't like your head." Enar drew back his sword, half in threat, half in jest. The sniveling creature wasn't a worthy opponent, but he had tried to capture Lily and for that deserved to die. No one hurt his woman on his watch.

Squeaking, the man jumped back. "May the Goddess curse you!" He turned and fled, disappearing like the rest of the crowd.

Enar shrugged off the curse, sheathing Blood Seeker, confident the Goddess had better things to do than grant the hideous little man his curse. Just to be on the safe side, though, he'd have one of the priestesses bless him when he returned home.

"Thank you."

He whirled at the sound of Lily's voice, its timbre sliding over his skin, making his erection stiffen further. She stood at the foot of the stairs, her pale hair falling over her shoulders, looking at him like he was some great hero.

A man could become accustomed to that look.

He wanted her, wanted to finish what they started, wanted to sink himself inside her wet core until they both screamed their release.

Although he should probably go get Thoren's and his bags from the inn and meet up with his friend. There would be plenty of time for him to make Lily scream her pleasure later.

He walked toward her, amazed she wanted him to take her away from her town, her life. Since when had a claimed woman been happy to leave?

Maybe he should skip the blessing from the priestess as the Goddess clearly favored him by giving him such a delectable woman.

"I can't believe you chased off the priest." Lily beamed, her eyes wide.

"Priest?" Enar felt his eyebrows touch his hairline. "Where are the priestesses?"

"What priestesses? Women can't know the ways of the Goddess without the interpretation of a man."

"How under the sun do males discern the will of the Goddess without priestesses?"

Her brows met as her head tilted. "You have priestesses? Women are allowed to hear the thoughts of the Goddess?"

Enar gestured for her to go up the stairs. He watched the sway of her hips as she walked, imagining what they would feel like against his groin as he thrust into her. "We have no priests. Females are needed for the males to see the will of the Goddess. Males can't discern the truth without females. Maybe that's why your town is so backward."

"Excuse me?"

Way to go Enar, insult her why don't you? "No offense, but things are just plain strange here. Like the priests. Everyone knows you can't have priests. Males don't hear the Goddess correctly, which leads to problems. That's why you need priestesses."

"So women are looked favorably upon where you're from?" She turned and pierced him with her blue gaze.

Enar inspected a piece of dirt on his boot. "Draconi females are considered equals with their males. Don't you need to be packing?"

She stared at him for a moment before picking up her bag, stuffing her clothes inside.

Whew. He almost got caught. Not that he'd lied, Draconi women were considered equals. Lily just didn't realize he wasn't Draconi. Probably wouldn't do her any good to know the Watchers' women were all captured from various towns and forced to live the rest of their lives serving their new masters and bearing children.

All but his mother, who managed to take some matters into her own hands. Yet another thing Lily didn't need to trouble herself about.

Not yet anyway.

Enar ran his fingers through his hair as he watched Lily place her clothes in a bag. Allowing a captured woman to bring her things was out of the norm for Watchers. Once he made it home, he'd be laughed out of town for his kindness.

Good thing he was used to it.

Lily didn't have much to pack. With the exception of the armoire and bed, the room was bare. He thought women liked decorating, putting little touches of themselves on everything. But not his woman. Although the closer he looked at the walls, he realized pictures had once dotted them.

"What happened to the pictures?" Enar pointed to a bare spot on the wall where the surrounding paint had lightened.

Lily blushed, grabbing her bag. "I'm done here. Don't we need to pick up your things?"

"We do." He gestured for her to walk in front of him. He'd let her have her pride, even though it tore him up inside that in order to live, she sold her pictures.

When they got to the back door, Lily took out the key. Holding it in her palm, she stared at it for a bit and then left the key on the counter by the door. He pulled the door shut behind them and followed her across the yard. Before she got to the gate, she turned, her front teeth capturing her lower lip. She took a deep breath.

"I have a favor."

"All right." Did he actually agree before he heard what she wanted? By all things holy, he was turning into a sap.

"Would you mind stopping by Tom the Shopkeeper's store and getting back my paintbrushes?"

Enar shrugged, relieved the favor was a small thing, amazed he wanted to grant this woman all her wishes. Ensuring she'd never want for anything again seemed to be his new goal in life, despite knowing the Watchers frowned upon exhibitions of kindness. They'd made sport of him since he was a child, what was one more chuckle?

Chapter 4

Lily ran her fingers over her box of paintbrushes, feeling the smoothness of the wood, knowing she'd never have to sell them again. The look on Old Tom's face when Enar demanded the paintbrushes back would be permanently engraved in her memory. She grinned. Clearly, bargaining successfully involved taking with her someone the size of a mountain loaded down with enough weapons to supply a garrison. For once Tom agreed to her asking price, one silver, the same coin he paid her with earlier.

She couldn't put the box down.

Not on the walk to the inn, or when they got Enar's and Thoren's horses out of the stables, not even now, as they led the horses to Keara's. As much as she didn't want anything to bind her to her old life, she needed a reminder of her parents love for her, needed to remember the joy permeating her soul when she opened the box for the first time. Despite their dislike of each other, her parents had loved her deeply and she missed them.

What would they say about her current partner?

Lily glanced at Enar as he led the horses, glaring at anyone daring to look their way. Not many dared. Most took one look at Enar and pressed against buildings, backs to the stones, white shining in wide-opened eyes, in an attempt to get out of his way.

Not that she blamed them. Enar's glare could ignite wet wood.

"Do you enjoy glaring at everyone?"

"What? You think I need to be smiling and waving at them?"

"No. I was just wondering."

"You like asking questions." A statement, not a query.

"How else am I supposed to learn?"

He shrugged, then leaned over, his voice dropped to almost a whisper. "If I don't glare at them, then they won't take my protection of you seriously. Understand?"

"Ah." She nodded.

A woman could learn to like that kind of protection. A woman could learn to like Enar.

No, no, no. She was not traveling down that road. All that liking business led to broken dreams, broken feelings, broken hearts. Not for her.

So why wasn't her heart getting on board with her head?

Not even the knowledge that for all intents and purposes he was her captor, her potential torturer, swayed those treacherous feelings that threatened to overwhelm her common sense. The bloody things seemed to revel with the evidence he didn't mind her odd coloring and didn't think her a witch.

Provided he told the truth about that.

He had defended her. Came to her rescue. That boded well for her future.

And if it didn't, she had two legs. Last time she checked, her two legs had no problem running.

As they neared Keara's shop, the buildings seemed

to close in on them, blocking out the light as if they were storm clouds covering the sun. Winding streets grew narrow and Lily began to feel prickles racing against her nape, their staccato beat warning of evil intent.

"Do you feel that?" Lily whispered to Enar, doubting he could feel the same thing she did. No one but her mother had ever been able to.

"What?"

"It feels like someone's watching us."

"They have been, but it's different here. Is that what you mean?"

He knew what she meant. What were the chances of that? "Yes! There's something not right down this alley. I'm surprised you feel it."

His head tilted to the side, brows pinched as his gaze pierced hers. "What you sense is a group of soldiers heading this way."

"Soldiers?" She cleared her throat in an effort to get her voice to return to normal. "We must hurry inside. Soldiers aren't a good thing. What if they kill us?" In an instant her throat dried up like earth in a drought, as she thought about Lord Simon's regiment heading their way.

Enar snorted, shaking his head. "Don't think that's going to be happening."

"How do you know?"

"I'm insulted, woman. Enough of this silly talk. Open the gate."

Lily pushed the gate to Keara's yard open, inhaling the fragrance from the herb garden, while Enar led in the horses. As soon as he entered, she slipped the box containing her paintbrushes into her cloak pocket and locked the gate. Probably a futile effort as a lock would not keep out a determined soldier, but it made her feel better. Lord Simon controlled the only soldiers in town and he would stop at nothing to get his hands on something he wanted. And he wanted Keara.

Enar's strength and sword gave a man a fright and she supposed Thoren was equal to Enar in strength, but not even those two would be able to overpower the contingent of soldiers.

Her Mountain Man and his scrumptious kisses were for naught, she would die before he even got the chance to crush her. And after those kisses she looked forward to being crushed. Bedding him did not mean she had to hand him her heart in a box. Unfortunately, she might never get to discover what he'd be like in bed. If the prickles meant what she thought they did, her friend would be taken and the two men who saved them would lose their lives in the process.

Clearly leaving town shouldn't have been crossed off the to-do list.

Once they secured the horses to the hitching post, Enar grabbed Lily's hand as he strode into Keara's shop. Keara stood in the middle of the back room of the shop, a packed bag at her feet, surrounded by Jamie and Thoren. The women stared at each other, their fear mirrored in each other's eyes and in the sharp scent of their sweat.

"Company?" Thoren stepped toward Enar.

"A group of men-at-arms heading this way. And they aren't being too quiet about it."

"Lord Simon!" Keara whispered. "We've got to leave before he gets here! He'll kill you!" Keara spoke to Thoren, motioning toward the back door.

"I said I would protect you." Thoren glared at Keara, his forehead furrowed into rows.

Enar had said the same thing to her, but everyone knew men exaggerated their sword-wielding abilities, among other things. Although she had to admit the two men overwhelmed Keara's shop, making the room seem smaller. Perhaps that impression boded well for them surviving.

Lily heard the noise of footsteps in the alley, closing in on the yard, more murmurs from the front of the shop. She swallowed, running her tongue around her dry mouth, trying to stop drawing in air like a bellows. If she kept it up, she'd hyperventilate.

The noises stopped as the soldiers paused, obviously waiting for the command to storm the shop. Lily felt her heart stop pumping and then Thoren reached into his pocket, pitching Enar a round ball. "Take the boy!"

Holding Lily tight around the waist, Enar grabbed Jamie against him as he squeezed the ball, causing the air to shimmer around them. Keara screamed, staring at them wide-eyed. Thoren lunged for Keara, clasping a hand over her mouth, murmuring in some language Lily didn't understand before both disappeared from view.

Enar clamped a hand over her mouth before the squeak she emitted became a scream. Where did they go? Was she invisible to them, like they were to her? If so, that would explain Keara's scream when Enar squeezed the ball.

And a good thing they were invisible since with a bang the front and back doors burst open, allowing soldiers from Lord Simon's regiment to spill in.

She glanced down, noting Jamie possessed the

good sense to remain quiet without the benefit of Enar's hand clamped over his mouth. Smart boy. She couldn't see Keara or Thoren, but knew they still stood in the last place she saw them. Their energy waves reached her, assuring her of their presence.

Enar dropped his hand from her mouth and she turned, pressing her face against his chest, breathing in the pleasing scent of sweaty man. He rubbed his hand across her back, soothing her, not enough to make her forget the situation, but enough to calm her breathing.

With her face buried in Enar's shirt, she heard Lord Simon storm in, directing his men to search upstairs while squeaking chair legs indicated he sat at the table beside where she last saw Keara and Thoren. As her breathing hitched, Enar stroked her back faster. Part of her wanted to continue burying her face in his chest and not see what happened, while another part wanted to look death in the eye.

Or maybe she could do both.

Lily left her face pressed against Enar's chest, and opened the eye that faced the room. Lord Simon sat at the table, eyes scanning for any sign of them. Enar's fingers ran down her spine then up, down then up, stilling her tremors. She felt safe in his arms, held by his strength.

The soldiers began spilling back into the room, each man bringing more of a scowl to Lord Simon's face.

"Sir, we checked outside, there're horses. Look like they've been ridden, but we don't find evidence of people. They ain't outside, sir."

"Sir, they ain't upstairs either." Boots clomped against wood as the soldiers strode downstairs.

"They were just here, you lily-livered sons of goats, I heard them! Now search again. Tear up the floors if you have to, they have to be someplace!" Lord Simon jumped to his feet, gesturing at something on the floor. "See here. It's a bag, packed and ready to go. They have to be here, search again!"

The men hustled, kicking the rugs around until they located the trap door to the cellar.

Lily stared at Keara's bag lying in the middle of the room. If Keara's man could make them all disappear, shouldn't he be able to make a bag vanish? And how did he manage to make them all disappear anyway?

The only way she knew of to make things disappear was with magic, and she couldn't work magic. Magic was different, like her white hair and Keara's red locks, and different was evil. Did that mean the man who had claimed Keara was evil? What about Enar?

Who and what were these men?

Perhaps she had more to fear than being crushed by Enar. What if the men planned some nefarious ritual death for them? Instead of rescuing them, they were leading the women, and Jamie also, to their deaths? Painful deaths at that. What if this invisible spell Thoren cast wore off and Lord Simon killed them right here? What if...

She could kill herself worrying about what-ifs. Her heart pounded hard enough already without the extra thoughts. Might as well live in the moment and face death once it came closer.

Lily slowly looked around, afraid if she moved too fast whatever magic kept them invisible would snap and cause them to be seen. Lord Simon's men stomped up from the cellar and in through the back door, making enough noise to obliterate the loud thumping of her heart. Which was a good thing considering her tunic fluttered with its pounding beat.

"Nothing down here, sir."

"Well, search again. They have to be somewhere."

"Maybe, sir, they left some other way. Because, no offense sir, but they ain't here."

Lord Simon glared at the soldiers and shoved a strand of hair behind his ear. "They can't be far, their horses are still outside. Peter and Markus, take your men and search the area. Hun and Geo, guard the front with me. The rest of you hide in the yard. If they come back for the horses, take them. I only want the apothecary. The rest are expendable."

What a donkey's arse. Why did Lord Simon want Keara badly enough to lie in wait for her? It wasn't done. Nobility did not marry shopkeepers and yet the lord had been chasing Keara for the last several weeks.

They only needed to make it through the next few minutes. Which they just might do, seeing how Lord Simon marched out of the shop, stopping in the doorway to stand with legs wide and arms crossed. His men took up a post on either side, generating stares from the few passersby. Lily craned her neck watching. Being invisible was a lot better now that he left the shop.

She looked to where Keara and Thoren had stood, concentrating on their energy patterns, the only evidence she saw indicating their position. Then the patterns began to move into the front room. Lily's hand slapped over her mouth as a satchel floated out from under the counter and books flew from the shelves into the bag.

Knowing her invisible friend dumped the books into the bag didn't make it any less strange.

Her teeth bit into her finger and she tasted blood when the satchel disappeared. Apparently Keara had no hand across her face as she gasped loud enough to draw Lord Simon's attention.

"Did you hear that?" he asked his men.

"No, sir."

"Didn't hear nothing, sir."

He stared right where her friend must be, even though Lily could no longer see Keara's energy pattern. The light in the main part of the shop was such she had a hard time seeing Thoren and Keara's auras, but she thought they still stood right by where the satchel last sat. Good thing Simon hadn't seen that disappear.

Lily bit back a laugh. She must be losing her mind. Maybe none of this happened. Maybe the whole day was a bad dream. People did not become invisible and bags did not disappear. For that matter, necklaces didn't stay put around one's neck until the giver died either. Most definitely, she was dreaming.

Closing her eyes, she buried her face into Enar's chest. Except this didn't feel like her pillow, nor did it smell like her pillow. She opened her eyes, noting nothing changed. She still stood in Keara's shop in the strong arms of a giant who gave delectable kisses. Her body reacted to her surroundings with a pounding heart and trembling limbs, making it hard for her to deny her circumstances. Apparently she wasn't crazy.

Although in these circumstances crazy would almost be preferable to magic-wielding giant men.

"Is everything in the bags on the horses?" Thoren's voice whispered out of nowhere.

"Yes. Packed and ready to go." Lily felt Enar's voice rumbling against her ear.

She turned her head, facing where the voice sounded, relieved to see Thoren's aura even if she couldn't see his body. She saw his aura move, what looked like his hand flick toward the open back door. Lily blinked when the bags on the horses disappeared. Then Keara's bag, the one sitting in the middle of the room, vanished. Shaking her head, Lily bit back a laugh. The events of the last few minutes had jaded her against disappearing bags. What would happen next? Men turning into dragons?

"Is there any way out of here besides the front or the back door?" Thoren's disembodied voice whispered.

"There're the sewers in the cellar." Lily blinked at Jamie when he spoke. "Leads to the south river."

How did a small boy know where the thieves hid? Just another thing to add to her list of unusual happenings. The previously non-existent list had grown enormous in the course of one afternoon.

"To the cellar then. Jamie, you'll lead once we're at the bottom."

****

Once down the stairs and out of sight of the open trapdoor, Enar handed the invisibility ball back to Thoren, returning to his visible self. Blood Seeker hummed against his back, ready for a fight, while Lily clung to his arm. His woman shook through the entire encounter with the bastard who called himself a lord. The harder Lily shook, the harder Enar's chest hurt. To stop the unusual, and heretofore never experienced, pain he had resorted to stroking Lily's back, which lessened her tremors and in the process reduced the pain in his chest.

Enar cursed as he stubbed his toe against an unseen object while he followed Thoren through the damp darkness. What he would give to have perfect night vision like his friend. Sounds from the soldiers drifted down like pieces of dirt and he felt Lily's hand tremble as she clutched his arm tighter.

That strange pain in his chest started up again and he rubbed his thumb against the smoothness of Lily's hand to assuage it. Maybe one of the Draconi healer priestesses would know what was wrong with his chest.

At least he knew the antidote for his pain.

Enar squinted, barely seeing Jamie standing in front of a small iron door built into the stone wall. And what a stench wafted through the opening. Human excrement mixed with dead animal. Everyone caught a whiff of the rank smell and started coughing. Surely not through there. He thought the stench almost unbearable, but Thoren must be suffering with his heightened Draconi sense of smell.

What had he done to deserve this torture?

Not only would his nose hairs be singed off, his boots would be ruined tromping through all that muck.

Jamie ducked through the opening, standing in the smelly, rock-lined tube. "You'll get used to it. Come on!"

Goddess's teeth. The dragon was going in. Thoren ducked through the door, doubling over as he entered the sewer tunnel. Enar cursed, bending his legs in a poor attempt to mimic the waddle of a duck, his eyes streaming tears from the stench. "Warriors are not meant to crawl around sewers."

"Nothing besides rats and small boys are designed for it, friend." Thoren patted Enar's shoulder.

Enar snorted. A small click echoed through the tunnel as Jamie pulled the iron door shut. Darkness settled, broken by the trickle of water under their feet and the thick scent of sewage in the air around them.

"Jamie, in front." Thoren led, Enar bringing up the rear in his formidable duck walk.

Jamie splashed by the others to stand in front of Thoren. Thoren worked his magic, forming a blue flame that danced in his palm, illuminating the dank walls of the tunnel. The light held steady for a moment and then flickered, growing brighter before returning to its normal flame.

Since when did Thoren not manage a steady, burning flame? *Oh, he forgot*. Finding his mate and denying the find would do that to a Draconi male.

"Best keep it down, Draconi. I have no desire to burn in this tunnel." Enar chuckled, wondering when his friend would realize Keara was his mate. Thoren's rock-steady flame-in-the-palm routine didn't work too well when the red-haired apothecary touched him.

And she seemed to touch Thoren a lot if the flickering flame was any indication.

Lily touched him a lot too, her palm sweaty in his. Once they got out of this odorous place he would lay claim to her. He smiled, imaging her lush red lips locked around his shaft, suckling, drawing him deeper as she swallowed him down. Imagined making her peak from his touch.

Concentrate on the task at hand, Enar. He reached

49

down, adjusting himself. Duck walking was difficult enough without a stiff shaft in the way.

He watched Lily's pale hair glow in the dim light. She was the epitome of his race's beauty, fair haired and fair skinned. Many Watchers had claimed blonde women, but none of those women possessed the pale skin his Lily did. His. He liked how it felt, knowing she belonged to him, knowing she depended upon him.

Instead of being ridiculed, he would be praised for his choice of a woman. He would protect Lily, not allowing anyone to harm her. Unlike how the other Watchers treated their claims. Bile rose in his throat and he swallowed hard. Some things he couldn't do no matter who laughed at him, no matter if his father never spoke another word to him.

"Almost there," Jamie said, rousing him out of his mind and back into their situation.

"Goddess be praised," Enar muttered. Torture time coming to an end.

The tunnel burst open into the side of the town's wall, the sewage stream falling over the edge into the river below. Thoren closed his hand, extinguishing the flame, before standing next to the opening. Enar felt the pulse of his friend's magic as Thoren reached out with his senses, feeling up along the wall and out across the ground, checking for the presence of humans.

"All clear. Enar, the bags are on the ridge where we first entered this valley. I'll lead if you'll guard the rear. They weren't following us, but they might have figured out where we went," Thoren said as he helped Keara step the few feet from the tunnel to the river.

Enar followed him, jumping calf deep into the river, soaking his boots. Ruined. If the excrement from the sewers didn't do them in, the drenching in the river would. Served him right for being so vain about his clothing.

Enar turned, offering his hand to his woman, helping her the two feet she needed to step. Lily's sweat-drenched hand grasped his tightly, refusing to let go. He stood a little taller knowing she must think him a capable leader.

Funny what respect from a woman, albeit a claimed one, could do to a male.

"Where are we going?" Lily touched his arm as they walked, a light touch, but one that nonetheless went straight to his groin.

What was it about Lily that made him feel like a randy bull in a pen full of heifers? Every touch, every movement, every look his way and he felt as if he'd been sucker punched in the chest. Since when did he feel this way about a woman?

Must be the claiming necklace. Yes, that was it. Somehow the magic in the necklace crept out and affected him.

"Enar?"

Had she asked a question? *Think with the head on your shoulders, Enar.*

"As Thoren said, we're camping in a clearing. We'll stay there tonight and leave in the morning."

"I meant, where are we going to go tomorrow? Where are you taking me?"

She didn't really want to know the answer to that. "We will go to Draconia. To return Keara to her people." There, no lies from him. Truth evasion, but no outright lies. Wasn't he an outstanding reconnaissance specialist?

"Who are her people?"

"The Draconi."

"The Draconi? The ones you were telling me about earlier who left their children behind?"

"They don't all leave their children behind, only a few of the males."

"Ah. So Keara is one of those Halflings you were talking about?"

"She is."

"So you were sent here to find her?"

"No. The Council didn't tell us about her. We were sent after a male Halfling."

"Oh. So what's so special about these Halflings that you have to return them to Draconia?"

"They possess magical powers. And the males have other abilities."

"Really? Like what?"

"Male Draconi are shapeshifters."

"Shapeshifters?" Mouth gaping, she stopped, froze right up like prey to a predator.

"Keep moving, woman. Yes, Thoren can change shapes."

She lengthened her strides to catch him. "Into what?"

"A dragon."

"A dragon?" she squeaked.

Enar raised a brow as he glanced down at Lily.

"Really? So he can turn into a dragon? Can you?"

He wished. Riding on Thoren in dragon form set his spirit free. To float above the clouds, wind racing through his hair, left him relaxed, calm. If only he had more moments like those.

"Of course not. Do I look like a dragon?"

"I have no idea what a dragon looks like. Thoren looks like a man."

"Dragons are big creatures. But they normally stay in human form."

She stared at Thoren for a couple of steps before turning back to Enar. "If you're not Draconi, then what are you?"

"A Watcher."

"A Watcher? What's that?"

"Woman, you talk too much. Hush, now."

Her glare felt like it pierced his skin. Her eyes narrowed, her nose shot upward and she strode forward to walk with Jamie.

Did he hurt her feelings? He needed to remedy that. Son of a goat. What was he thinking?

If anything happened to Lily, he'd pull a demented-dragon act and raze everything to the ground.

He clearly had a problem if his claim affected him this way. Maybe it meant he needed to join with her. Perhaps his crazed thoughts about her would disappear after he took her.

That had to be it. Because if taking her to his bedroll didn't solve all those feelings pinging around inside his chest, he had a real problem.

Chapter 5

They arrived at the campsite as twilight approached. After a quick dinner using no fire, Thoren laid wards, the magic preventing anything non-magical from entering or leaving the campsite. Enar walked about the site with him, wishing, not for the first time, he had been born Draconi. What he wouldn't give to be like Thoren, to use magic as effortlessly as most people breathed. Instead, he only possessed the weak magic of his mother.

Something he hid well, considering Watchers weren't supposed to possess magical abilities.

Besides using a persuasive smile at Draconi females until they joined with him, he wasn't sure what his middling magic could do.

No sense wondering over the unknown. If the Goddess wanted him to know, then he would. Until then...

His eye caught sight of Lily sitting on a downed tree trunk with Keara, holding her friend's hand. His woman's pink tongue licked over her lips as she watched him from hooded lids.

And just like that his shaft strained at his laces, wanting to be free.

Mighty inconvenient of Thoren to make him help lay wards when he could be spending time with his woman.

"I heard that thought." Thoren waved his hand over another stone, turning the rock into a ward.

"What thought?"

"Uh-huh. Don't play all innocent with me."

"You know me better than that."

"You're right, I do."

"You shouldn't eavesdrop on me."

"Sorry. Sometimes you broadcast your thoughts."

"Sometimes?" *How embarrassing.*

"On occasion."

"You mean besides when I'm mind-speaking to you?"

"Yes."

Goddess's toes. "Keep it to the mind-speaking. My thoughts are my own."

"I know. But sometimes I just can't help it."

Sure you can't. "So, how's Keara?"

Thoren shrugged and laid another ward. "How's Lily?"

"Glad to be away from the town."

"I can imagine."

"Can you believe they have priests?"

Thoren cocked an eyebrow. "Priests?"

"Yes. No priestesses, just priests. No wonder the townsfolk were so backward. And they think anything out of the norm is evil. Good thing we're taking the females away from here."

"You're right. The sooner we can return to Draconia the better." Thoren walked ten paces, picked up another rock and cast a ward spell over it.

Enar glanced at Lily. His perfect woman. Given to him by the Goddess. He could never hurt Lily on purpose. Which was something he never understood about his father, or any other Watcher for that matter. How they could abuse their women was beyond him. His woman was a gift from the Goddess, how could he even think of hurting her?

Bedding her, definitely, but hurting her, never.

After what seemed like an eternity, Thoren finished laying wards. Enar breathed a sigh of relief as they walked to where Lily and Keara sat on the log.

Lily raised her eyes to his, her face paler than normal. She licked her lips, her little pink tongue popping out as if to meet his shaft, and swallowed. A streak of lust shot through his body, ending between his legs.

Oh yes, they would have some fun tonight.

"Come, Lily. You will sleep with me." He held out his hand, waiting as Lily straightened her shoulders, placing her small palm in his.

Enar led her to his bedroll. He grabbed the invisibility blanket and motioned for Lily to lie down. Yanking the blanket over them, he lay beside her.

"This blanket is see-through!" she whispered, holding her hand to it. "And it doesn't touch my legs even though it's lying on them. What is this?"

"It's an invisibility blanket. We can see out of it, but to anyone looking at us, we appear like a rock. Enough talking, woman. Tonight you have the privilege of knowing what it's like to belong to a Watcher."

Her muscles contracted, arms stiffening at his words, her eyes shutting hard enough to wrinkle their corners.

Nice words, Enar. Try not to scare her next time.

Slow, he'd have to move slow, lest he frighten her too badly. He needed to ease her into her new life. Not scare her away.

He kissed her nose, smiling as her lids flew open. "You enjoyed me earlier, you'll enjoy it now. Just a little kiss here," he pecked her cheek, "then here," he pecked her other cheek, "and let's not forget here." Covering her lips with his, he kissed her, running his hand down her side until she relaxed against him.

Trailing kisses down her neck, he lightly nipped her silky skin, pleased when she moaned. Too much clothing lay between his skin and hers, but if he ripped off their clothes the way he wanted, she'd probably freeze in fright. A frightened woman was the last thing he wanted in his bed.

Why was he thinking like this? What was it about his claim that made him care how she felt?

The why of it didn't matter. Only the woman lying beside him mattered.

Running his hand down her hip, he found the edge of her tunic and slipped his fingers underneath. Her breathing stopped the instant his hand touched the smooth skin of her belly, her body tensing. He gave a mental curse. How much slower could he go? Maybe he could distract her, overwhelm her with pleasure so she welcomed his hand on her hip. He had no choice but to kiss her, delving deep into her mouth, tangling his tongue with hers until she relaxed, her fingers curling into his shirt.

Enar let his fingers roam, walking the ladder of her prominent ribs until he reached her breast. What he would give to see the color of her nipples, to see what his fingers felt. He imagined the color of pale pink roses covering her pebbly nubs. Tomorrow he'd have a look. For now he was content with the texture of her skin beneath his fingers.

He drew small circles around the peak, lightly touching until he reached the tip. Lily moaned when he rolled her nipple between his thumb and finger, the sound vibrating across his lips. He broke the kiss, continuing to play with her nipple.

Patience was never one of his virtues. "Take your tunic off, before I rip it."

****

Lily froze, all the pleasurable feelings zipping around her body coming to a complete halt at his words. Despite the dark, she saw lust ravaging his features, heard it in his voice. She had no doubt he would rip her tunic to get at her.

In truth, part of her wanted him to.

But the reality was, she didn't have many clothes and losing one that way wasn't worth it. A bit frightened, and yet tingling with excitement, she sat up, the blanket hovering around her as she removed her tunic. What was more bizarre, a hovering invisibility blanket or the fact Enar wanted her despite her coloring?

Enar stared at her breasts, palming one, the calluses in his hand scraping against her swollen nipples, shooting tendrils of fire through her veins.

"Exquisite."

He pushed gently against her shoulder and she laid spread below him, staring at his face as the moonlit shadows danced across it. Enar scared and excited her at the same time. Her belly knotted, blood pulsed through her veins, pounded in her chest. She knew the basics of this act, but not the specifics. Would he crush her? Would he care if he hurt her?

He was being gentle. For the moment anyway.

Lily looked into his eyes, into the blue pools, now black in the moonlight. Never in her wildest imaginings did she think her innocence would be lost to a stranger. Or to anyone for that matter. She figured she'd die with all parts intact. The priests, and all other men she knew, had never been interested in her body for anything other than ridding it of its spirit.

What was he waiting for? Enar stared at her breasts, flicking a thumb across the nipples, his brows drawn together. She raised her head, glancing down. Had he found something wrong with her? Her gaze met his and she felt heat rise in her cheeks.

"What color are they?" His voice rasped as his middle finger flicked across one of her nipples.

"What?"

The finger flicked again and she bit her lip to stifle the gasp. "What color are they?"

She felt the heat explode in her face. How embarrassing. "Umm. Pink?"

"Like a rose?"

"Umm. Sure."

"I knew it. You are truly exquisite." He glanced at her through hooded lids as his head lowered, his tongue reaching toward her nipple, then circling her bud before drawing it into his mouth.

Embarrassment forgotten in the sensations, she closed her eyes, reveling in the pleasure that swept through her with each lick of his tongue, each swipe of his fingers. Arching her back, she held his head against her breasts as his tongue played with one peak and then the other.

The rasp of his unshaven beard against her

sensitive skin drew another shudder from her. The man was magic. Each stroke of his hand, each lick of his tongue brought her closer to begging him to crush her. She wanted it, she needed to feel his body press against hers.

She wanted it until she felt him loosen the tie of her trousers and slip his hand inside, cupping her most private parts. Then the reality of the situation hit her like a pile of grain. She stiffened, shoving his hand away.

Lily tried to roll away, but he threw a leg over both of hers, holding her in place.

"What is wrong, woman? You want me. My fingers are coated with your dew."

How mortifying! He'd felt the unusual wetness coating her woman parts and then remarked on it. She clasped a hand over her face.

****

Enar stared at his woman, sexual heat throbbing against his veins. He wanted nothing more than to bury himself inside her and the slickness his fingers felt meant she wanted the same. So why had she pushed him away? And now she lay with her hand hiding her face as if embarrassed. Why should she be embarrassed? Surely she'd been with a man before.

Then he remembered the priest and the empty shelves in her store. The thinness of her ribs indicative of not enough to eat. The way he had to threaten the shopkeeper to return her paintbrushes.

Maybe she had never known a man's touch. Maybe he would be her first.

Another one of those strange feelings causing an ache in his chest crashed into him. He rubbed his chest as he peered at her.

"Lily, how many men have you joined with?"

She put her other hand over her face and shook her head, giving him all the response he needed.

His. She would only belong to him. His touch would be the only one she would know. What a responsibility. If he erred this time she might never welcome him to her bed. Totally unacceptable.

He kissed her cheek, pulling her hand down. She closed her eyes against his gaze.

"Lily, let me," *swive*, no she might not like that word, what about, "pleasure you."

Her eyes flew open. "But, there's something...wrong...with me...down there."

Enar thought about checking out what was wrong, he hadn't felt anything out of the ordinary, but his hand hadn't felt all there was to feel about her sweet core either. "Like what?"

"It's all, umm, well you felt it."

"Wet?"

She put her hand over her face again, nodding.

Enar snorted. "Woman, that's supposed to happen. Means you want me to swi-um, pleasure you."

Lily dropped her hand, staring at him. "Seriously?"

"Didn't you enjoy my touches?"

He couldn't be certain in the dark, but he thought a blush crept across her cheeks.

"They were nice. But you'll crush me. You're much bigger than I am."

Ah, the real problem. "Nonsense. I'll fit you fine. Let me show you just how fine."

She stared into his eyes as if trying to discern whether or not he told the truth. After a moment, during which Enar thought he might pass out from holding his breath, she nodded. He smiled, running a hand down her cheek, feeling the smoothness of her skin.

Making a woman so crazy with pleasure she forgot her surroundings was a lot of work. But someone had to do it and Enar felt up to the task.

He kissed her lips, when they opened to him, he tangled his tongue with hers until the tension left her body. She turned toward him, clasping her fingers in his hair, holding his head. He recognized the feeling in his chest this time, pride. His woman wanted him.

Probably not as much as he wanted her though. His staff ached, straining against the leather ties, wanting to find its home. If she had been anyone else, he would already be in her.

But he wanted to savor his woman, not frighten her.

Running his hand down her bare skin to her hip, he kissed down her throat, nipping the pulse point in her neck. A little moan left her lips as she tilted her head, allowing him better access to her throat. Ignoring her silent plea, he kissed up to her ear, swirling his tongue around the rim, nipping the lobe. She jumped, her exhale a sigh of pleasure.

He'd have to remember her ears were so sensitive. Wonder what else was sensitive?

Nothing for it but to find out.

Tracing the path he took earlier, Enar kissed the silky skin of her chest, trailing his way to one nipple. Happy to note it met his questing lips all perky, he drew it into his mouth, flicking his tongue across the bud. Lily arched her back, clasping his head to her. He worked her other nipple with his fingers, rolling the tender nub, scraping lightly with his nail. Then he switched sides, caressing with his lips and tongue what his fingers had touched, while his fingers rolled her wet nipple, pinching lightly. He continued from one side to the other until she cried out, her hips arching, beckoning him in the age-old way of women.

He took the offer.

This time she made no protests when his hand snuck beneath the band of her trousers. Her springy curls were damp with her dew, the best welcome in the world. Unfortunately her trousers were in the way of her sweet core.

It took a lot of willpower for him to remove his hand from her, but he managed, knowing he would be rewarded for it in a bit.

"Please," Lily tried to hold his hand against her. "I'm not scared anymore."

He was the man. "The trousers need off."

She hooked her fingers in the waistband and wiggled out of them, lying nude for his viewing pleasure. Shame he couldn't see her clearly in the dark. Not that he needed to for what he had in mind. Tomorrow he would look at her, and the day after that. She was his forever, what was one night?

"You are beautiful." What he could see of her.

He bent to her lips, feeling the press of her body against his clothing. His clothing? Why was that still on? Best get rid of the stupid things lest they get even more in the way. She helped him pull his shirt off, leaving him to his leathers. His staff sprang free of the confines, jutting away from his body.

Enar rolled, pulling Lily against him, pressing his staff against her belly, kissing her deeply. He kissed his way down her body, over the smooth skin of her stomach, until he came to her damp curls. She stiffened. Before she could voice whatever censure she had in mind, he took her into his mouth, lapping at her folds. She tasted of honey and spice, a scent belonging to her alone.

He circled her folds with his tongue, lapping up her cream, judging her desires by her sighs and soft moans. Sucking on her bud, he thrust a finger into her passage. Son of a goat, she was small. At least she was wet. A second finger joined the first, thrusting in, pulling out. His tongue flicked her clit as she clutched his hair.

She peaked, crying out, spasming around his fingers. Crawling up her body, he entered slowly, pushing past her barrier, giving her time to stretch, to adjust to his size. Not that he was a braggart, but the Goddess had seen fit to endow him with a large staff. One he learned to use for a woman's pleasure. One he slipped, inch by inch into Lily's unused passage until he was seated to the hilt. Even in the dark he could see her eyes wide open as she stared at him, see the white of her teeth as she bit into her lip. He remained still, allowing her time to adjust to him. She took a deep breath and released her teeth's grip on her lip.

"Oh, my. You are huge."

Balancing on his elbows, he pecked her forehead, liking her words. "It is a gift. Do you hurt?"

"A little, but not much. So this is it?" She wiggled a bit as if trying to get comfortable.

Enar gave her another peck on the forehead as he began to move. "Not even close, woman."

He smiled as she blinked, mouth opening. "Oh. That feels good."

"It'll feel better."

He thrust into her, loving the feel of her core sucking at him, of her ankles clasped around his waist. Close, so close to finishing, his balls pulled up tight, waiting to release his seed. Reaching between their bodies, he touched her clit, massaging it as he thrust into her. She moaned and he rubbed harder, quickening his pace. Her hips bucked against his as she cried out, raking her nails down his back, her core clenching around him, milking his seed, sending him into the biggest orgasm of his life.

An orgasm that continued long past when it should have stopped.

What was happening to him?

With a final cry, he dropped his head to her shoulder, still shuddering in the aftermath. Her legs dropped from his waist, her hands pushing gently at his shoulder. He rolled to the side, taking her with him, still in her, his staff unwilling to move from her core.

Maybe he should have spent more time listening to Watchers talk about the first time they took their claims. Until he saw Lily he hadn't planned on claiming a woman. He carried the necklace because it had been given to him at the same time as Blood Seeker, when he was deemed a man. Enar preferred the Draconi way of bonding, not the Watcher's way.

Maybe that was because he had spent more of his childhood with Thoren's family than his own.

He'd have to ask someone about why he couldn't pull free of her core. Lily obviously didn't realize anything was wrong, she snuggled against him, her fingers raking lightly against the hair on his chest. He felt his staff stiffening with each touch of her hand despite his unease over the end of their joining.

"That was nice. You didn't crush me."

"Humph. Told you, woman."

"I'm sleepy...oh!" Her gaze flew to his as he twitched inside her. "Guess you're not."

He kissed her, moving his hips, reaching his hand between them to rub her swollen clit. It took three strokes and she spasmed around his staff, the movement of her inner walls causing his release. This time, he was happy to note, he pulled free of her sweet core.

"Mmm. Is it always like that?" Pleasure-drenched eyes turned to his.

"Like what?" Perhaps she had noted the odd way his staff refused to pull free of her body.

"That good."

Or not. "Only when you're with me." He arranged her head against his arm, stroking her back until she relaxed against him.

Despite his tiredness, his mind raced, chasing away sleep. What had he been told about the necklace, about claiming women? Nothing odd he remembered. Put the necklace around the neck of the woman you wished to claim and she was yours. Many Watchers had more than one woman, ensuring multiple sons. Enar only wanted the woman lying in his arms. But he'd like to know why his staff wouldn't pull free. Maybe he should just be happy he had tumbled a woman twice in a row and let it go at that.

Enar shoved the niggling little voice telling him something special had occurred to the back of his mind and fell asleep, holding his woman against his side.

Chapter 6

Lily stood by Keara, watching as Enar and Thoren walked out of the warded campsite to find Jamie. Sunlight glittered off the dew coating the leaves and grass as bird song greeted the morning. Lily felt a chill lodge in her stomach. Alone, with only Thoren's wards to protect them.

As if those wards worked. No one in their group seemed affected by the wards, except for her. Everyone else walked through them like a curtain in a doorway. With her though, the curtain became an invisible wall blocking her path.

Even Jamie could walk through the wards, as he proved by wandering off in the middle of the night. If he and the others could do it, what was stopping Lord Simon and his soldiers from walking through the wards? How safe were they if those wards didn't work? They weren't. At all. And yet, they continued to stand behind the wards.

Alone.

Before they could continue on their journey to who-knows-where, the men had to find Jamie. What was the boy thinking to wander off in the middle of the night and get lost? If not for his disappearing act, they would be far away from River's Run instead of hanging out in the woods behind wards.

"I can't believe Jamie is a Halfling like me and can

walk through Thoren's wards." Keara pushed a strand of wind-blown hair behind her ear.

"Sorry, but I wasn't paying attention earlier. Jamie's a what?"

"A Halfling. Half Draconi like Thoren and half human. Just like me." Keara's voice took on the high-pitched tone of complete excitement.

Good thing one of them was excited.

"Does that explain why he walked through those wards?"

"Yes. That explains why you can't. The wards are against non-magical beings. So you don't have magic, unlike the rest of us. It's odd to think I possess magic."

Wasn't that the truth. "No offense, but I'll let you keep the magic." Seeing visions was bad enough. Compound the visions with magical powers and she would be one crazy woman.

"Do you think they can find Jamie?"

Two men against one small boy? "Yes."

Keara stared at the trees that swallowed Enar and Thoren. "I hope they do too. What about you?"

"Of course. What do you take me for?" Lily turned and walked toward the invisibility blanket. Now that thing she trusted, much more so than the so-called wards.

Keara grabbed her arm before she reached the blanket. "That's not what I meant. I meant, how are you, love?"

"Fine. Why?"

Keara waved a hand. "Last night. I thought Enar might have hurt you. Did he?"

Lily felt her lips curve as her thoughts turned to the night before. Hurt would not be the word that came to mind. "No. It was nothing like that. You? Did Thoren hurt you?"

"No. We just talked." Keara gave her a piercing stare and Lily felt her cheeks heat.

Talking in detail about last night did not make it onto her to-do list.

"That's good. I'm glad he didn't hurt you. Do you think it will be onerous to be his wife?"

"He doesn't think I am his wife. Something about rituals and whatnot and since we had no ritual, therefore no marriage. You?"

Lily shrugged. "Don't know what he wants. Well, that's not right." Heat poured back into her cheeks. "I mean, I know some of what he wants, but I'm not sure what all being his claim involves." She suspected last night's activities made up most of her claim duties. But she refused to voice the thought. Keara might be her best friend, but even friends had their limits.

"I'm sure it will be all right. If not, you can stay with us." Keara's brows knitted. "Wherever that might be. Draconia. Have you heard of it?"

Lily shook her head as she pulled the invisibility blanket around her shoulders. "Enar only said we're going there. Where is it?"

"Thoren said about two weeks from here. On foot. Are they crazy?"

"Two weeks?"

"Yes."

"Definitely crazy. Maybe they'll bring back the horses while they're out looking for Jamie."

Keara ran a hand over her head and started pacing. Lily watched in silence as her friend tromped one way and then the other, wearing a path in the grass. Keara finally stopped and looked toward the town. As if she spoke, Lily knew what Keara planned. Knew it for the bad idea it was, knew she could do nothing to stop her friend.

Keara headed her way and Lily pulled the blanket off her head. "Don't even think about leaving me here alone."

"You have the blanket. No one can see you. Jamie needs me. The men don't know their way around these woods. What if they get lost?"

Keara had gone daft. As if she could do a better job of searching for Jamie than the men could. "They won't get lost. You on the other hand..."

"Don't be ridiculous. I grew up around here. Grandmother used to take me to these woods for herbs. I'm going to find Jamie. He needs me."

"And I don't?"

"You have the blanket. And you're sitting in the wards. Jamie's by himself in the woods. What if something happened to him? I can't leave him alone out there!" Keara gestured to the woods.

"Are you sure nothing can get to me?"

"Thoren said nothing non-Draconi can get through those wards. You can't get out can you?"

"No."

"Then nothing can get in to you. You're safe. Jamie needs me."

"Thoren won't be happy about it." Maybe that would persuade her. As Lily's doubts about the security of the wards didn't seem to be doing much good.

Keara sighed. "I know. But I have to. You understand, don't you?"

"I understand." If Enar wandered off, she would go

search for him, and she had just met the man. Jamie was Keara's apprentice, whom she thought of as her child. Of course she'd want to look for him, no matter how dangerous. "Don't worry about me. I'll hide under this invisibility blanket." She pulled the blanket over her head, disappearing from view. "Be safe."

"Thanks, love. I won't be long."

Like the men before her, Keara walked through the wards, disappearing into the woods. Although she understood her friend, she disagreed with Keara leaving. Lily knew without a doubt Lord Simon still looked for Keara. Once the lord had an idea or obsession nothing got in his way until he saw it through.

And despite their social statuses, Keara was his current obsession.

Oddities were gaining the upper ground in her life.

Lily leaned back against the tree, feeling the scratch of the bark through the blanket and her tunic. Unlike the wards, she knew the tree existed and it grounded her in the moment. She watched as the sun skipped across the sky like stones thrown across the still waters of a pond. If only she had paints, canvas and an easel, she could escape reality.

Being by herself gave her time to think about the preceding night's events. Who was she fooling? Being alone gave her time to think of Enar and the things he'd done to her body. Things she refused to discuss with her best friend. Things that caused a whole host of problems, which she also refused to discuss with Keara.

For instance, her self-talk about remaining aloof being thrown into the woods when his lips touched hers. Or maybe it was when his hands traced down her side. Or touched her core. Lily shook her head, trying to gather up the pieces of her scattered-to-the-winds barrier and rebuild it around her heart.

Which was a little hard to do when the reasons for her heart to tumble for him stood in his favor. She definitely liked Enar's kisses and what his tongue, hands and various body parts made her feel. And he took her away from River's Run. If only she knew what her new life would be like. He seemed to be hiding something about where he was from.

And with that realization the mortar between her bricks began to harden.

His lack of forthcoming presented a problem. If he lied about her new life, then she couldn't trust him.

And she wanted to trust him.

Well, the part of her heart that was clearly having issues with the remain-aloof plan wanted to trust him. The rest of her chinked another metaphorical brick into place.

Sudden pain shot through her skull, catching her off-guard as she clenched her eyes shut. Lily dropped the blanket, grasping her head with both hands in a vain attempt to stop what felt like shooting arrows from piercing further. Oh no, please Goddess no. Don't let it be about Keara.

Her vision grayed and despite her plea she saw Keara surrounded by Lord Simon and his soldiers. They bound her friend's hands and feet, threw her over a soldier's shoulder and slapped her face. The lot of them walked through a door in the wall of the town, carrying Keara into the inky blackness. Lily screamed but the door slammed in her face, sealing off entrance.

The pain stopped shooting through her skull, her

vision returning in increments. Lily curled into a ball on the grass, hands clutching her head.

Stupid visions. Why couldn't she have seen this before Keara walked out of the wards? Her visions were fickle things, coming as they wanted, leaving her either puzzled at the scenes, or frustrated as she saw, but could not help.

What good were visions if she couldn't act on them? Or if no one believed her when she told them about the scenes? Lily smacked the grass with her palm.

How could she help her friend when she remained stuck behind invisible walls?

Lily shook. Lord Simon had Keara in his clutches and the only ones who could get her out were off chasing a small boy around the woods. Lily jumped up and ran full force into the barrier, beating her hands against it, hoping it would break. Her hands turned red, stinging, her voice grew hoarse and still no one heard her screams.

She sank against the invisible wall, tears rimming her eyes. Her friend was lost, as good as dead.

And she could do nothing about it.

****

Enar grasped Jamie's shoulder, holding the little imp in place as they walked back to their campsite.

"You know, you don't have to hold me. I won't run off."

"What? So we chased you around because we needed running practice?"

"Come on. Please?"

Enar glared at the Halfling and tightened his grip.

"Fine." Jamie huffed.

Trouble came in small packages. Packages shaped

like a boy. Surely he and Thoren hadn't been this much trouble as boys. A vivid memory of Thoren's mother yelling at them came to mind. Enar scrunched his eyebrows. No, they hadn't been this much trouble. Unlike Jamie, they had never wandered off through wards, gotten captured, and needed to be rescued.

Not once. No one ever needed to rescue them.

And to top things off, Keara had chased after Jamie and gotten herself captured. What a mess.

Enar's gaze locked on Thoren's back, Keara's red locks hanging over his arm as he carried her. It wasn't until they found Jamie with Lord Simon's henchmen that they realized Keara had been captured by the lord too.

"How is she doing?"

Thoren continued forward, speaking over his shoulder to Enar. "Same. She still hasn't moved."

Enar grunted. He'd love to kill Simon for hurting Keara. She had been drugged with some potion rendering her incapable of voluntary movement, susceptible to commands by the one who gave her the drug. Her free will vanished while under the power of the potion.

Good thing they found her. Maybe now Thoren realized she was his mate. Or not. His best friend had a habit of being hardheaded.

Branches brushed against his arm as they walked through the woods, leaving the town. Again. At least his woman remained safe behind Thoren's wards. Where they left her. Hopefully. Enar swallowed and rubbed the achy spot on his chest. What if Lily wasn't at the campsite? If anything happened to his woman, he'd kill the cause of it. She belonged to him. With any luck she'd enjoy being his claim.

At least until he returned her to his people. Then she'd loathe him. And not taking her back wasn't an option. Right?

A sound like distant thunder interrupted Enar's thoughts.

"Dragon wings!" Jamie turned and Enar almost lost his grip on the boy's shoulder. Almost.

Enar peered at the sky, but saw a bramble of tree limbs instead. Not that he could see the dragon. The male flew in full camouflage mode, invisible against the backdrop of clouds and sky. Instead of being reconnaissance specialists, today he and Thoren turned into rescue specialists. First Jamie, then Keara and finally a grown male Draconi unable to change from his dragon form.

They found the dragon in a titanium-lined cell deep within the cellar of Lord Simon's house. How a mere human managed to capture and keep a Draconi for years defied belief. And yet, the male sat behind titanium bars, unable to perform magic to free himself. The bane of Draconi, titanium rendered their magic useless.

Good thing Enar possessed no such failings. If he got screwed over, it was his own stupid fault.

"I want to fly!" Jamie pointed up, waving his arm at where the dragon presumably soared.

"Boys don't fly. And since you're a Halfling, you might not ever fly."

Jamie turned and snarled. "I will so fly. My daddy said so. Just you wait and see."

"Who's your father?"

The boy's eyes narrowed. "No one."

"No one? Everyone has a father." *Even though some of us wish we didn't.*

Jamie looked down at the ground and sniffed. A couple of sniffs later and Enar gave up expecting an answer. Plenty of time remained to discover Jamie's parentage. Two whole weeks of walking, in fact.

By the time they arrived in Draconia, Enar would know everything about Jamie's life.

He hoped.

As they approached the campsite, Enar heard the faint hum of the wards. Would his woman be where he left her? Of course she would. As a non-magical being, how could she be elsewhere?

But what if somehow she managed to get through the wards? What if she wasn't all right?

She will be where you left her.

So where was she? Scanning the campsite, he saw a lump on the ground. He squinted, trying to see if Lily hid under the invisibility blanket.

The lump squirmed, Lily's too-thin body coming in view as she dropped the blanket, running toward them. Enar rubbed his chest as she ran, exhaling a breath he didn't realize he held, and sent up a prayer of thanks she remained unharmed. He shoved Jamie through the wards and took a deep breath before thrusting himself through the invisible barrier.

Pain erupted from his pores, dragging at his body as he broke through the magic. He should have waited for Thoren to touch him as he walked through the wards, but he wanted to hold his woman, to ensure she remained unharmed. Looks could be deceiving.

She apparently had other ideas as she veered toward Thoren.

"Keara!" Lily ran to where Thoren placed Keara on the ground, touching her friend lightly on the arm, peering into Keara's vacant staring eyes. "Dear Goddess, what happened to her?"

"She's been drugged and can't move," Thoren said.

Enar walked to Lily, meaning to hold her in his arms, to feel her against him. Before he could reach her, a loud blast of dragon song rent the air, followed by a thud as the male Draconi landed in the middle of their camp, dropping his invisibility shield.

The wings might be a little underused. The dragon's voice thundered through their minds as he shook the grass off his scales, flinging it against the wall of the wards. Lily screamed, leaping up and running to Enar, who caught her, clamping a hand over her mouth.

"Shh, woman. It's just, um...I didn't catch your name?"

The dragon paused, as if he didn't know his name. Which, after being locked in a magic-prohibiting titanium cell, might well be the case. The male took a quick breath, a twitch crossing his lips. *Fafnir. And yours?*

Guess the dragon knew his name after all. Although from his expression, Enar swore the dragon lied. "Enar. And this is my woman, Lily." Enar wrapped an arm around Lily's bony shoulders. It took all his will not to run his hands over her, to ensure she truly was unharmed. Eyes could make mistakes.

"My apologies, friend, for not asking earlier. I'm Thoren. The Halfling female is Keara, and you've already met Jamie." Was that a blush on his friend's face? Rather embarrassing not to know the name of the

Draconi they freed.

Fafnir waved a front limb to and fro, dismissing Thoren's apology, while Lily pulled out of Enar's embrace and rushed back to her friend's side. Away from him. His mouth tightened. She did not just walk away from him. Enar watched Lily kneel beside Keara, gathering her friend's hand into both of hers, and felt a brush of air where she had stood. Her eyes searched Keara's face and she gave her friend her total concentration. Even Fafnir shuffling to where Thoren knelt on the other side of Keara didn't faze her.

Fafnir stared into Keara's flaccid face. Two seconds later his eye-ridges popped halfway up his forehead.

How did she get to Cautasia?

"Her father abandoned her mother before she was born. She's lived in River's Run her entire life," Thoren said.

Fafnir took a step back, eyes wide, mouth slack. *No.*

"What's surprising is no word of her got back to us. We heard about Jamie, but not her."

The dragon shook his head, looking like someone pole-axed him. The whole situation shocked Enar too. But at least his woman was fine, even if she did refuse to stand beside him. He couldn't say the same about Keara.

"It's bizarre, I agree," Thoren placed a hand on Fafnir's foreleg. "She'll be all right."

Fafnir looked at Thoren, blinking...was that tears? Did male Draconi cry? Watchers sure didn't. Totally un-warrior-like. However, if he'd spent the last who-knows-how-long in a cell going crazy, he might shed a few tears too when released.

Provided no one was around to see his eyes leak.

All he wanted to do now was pull his woman into his arms and run his hands over her. He needed to lay her down, strip off her clothing, feel the caress of her skin against his. None of which he could do with her out of touching distance.

No problem. He'd move to where he could touch her.

Placing his hands on her shoulders, he felt bones poking against his fingers and a snarl pulled his lip. How dare that town treat his woman so badly she lacked enough food to eat. A part of him wanted to storm back and kill the whole lot of them, starting with the sniveling priests.

Thoren's voice echoing in his mind cut through his thoughts, pulling his attention back to Keara.

She moved!

Enar focused on Keara until he saw a faint twitch of her lids, small enough to be almost unnoticeable. Was the drug wearing off? *Move again, come on, move.* Keara blinked, turning her head toward Thoren.

Yes! It looked like Keara would recover. Lily's bones poked against his hands as she shifted, turning her head to meet his gaze. With a quick grin, she faced Keara.

"I think she'll be fine," Lily said.

"You had us worried there for a moment." Thoren grasped Keara's hand.

Enar looked at the sky. If they wanted to go, they needed to do so while daylight still prevailed. "The sun is overhead. Do we stay or go?"

"It would be better to get farther away from here,

but she is still weak. I'm not sure she should be moved." Concern laced Thoren's voice as he tilted his head to the sky.

I don't want to stay here. Can you still hear me? They'll find us. If we stay here we'll be caught. Can you still hear me? Please say yes.

Enar rubbed the side of his head as Keara's voice slammed through his mind. "Even I can hear you, female. Tone down the mental screams." Thoren needed to teach her control over mind-speaking and the sooner the better.

"It is a little loud," Thoren smiled at her, "but we'll work on it. You just need to be taught."

Fine. But we can't stay here. They'll find us.

"She has a point." As loathe as he was to admit it, they needed to get as far away from this place as possible. Less chance of him having to crawl through sewers again.

"What are you talking about?" Lily looked from one face to another, wrinkles creasing her forehead.

"You can't hear her?" Was there something wrong with his exquisite woman? Keara's screaming mind-speaking attempt at communication had everyone else wincing.

Lily's jaw clenched. "She's not speaking."

"Draconi can mind-speak, Lily," Thoren explained.

Enar gave himself a mental smack. Why hadn't he thought of that? Humans couldn't mind-speak, which meant nothing was wrong with Lily after all. Thank the Goddess.

"Truthfully?" Lily's brows shot up.

"Yes. Keara is speaking to us, telling us to leave."

"Sounds good to me."

"True. But by the time she can move, it will be dark, and our campsite is warded from intruders. Only Draconi can get in and besides us, there aren't any around."

There was one working with Lord Simon. He offered Simon money to capture me. He said he needed me to get revenge on his enemies.

"What?" Thoren exploded, eyes popping wide, lips peeling off his teeth. Ripples crept beneath his skin and he shook, as if trying to cast them off.

"Who?" Enar knelt beside Thoren, placing a hand on his arm, trying to calm his friend's inner dragon back into hiding.

"What did he look like?" Thoren growled.

*I don't know. He wore a cloak pulled over his head, but he had the Draconi mark and he said he needed me to get revenge on his enemies and that he needed to unlock my powers. I thought he was going to...*Keara stopped mid-sentence, a shudder cascading through her body.

"We move. Pack the campsite and make it quick." Thoren said.

"We can take him on. Finish this now." Pay them all back for hurting Lily and Keara.

"Not with the females and a boy. Even a warrior has to retreat some time. Besides, we'll be back."

Enar sucked down a couple of breaths, pushing the voice telling him to fight, to kill, to protect, into hiding. Thoren was right. Why risk the small chance they lost and something happened to Lily and Keara?

"And then they won't get away."

*****

Thoren's gaze met Lily's. "I'll be back. Lily, stay

with her."

Not a problem. She patted Keara's ice-cold hand. Her poor friend. What had Lord Simon done to her? Thoren mentioned a drug made her unable to move, but what kind of drug did that? In all the excitement Lily didn't get a chance to ask. Whatever the drug, the effects seemed to be wearing off. "What happened to you?"

Keara opened her mouth, tongue flopping in an effort to speak and getting nowhere fast. "Gwrph."

So much for talking.

"Sorry. I should have known. I'm so glad you're back. I was worried about you." Lily squeezed Keara's hand and wished she had the mind-speaking ability like everyone else. Then she could talk with her friend.

Then she could know what Enar really had planned for her.

Maybe it was a good thing she couldn't mind-speak.

A small squeeze pressed against her hand. Lily grinned. Soon Keara would be back to normal. She hoped. Jamie plopped beside her, out of breath, bouncing up and down. At least one of them was no worse for the adventure.

Or not. Was that a bruise and cut on the side of his head? Before she could ask what happened, all his excitement poured out in a rush of words.

"Guess what, guess what, guess what?" A bounce punctuated each question.

"What?" Where did he get all that energy? She was tired just watching him.

"They're going to let us ride Fafnir! It's apparently not done and a big deal, but Fafnir insisted and we get to ride! Isn't that grand?"

"Ride? On that, that, creature?" Could she sound anymore scared? *Calm down, Lily.*

"He's a dragon. Same as me. One day I can turn like that. That's grand, huh?"

Lily swallowed. *It'll be fine.* "Sure. Great. How are we supposed to stay on a...dragon?

"Duh. Hold on, silly. How're you doing Keara?"

Keara stared into Jamie's face, hers the expressionless mask of the drug, his a parade of emotions.

Lily crossed her arms, trying hard not to let the jealousy seep out through her voice. "Are you two talking again? That's rude to do that in front of me, you know."

"You're right. I think I'm needed over there." Jamie leapt to his feet and ran to where Enar and Thoren stood.

What did Keara say to him? Her best guess was Keara scolded him for running off last night. For the first time since Keara had placed her hands over Lily's eyes, banishing the black veil from her sight, allowing her to see, she felt a distance between them. Unlike the rest of their group, she couldn't mind-speak and remained oblivious to the other conversations. Excluded despite being in the company of friends.

And that dragon. *That huge, scaly, clawed dragon.* They wanted her to crawl on that thing and let it take her for a ride?

"I'm a little scared about riding on the dragon."

Wasn't that an understatement?

Keara's lips cranked upward. This time her tongue worked. "Good."

"Good? It's good I'm scared?"

"No." Keara took a breath, words sighing over her lips. "S'all...good."

"You mean it'll be all right?"

"Uh-huh."

"You're speaking. That's good, right?"

Keara smiled, the expressionless mask of her face cracking.

"Well, if you're not scared of the dragon, then neither am I." Lily pasted a grin on her lips and hoped to Goddess Keara didn't notice the lie written there. She might be more terrified of the dragon than a vengeful mob, but she'd crawl up his back and act normal if it was the last thing she did.

Which it might very well be.

"Lie."

So much for fooling Keara. Even drugged her friend could see right through her.

"What can I say? It's a bloody dragon!"

Keara's eyes twinkled. "S'all good."

"I know. It's just..." Lily's gaze followed Enar as he strode across the campsite, carrying her bag.

"Like?"

"Like?"

Keara's gaze tracked Enar and flitted back to Lily.

"Oh. Like." Lily tried to keep the blush off her face, to no avail. "It's complicated. So, how are you feeling?"

"Bedder."

"That's good." Lily watched as Enar piled bags by Fafnir.

Did she like him?

She definitely liked his kisses and his touch. She

felt her cheeks grow warm at the thought of his hands on her body, how he had turned her fear into longing. He didn't mind her odd appearance and he threatened a priest, make that two priests, on her behalf.

Maybe he was only being protective of what he saw as his, but the little part bricked in behind a wall wanted to believe he had some feelings for her.

Stupid part. It could get over those feelings now. She was not falling for him. She was not walking the path of her parents, miserable and longing for something more. She would remain aloof, untouched.

Lying to herself.

No, no, no. Not lying. Protecting. And by his lack of response to her questions, she knew he hid something about what being claimed meant.

But what?

Whatever he hid, she would unearth it. Just not now. Running from Lord Simon was not the time to discuss future responsibilities, or discover why her heart refused to line up behind her decision.

"Lily! Come here." Enar stood by the red-scaled beast, his fingers waggling at her.

Would coming at his bidding be her lot in life?

"Will you be all right?" Lily touched Keara's shoulder. "I'm being summoned."

Keara cracked a grin. "Uh-huh."

Giving Keara's hand one last pat, Lily drew her feet under her and stood. The red-scaled creature grew larger as she approached.

Dragons do not scare me. Dragons do not scare me.

Someone needed to give her a lesson on becoming a better liar.

Enar placed his palm against her mid-back and she did her best not to melt into his touch. Now was not the time for melting.

"You're up first." He pointed at the dragon. "We'll tie Keara to you and then have Jamie sit behind her to make sure she stays on Fafnir's back."

Spots appeared at the edge of her vision and she swayed. So much for self-talk helping her get on the dragon. At least the creature held still, its only movement the ripple of scales as it breathed.

"What's wrong, woman? Don't tell me you're scared of a dragon?"

Air hissed through her teeth as she straightened her shoulders. "Of course I'm not scared of the dragon." See, she could lie. "I've just never flown before."

Enar's eyes lit up. "Flying is the best thing you'll ever do upright. Riding the air currents, feeling the rush of wind in your face. Knowing you're the biggest thing out there. Nothing, well, almost nothing, compares."

"You really like it?"

"Didn't I just say that? Now let me help you onto Fafnir."

Large hands encircled her waist and lifted her, his touch warming the chill in her stomach. She reached for the spine of the dragon and scrambled up the slippery scales until she straddled its back. Throwing her arms around its neck, she leaned against the cool scales and drew in a breath.

This isn't bad. I can do this. No problem. As long as the beast stayed firmly on the ground.

A touch like the beat of butterflies' wings brushed against her mind and she jumped, almost losing her grip.

Hello, Lily.

Was that the dragon? *Dragon?*

A chuckle drifted through her mind. *My name is Fafnir.*

How can I hear you?

I'm speaking to you.

Apparently smart-arses crossed all races. *But I can't mind-speak.*

True. But I can speak directly to you if I want.

How? And if that was true, why wasn't anyone else speaking to her this way?

I'm a Draconi. And one would have to project their thoughts directly to you. If you're conversing in a group and one doesn't mind-speak, it makes things difficult.

So I've discovered. I feel rather left out. She stroked a hand across his scales, feeling the cool hardness. Fafnir shifted. She jerked her hand back. *I'm sorry.*

Whatever for?

I thought I made you uncomfortable.

Nonsense. A dragon likes to be petted now and then.

In that case. Lily stroked a little higher up Fafnir's neck. A gentle sigh escaped the creature's snout.

As she ran her palm over Fafnir's scales, she glanced back to where Keara lay. Thoren picked Keara up and headed toward Fafnir, Enar in the lead. Long legs ate the distance between them. His gaze locked on hers, his blue eyes drawing her in, an invisible bond locking them together.

Fafnir turned his head, his feet stamping and the moment she shared with Enar cracked like dry ground in a drought. And here she thought she'd gotten used to the dragon, until he moved. What was he trying to do? Throw her off? She threw her arms around Fafnir's neck, and squeezed.

Is that Watcher treating you well, Lily?

What did that have to do with her trying to stay on his back? *You mean Enar?*

That giant Watcher.

Enar. And he's treating me fine. Why would Fafnir care how Enar treated her? What was she to the dragon? Although she had to admit, people, or in this case a creature, caring for her felt good.

Fafnir tossed his head, steam rising from his nostrils. *If he doesn't, you let me know and I'll take care of him for you.* The words growled through her mind, setting off a string of shivers cascading down her spine.

First Enar and now Fafnir. Being cared for felt good, but odd, like walking through a dreamland of honey treats. *I don't think that will be necessary. He treats me well.*

It might become necessary. Keep me in mind.

What did one say to that? *All right.*

"Lily! Thoren's going to tie Keara to you." Enar's big palm patted her foot.

"And how am I supposed to hold us both up? I can barely hold on myself!" And wouldn't it be grand if they both took a nose dive off Fafnir's back?

Enar's brows slammed down. "How can you not hold on?"

Do not worry, Little One. I will wrap you in a spell.

"You can do that?"

"I can do what?" Enar squeezed her foot, a gentle tightening.

"What?" She looked at him for a second before realizing she had spoken out loud instead of in her mind. "Oh, sorry. I was talking to Fafnir."

Enar opened his mouth, but Thoren interrupted him.

"Lily, don't move."

She froze, looking down at Thoren. His lips moved and then Keara lifted out of his arms and floated until she landed behind Lily. And why not? Yet another odd occurrence she now considered normal. Flying dragons, invisible walls, friends who floated through the air. What next? Priestesses asking her to join their rituals?

Jamie came running, carrying a long strand of rope. "Hey! I found it!"

"Great. Now get up there and tie Keara to Lily." Thoren gestured to Lily and Keara and before she could blink, Jamie sat astride Fafnir.

How did the imp move so fast? Lily twisted around, staring at Jamie. Maybe he sprouted wings. No, no wings, just over-excited boy.

Despite constant input from Thoren and Enar, they managed to tie Keara to Lily, but her doubts remained about not falling off. If Fafnir could cast a spell to hold her in place, why did they have to tie Keara to her?

Because her mate feels safer that way.

Lily jumped as Fafnir's voice echoed in her mind. *Didn't anyone teach you it's rude to read minds?*

He chuckled. *You have loud thoughts.*

Her words choked in her throat as movement to the side caught her eye. The air around Thoren shimmered, waving around his body like steam. He threw his head back, ripples coursing under his skin, moving in a rhythmic motion. His clothes disappeared, replaced by red scales glinting in the afternoon sun. Arms and legs lengthened, his face elongated. The air warped around him, obscuring his body, expanding outward. And as soon as the air covered him, it disappeared, leaving a huge dragon in its place.

Her mouth dropped open. Impossible. Thoren had disappeared into scales, claws and huge teeth. The dragon he became shook its head, glanced at Fafnir and puffed out its chest. Red scales rippled in the sunlight as he stamped his feet.

Now she'd seen everything. A man who turned into a dragon. What was this world coming to? Lily had a feeling she'd see more odd things before this journey to her new home ended.

She watched Enar tie their baggage onto Thoren's back before climbing on, watched his muscles tense and release as he pulled himself into a sitting position. Heat washed through her as she remembered him the night before, moving above her, inside her.

Ready? She felt Fafnir's spell as it wrapped around her, a solid cage anchoring her to his back.

With a stomach-lurching hop, Fafnir expanded his wings, his muscles bunching under her thighs as he leapt into the air. Oh Goddess, she was airborne. What if she fell off? What if they fell out of the sky? Her eyes ached from squeezing the lids so hard together.

A wave of heat passed through her, nausea threatened to overwhelm her.

"This is fun!" Jamie hollered. "Fly higher!"

Oh, please no.

Lily. Fafnir's voice echoed inside her head. *Try to relax. You won't fall off. I promise.*

Are you sure?

A Draconi doesn't give promises lightly. Now, take deep breaths. In through your nose, out through your mouth. That's good.

In through the nose, out through the mouth. Lily felt her nausea recede, the heat in her body dissipate in the cool wind brushing against her face. Her eyelids felt like stones, but she managed to raise them enough to see clouds like puffy balls floating beneath Fafnir's flapping wings. The ground looked different from the air, fields and trees stood out in patterns, like a patchwork quilt.

A quick glance showed Enar sitting on Thoren's back, head tilted to the wind, a look of pure pleasure on his face. As if he felt her stare, he turned toward her, a smile spreading across his lips.

Her stomach lurched, but this time it had nothing to do with being airborne. Her eyes locked to Enar's and time seemed to stop. Nothing mattered but him and her. And then they flew into a cloud and the moment disappeared as Enar vanished from view.

Lily closed her eyes and saw her life in River's Run. Her miserable, in-fear-of-death life. Priests chasing her, threatening her. Her parent's deaths. The failure of her shop, her livelihood. The only decent thing that happened to her was Keara, the other village outcast. What possessed Keara to grab hold of Lily when they were children, whisper in her ear that she could cure her blindness and then proceed to do so, Lily would never know, but she remained forever in Keara's debt.

She didn't even want to imagine how bad her life would have been if she'd been outcast and blind.

But she never needed to worry about being an

outcast again. Enar took her away from it all.

Never mind she didn't know where Enar was taking her, or what he expected from her, or how things would be once she got there.

Maybe the priests weren't so bad after all.

What was she thinking? The unknown with Enar was better than being starved to death or hung for being different. And she got an attentive bed partner in the bargain.

But he hid something from her about her new life. Why? Why was answering her questions so difficult? Lily felt a chill run across her skin that had nothing to do with Fafnir banking to the right. What if Enar's town was worse than River's Run?

No. She refused to believe it. Everything would be fine. She glanced at Enar, watching him ride through the clouds as if he owned them. Would he defend her in front of the town's priests if he meant to take her to a place equally as intolerant? Of course not.

Or would he? What did she really know about him besides his skills in the bedroll?

A big fat nothing.

But she wanted to believe he wouldn't deceive her in that way. Hope sustained her. Hope always had. Enar grinned at her and she felt her lips turn up in return.

Gods. Every time that man looked at her, her insides turned to mush. She buried her head in Fafnir's neck. She did not want to think about what it meant. No, she did not. It was better to focus on where she was going and what would be expected of her once she arrived. And as soon as they landed, Enar would answer her questions.

She hoped.

Chapter 7

Dear Goddess, how many questions did a claim have?

Enar stared at Lily, watching her mouth move. A total waste of her lips, which would be put to better use encircling his staff. Lifting her off Fafnir's back caused her lips to move like branches in a storm. Setting her on the ground hadn't helped matters.

"What?"

Small fists slammed against her waist. "I said, where in Draconia are you taking me?"

"To my home. How did you like flying? Was it as bad as you thought?" There, if she was going to talk, she could at least talk about a topic he was willing to discuss.

Narrowed eyes regarded him and he felt the puff of air from her sigh. "It wasn't as bad as I thought, although I almost threw up. Fafnir's really nice, but you're avoiding the question."

He cursed under his breath. Just when he'd thought he was in the clear. "Watchers live in our settlement several hours from the Draconi Temple. Enough with the questions, woman, we need to help prepare dinner."

He pointed in the direction the others had taken, motioning Lily in front of him. With a huff and a glare she marched to where Thoren started a fire. Enar ran his hand through his hair, yanking strands out of the leather bind. Gathering the loose strands together, he tied them back off his face. Flying always loosened the things.

Ah, flying. Now that was an activity he could do every day. Soaring above the clouds, looking down at the patches of ground, knowing he was the biggest, baddest thing around. Wait. Where did that thought come from? Thoren was the biggest thing around when in dragon form, not him. And yet, flying made him feel as if he possessed the wingspan of a dragon, as if he dominated the world.

He'd give up being a Watcher if it meant he could be a dragon.

And how bizarre was that? No other Watcher he knew wanted to be a Draconi.

Lily bent over, picking up dried sticks, the firm globes of her arse beckoning, and faster than he could blink his thoughts fled, replaced by a longing that made his balls ache. He wanted her. Wanted her to care for him, wanted her to need him like he needed her.

Goddess's teeth, what was wrong with him?

He'd obviously been around Thoren too long.

Keara joined Lily in her quest for sticks. It seemed as if the red-headed Halfling had recovered from her ordeal. Bruises dotted her face and he felt a cold ball of rage twist in his stomach. He understood the battle Thoren must be going through, the fight within to stay and kill the ones who harmed Keara warring with the urge to get her to safety.

If Lily had been kidnapped instead of Keara, he wouldn't have hesitated to unleash his anger on the ones who hurt her. If he didn't know any better, he'd think he was falling for his claim.

What a thought.

Throughout dinner Enar stared at Lily, unable to get her questions out of his mind. He refused to tell her what things were like in his village, how Watchers treated their women. But how long could he avoid her questions?

Lily's white head bent toward Keara's red one as they sat together on a log, chewing on their dinner of jerky. Undoubtedly sharing secrets he wished she'd share with him.

He mentally banged his head. Why did he have such feelings for his claim?

Luckily Thoren slammed a hand against his knee, derailing his thoughts.

"What's going on, friend?"

Oh, let's see, I care about my claim and it's scaring me half to death. "Nothing much. Glad to see Keara's better."

"So am I. They'll die for it."

"As it should be."

Thoren ran a hand through his hair. "How's Lily?"

"Fine. She seemed to like flying."

"Good."

Thoren did another hand-through-the-hair routine. Since when did his best friend get nervous? He followed his friend's gaze until it landed on Keara. Oh. That explained things. No doubt Thoren had the night's activities front and foremost in his mind.

"Keara," Thoren's voice broke through the flickering flames of the fires, causing all sets of eyes to turn to him. "I need to speak to you. Would you follow me?" Standing, he gestured toward the woods behind the campsite.

With any luck, tonight Thoren would realize Keara

was his mate. Provided the knowledge got through his best friend's thick skull.

A hiss and barely audible growl snapped his head toward Fafnir. The dragon stopped munching on a deer carcass, staring at where Thoren and Keara disappeared into the wooded darkness. A small stream of smoke trickled out his nostrils. Growling again, steam circling his snout, the dragon grabbed his dinner and leapt into the air, wings flapping eddies of dirt and grass.

"What's wrong with him?" Lily sat across the flames from Enar.

"Why did he fly off like that?" Jamie asked.

"Why do you think I know?" Enar shrugged, wondering the same as the others. He didn't know Fafnir, but the dragon's actions seemed strange.

Maybe it had something to do with spending all those years locked in a cell.

Enar shivered. How the dragon managed not to go crazy from years of no exercise was over his head. So if Fafnir wanted to fly off in the middle of dinner, more power to him.

"I'll go refill the water bags." Lily gestured in the direction of the stream flowing several yards past the tree line as she rose and grabbed the bags.

Her dark clothing disappeared into the shadows, her white hair bobbing like a lantern in the darkness until the thick trunk of a tree swallowed her from view. Enar felt a cold pit form in his stomach. What if something happened to her? What if the Draconi Keara saw in River's Run followed them and took Lily?

"Jamie, you are not allowed to leave this campsite. If you need to relieve yourself, go no farther than that tree there," he pointed to a tree at the edge of clearing, one that stood in the light of the fire, "Do you understand?"

"Yes. Where are you going?"

"To make sure Lily is all right." Standing, he strode in the direction Lily went. "I'll be back."

"Enjoy your alone time."

Enar stopped and turned to see Jamie's lips fighting a battle not to smile. "What?" What did a boy his age know about "alone time"? "Never mind." Slicing his hand through the air, he turned in the direction he'd been heading and followed Lily to the stream.

She knelt beside the small stream, a water bag immersed in the slow-moving water, the smell of dead vegetation thick in the air. He watched her for a moment, his claim, his exquisite woman. A snap of a twig under his foot caused her to jump, dropping the bag in the water.

"Enar! What are you doing here?" She glared at him before retrieving the bag from the stream. "Besides getting me wet?"

His lips twisted. Oh yes, he'd like to get her wet. Just not in the way she referred.

Huffing something that sounded suspiciously like, "men," Lily marched over to him, wet water bag dripping, and slapped the bag against his chest.

"Hold that, please."

Turning, she marched back to where the other bag lay and proceeded to soak it in the stream, filling it.

Enar looked at the dripping bag clutched against his chest and stared at the petite woman who put it there. His woman seemed to have a spark of fire in her. Like his mother.

He shook his head at the thought, vanquishing it. He didn't want to think of his mother or where she lived. Those thoughts led back to Lily's questions.

"Why did you follow me?"

He shrugged and blurted out the first thing that came to mind, "Alone time."

She pulled the bag out of the stream and turned to stare at him. Thin light dappled her face, obscuring her expression, but he thought he saw a brow rise. The water bag dripped on his ruined leather shoes as he crossed his arms and stared back. She didn't need to know that was the second idiotic thing he'd said in the last two days, right behind, "sure you can pack a bag."

"Alone time?" Her lip quirked.

"That's what I just said." And wished he could take back.

"Hmm. Here? In the woods? With no invisibility blanket? Where anyone can see us?"

He shrugged, shifting the water bag so it no longer dripped on his boots.

"I think I need to get the water back to the campsite. Then we need to make sure Jamie gets under his blanket and stays put so we don't have a repeat of this morning. Then we can see about alone time. All right?"

She didn't move, remained kneeling by the stream, her words belaying her unease. Enar dropped his arms and tried his best not to look frightening.

"That is acceptable." Why couldn't he have just said he was worried about her? Because Watchers didn't worry about their claims. "You go first." He gestured for her to walk in front of him.

Where he could watch the sway of her hips as she

stalked past him, grabbing the water bag from his hand as she went.

He needed to learn how to talk to her. How to tell her what he felt. How did he explain how worried he had been?

Lily placed the water bags with the rest of their things and walked to where Jamie sat on a log staring into the fire. Enar didn't hear what she said to the boy, but Jamie crawled into his bedroll with a glance to Enar.

"Alone time," the imp mouthed, grinning as he pulled the blanket over his head, disappearing from view.

Enar shook his head. Jamie was trouble as only a boy his age could be. Good thing flying meant they'd be home in the next day or so and Jamie would no longer be his responsibility.

Lily, though, would still be his. *His.* Enar grinned, watching his woman straighten her shoulders as if about to go into battle. Without meeting his gaze, she marched to the invisibility blanket and bedroll, spreading them on the ground. She sat down and pulled off her shoes.

Meeting his gaze, she shook the corner of the blanket. "You coming or what?"

A willing woman was all the encouragement he needed.

****

Lily watched Enar stalk toward her like a dog about to receive its favorite treat. Except in this case, she was the treat. What was she thinking to offer herself to him like she had? She knew the answer. She wanted more of his kisses and touch.

Even if he was lying to her.

Discovering what he hid was second on her to-do list. Right after seduce him witless. Did she just put that on her list?

Obviously.

Check her out. Going from scared of bedroll romping to wanting more of it in less than a day.

Must be some sort of record.

Heat licked through her veins as Enar sat beside her on the bedroll, pulling off his boots. Despite his secrets, she wanted him like she wanted her next meal. She wanted to be his lover. His friend. His companion of the heart.

And that scared her more than anything else she had experienced over the last day. That road led to heartache, to despair. So why did she have the feeling her feet pointed down that path?

Enar ran a finger down her cheek, turning her to face him. "Hello, lovely."

"Hello, handsome."

His thumb ran across her lips as his gaze met hers, drawing her in, the sounds of night fading until only the two of them remained. His lips replaced his thumb, pressing against hers as gentle as a butterfly resting on a flower.

She opened for him, touching her tongue against his, and then he took possession of her mouth. Tongue thrusting, tangling with hers in a dance as old as time, ravishing, possessing. Leaving no doubt she belonged to him.

His hands shoved her tunic up and she helped him remove it. He yanked his off and with one move had her lying on her back, the invisibility blanket covering them both. His lips returned to their possession, his hands stroking down her side to untie her trousers. She helped him pull them off, fumbling as she tried to untie the laces of his leathers. With a growl, he shoved her hands away, pulling on the strings until they gave way and his erection sprang free.

Propping himself up on his elbows, he thrust inside her, filling her, joining them together. Lily cried out at the invasion, but he caught the sound in his mouth. Last night was gentle, pleasant, but tonight as he pounded into her, he branded her his.

Possession.

Goddess help her, but that knowledge here, now, as he rode her hard, pushed her over the edge and she came screaming, joining her cries to his.

The weight of him collapsed upon her was like a blanket, warm and heavy. He lifted his head.

"Did I hurt you?"

"Not at all."

"Good." He nuzzled her neck as he rolled to his side, one arm draped across her waist. Possessive.

She liked being possessed by him. If only she knew what that possession meant for her future. Now was as good a time as any to ask.

"Enar?"

"Hmm?" He licked her lobe, drawing it into his mouth.

"What am I to you?"

His tongue stopped and he pulled back, looking at her, a crease between his brows deep enough to run a river through. "My claim?"

"Yes I know, but what else?"

"A very exquisite woman I'm happy to have as my

claim. Why?"

No time like the present. "Because I think you're hiding something about what my new life is going to be like and I want to know what it is." Lily held her breath as she stared into the dark orbs of his face.

Enar blinked before schooling his face into a blank shield. "If you can still talk, I haven't done a good enough job." He bent to kiss her, his lips warm upon hers.

She should push him away, refuse his kisses, insist on having a discussion. But his lips felt good, as his touches stroked her blood into a fire.

As the melody he wrote into her skin drew them together in a frenzied passion, her questions, like her thoughts, faded into oblivion.

Chapter 8

Enar flinched, eyes popping open. Tree branches shifted against one another, their leaves sounding like shaken paper. Moonlight glittered through the leaves, dappling the ground. What noise woke him?

A quick glance showed Lily curled on her side, one hand against his chest, her ribcage rising and falling as she breathed. A small tendril of tension released, although his chest still felt constricted.

What had he heard?

Jamie lay under the invisibility blanket, oblivious to whatever mysterious sound awakened Enar. He turned his head to the last place he'd seen Fafnir, but the dragon remained absent. For whatever reason, once Thoren and Keara had disappeared into the woods, Fafnir took to the air, vanishing in a rush of wind.

If the mystery noise didn't come from Lily, Jamie or Fafnir, what or who did it come from?

Thoren and Keara?

As if he was going to go traipsing into their little love nest.

The fine hairs stood up on his body, pulsing rhythmically, causing a sharp spear of sensation to lodge in his lower spine. Rolling out from Lily's hand, he crouched beside her, listening with both his ears and his body.

Magic. Strong, primal magic flooded the clearing,

tripping over his skin, prickling as it touched him. On a primal level, he recognized the source, recognized it as belonging to Thoren. But not solely Thoren's.

With an almost audible pop, the magic drew back, leaving him alone with a flickering fire and a sense of unease. But what about magic made him uneasy? He'd grown up with Draconi, magic didn't bother him at all. As a matter of fact, it made him relaxed, although he'd never admit that to anyone.

The sense of unease grew, pressing against him, insisting he seek the source of the magic. Great. Looked like he needed to intrude on Thoren's love nest after all.

Standing, he yanked on his leathers and with one last glance at Lily, left the clearing in search of Thoren.

Branches scratched the skin of his arms and he slapped them aside. The scent of magic grew stronger and he inhaled deeply, following his nose to Thoren. A roar slammed through his ears. He cursed. That was Thoren and it did not sound good.

Enar broke into a run, following the dying echoes of an anguished roar.

"Thoren?" His friend knelt in front of Keara, head thrown back, magic rippling in waves around him. The smell of fear and anger hung in the air, along with the musk of sex. Keara lay motionless, bare legs spread on a blanket.

Thoren snarled and flipped the blanket to cover Keara's naked form. Enar froze. Goddess's teeth. Scared and pissed off Draconi. Smothering scent of magic overlaying the musk of sex. Unconscious female. He cursed. Some love nest. He'd unknowingly walked right into the beginnings of an unholy chaos. One wrong word and Thoren was liable to breathe fire.

"You Changed. I smell the magic." The obvious seemed a good place to start. And less likely to cause a fireball lobbed his way than if he commented on Keara's prone position.

The Change. The time in a male Draconi's life when he came into his full powers. A ritual unknown to him had to occur or else the male Draconi would be locked in dragon form forever. Like Fafnir. Enar shivered. Sure, he'd love to turn into a dragon occasionally, but to be shaped like one forever? Not likely. Not even Thoren, who was a Draconi, wanted to be locked in dragon form forevermore.

The only thing he knew about the ritual was it involved a female and sex. Both of which Thoren seemed to have. Something though had clearly gone wrong. Not only did his gut scream it, but that anguished roar of Thoren's was the clincher. But what?

As if he was going to ask a distraught Draconi.

"Keara's injured." Thoren's eyes radiated fear.

"You hurt her?"

"Yes. No. She absorbed my magic."

"And that's bad?"

"She's supposed to throw it away, not absorb it. It might kill her. I need to get her to the Temple so the priestesses can perform a healing. Where's Fafnir? We need to leave now."

"Um. About Fafnir. I don't know where he is. He disappeared when you and Keara walked back here."

Thoren cursed. "I can't carry all of you and she needs help now."

"You go. We'll come later. It'll take us awhile, but we'll get there. Still have our feet."

Not that he wanted to use them, but he had no

105

choice. How long would the walk take? A week maybe? It was almost another day by air, which meant about a week or so walking. Would Lily be able to make it? She'd have to. Maybe if he kept the pace slow she wouldn't tire out as much.

Aargh! What was it about the woman that made his mind dwell on her? What kind of Watcher thought of his claim all the time?

Enar watched Thoren wrap the blanket around Keara before picking her up, holding her close to his chest. Enar slapped a hand over his heart. Stupid thing got all erratic when he thought of Lily hurt like Keara was.

Thoren strode through the woods, Enar following, to the clearing where Lily and Jamie slept by the fire. He placed Keara down, took a couple of steps away from her and turned into a dragon. Scales rippled as skin disappeared, muscles elongating into a beast.

See you soon, friend.

"May your journey be quick." Enar watched as Thoren gathered Keara into his talons, grasping her and the blanket. Two hops later and the wind caught his outstretched wings, lifting him into the air. With powerful strokes he headed toward the Temple, leaving them to follow on foot.

Enar ran both hands through his hair. Great jumping dragons. He was stuck with Jamie for a week. What was he supposed to do with a boy when all he wanted was some alone time with his claim?

There he went again, thinking of Lily. Good thing mind readers were non-existent among the Watchers, or he'd be teased without mercy.

What else was new? Since when had he gotten

along with any of the Watchers? This time would be different. He had Lily, the Watchers' perfect idea of a woman. Her alabaster skin and white hair would ensure the other men never made sport of him again. It might even go so far as to prove to his father he was worthy of the old man's attentions.

Aargh. He did not want to think about the old bastard now. Turning on his heel, he strode to where Thoren and Keara had camped. Their bags and bedding lay spread across the ground and he gathered it up. Yet more things for him to carry. On foot. Great.

After stuffing the last item into Thoren's bag, he tied the bag shut. A thought crossed his mind and he couldn't stop the smile turning his lips. He might have to walk all the way to the Draconi Temple, but he'd have plenty of alone time with Lily.

Seemed like Thoren did him a favor after all.

Chapter 9

This must be a dream. The floating balls of color were a dead giveaway, but the woman with long black hair and green eyes wearing white robes trimmed in gold sealed the deal. Lily met those green eyes, so like her friend Keara's, and tried not to flinch as the force of the woman's stare bored into her being.

Black eyebrows rose over wide eyes. "Ah. And who might you be?"

Something grabbed Lily's shoulder, shaking. Lily tried to shove it off, but it persisted.

The green-eyed woman smiled, a sadness pulling at the corners of her eyes. "We'll meet again, I'm sure."

"Lily! Wake up!" The shaking of her shoulder continued, the woman fading from view.

"Lily!"

With effort, Lily opened her eyes, looking into Enar's blue ones.

"Finally, woman. You had me worried. You wouldn't wake up." His thumb stroked her shoulder, the weight of his hand a pleasant warmth.

"Was dreaming." Although she suspected the woman in her dream was real. Alive and well.

Waiting for her.

Most visions came to her while awake. Not while she slept. And even if they did come to her when she was asleep, the people in the visions never spoke to her.

In the past, her dreams had been a foretelling of things to come. Not a way of chatting with strangers.

Who was the woman? Why did she think she'd meet Lily? What kind of a dream did she just have?

"Lily?" Enar patted her shoulder, his big hand gentle. "Snap out of it, woman. We need to leave."

"Oh, sorry." What did he expect? He woke her from a dream. Of course she was introspective.

Lily looked around the campsite, smelled the burnt remnants of the fire, smoke blending in with the gray dawn as it rose from blackened ashes. Jamie sat on the ground across from her, Keara's bag by his side.

"Where're Keara and Thoren?"

Enar's palm rubbed her shoulder. "Keara took a turn for the worse in the night."

"What?" Shoving off his hand, Lily sprang to her feet, heading in the direction she last saw Keara. "Why didn't anyone wake me? I could have helped." Even if it was to hold Keara's hand.

Enar grabbed her upper arm, pulling her to a stop. Lily whirled, eyes level with Enar's chest. "Thoren turned and flew her to the Draconi Temple for healing. There was no use in waking you. There was nothing you could have done."

"I could have said good-bye." Jerking out of his grasp, she threw her hands up chest level, palms facing inward.

He shook his head. "She wouldn't have heard you."

And like mist over water her anger evaporated. "Oh no! I thought she was better. I thought she would be all right. Are you telling me she's going to die?" Lily couldn't get her mind to stop tripping over the fact

Keara was injured. Only last night the two of them had sat together eating. She seemed fine then. What if she didn't make it? What if she died?

Enar shrugged. "I don't know. Come now, we need to leave."

"We can't leave. Fafnir isn't back." Jamie hopped to his feet, fists balled.

Judging by his expression, it looked like he already knew about Keara and was dealing with a lot of righteous anger.

"Fafnir knows how to find his way home. Pick up your bags."

"No! You're not in charge of me!" Jamie stamped his foot, eyes narrowed on Enar.

Enar crossed his arms and glared. Didn't say a word. Lily felt the frost of his glare and she wasn't even in its path. Poor Jamie. Although she had to give the normally shy apprentice credit. It took a full minute of frosty glaring before the boy's gaze dropped. She shivered.

"Fine. I'll pick up these bags. But you're still not in charge of me." With a huff, Jamie grabbed the bags and started to march off.

"Wrong direction. We head southeast, not west." Enar pointed to a clump of trees. "Go that way."

Jamie snarled, but switched directions.

"Don't just stand there, woman. Grab your things and let's go. Daylight is wasting."

Lily ran a hand through her tangled hair. "Can't I relieve myself?"

"As long as it doesn't take all day." He gestured to the woods as he turned in the direction Jamie went. "Jamie! Come back here!"

When Lily returned, the glaring continued with Jamie snarling at the edge of the camp ground. At least he hadn't wandered off. While Enar occupied himself with Jamie's attitude, she grabbed a comb from her pack and pulled it through her tangled hair.

Nothing like having smooth hair.

A quick braid followed by a tie and she stuffed the comb back into her pack, ready to leave. Ready to find her friend. Ready for Enar to tell her about her new life.

As if that would happen anytime soon.

Once she stood beside Enar, he started walking, Jamie running ahead, disappearing behind a strand of trees. At least they headed in the same direction as the boy.

"Are we going to get horses?" Her feet already hurt and they hadn't even left the campsite.

A snort was her reply. "You have a sense of humor."

"There is nothing humorous about wanting to ride. How far is Draconia anyway?"

"Maybe about a week from here. Give or take a few days."

"A week! And we're not stopping to get horses?" Was he crazy?

"We have feet. They work. And horses cost money."

"What? You're saying we don't have money?"

Enar shrugged. "Don't worry, woman. We have enough to eat. I won't let you starve."

Didn't that give her a ball of happiness? She shook the feeling off. Being told she needed to walk to Draconia, walk a bloody week, all day long every day, on top of learning about Keara, did not make her morning.

Although it wasn't as bad as being cheated out of her fair share.

Walking sure didn't endear her to Enar. Jamie was right, they should have waited for Fafnir to return. At least that way they could have all ridden.

"Why don't we wait for Fafnir?"

"Because I don't know if he's coming back. I don't know where he went and if we wait around we become sitting ducks for anyone who might want to do us harm. That's unacceptable."

"So we walk?"

"Yes."

"And it'll take a week?"

"Did I not just finish saying that?"

Definitely crazy. She hadn't walked for more than an hour in years. Maybe not since she was a child. And now he wanted her to stomp through the woods and grass for a whole week? What if Keara died while Lily was busy traipsing through the woods?

The man clearly had nothing between his ears.

Although she had to admit, his talented fingers and tongue made up for it.

Not that he would be getting any tonight after making her hike the whole day.

Lily adjusted her bag and marched after Enar. It could be worse. She could still be in River's Run.

****

Her legs hurt, her feet hurt, her eyes hurt from squinting in the sun and still they walked. No relief in sight, no conversation, no breeze, but at least they caught Jamie.

Shortly after leaving the campsite, Jamie ran off,

disappearing into the trees lining the dirt-packed trail they walked. They found him some time later, wandering through the trees, lost as a bird caught in a storm's updraft. For the time it took them to get back to the path, Jamie seemed relieved to see them. Now he chafed at Enar's grip on his shoulder, trying unsuccessfully to escape.

Considering how bad her feet hurt from traipsing around looking for the little imp, her normal sympathetic nature disappeared like steam over cooling water.

Jamie spun to the side in an apparent attempt to free himself. No such luck. Enar white-knuckled the boy's shirt, his glare forcing Jamie into submission.

For now.

That same glare had turned on her when she asked how far to go until they rested.

She still didn't have the answer, but had long since given up on hearing it.

Lily took a swig of lukewarm, leathery-tasting water. The sun beat down on her head, burning her skin despite her hood and cloak. Cool water sounded wonderful, but she didn't see or hear a stream. Lily sighed. At least the scenery looked pretty. Thigh-high prairie grass to her left, trees off to her right, light fluffy clouds floating through a crystal blue sky, Enar.

She stared at Enar's nicely formed backside and wondered, yet again, why he claimed her. For nighttime bedroll activities? And after walking the Goddess only knew how far, she did not look forward to that activity.

Then there was the little problem of what exactly her life would be like in his village. She knew next to nothing about his society and his unwillingness to talk to her about it made her expect the worst. Would she be shunned like she had been in River's Run? Vilified for her complexion? Would they think her a witch and try to burn her at the stake? Run her out of town? Turn Enar against her?

No, Enar would never let his own people hurt her.

And didn't that make her bricked-up heart leap into the air looking for an escape.

No, no, no. The knowledge she walked out of danger instead of into it did nothing but make her feel safe. *Safe.* Safe was good. Being safe meant not journeying down the road of infatuation. It meant observing but not getting involved.

And the observation noted Enar still hadn't informed her of what she could expect from her new life. If only he'd tell her about her future.

She'd have better luck getting him to stop walking.

Despite focusing on her feet and the pain therein, her thoughts kept returning to Enar. Probably because his fine arse continued to walk in front of her, muscular leather-clad legs eating long strides in the dirt. Lily took another swig of water, drawing her arm across her mouth. She couldn't help but think of being with him when he walked that way. Or any way.

He seemed to care for her. She remembered Enar's dagger pressed against the priest's neck, blood welling from the cut, the vibe of angry warrior spreading through the crowd gathered around them. He took his time in the bedroll, ensuring her pleasure before his own. But he never said why he captured her.

He needed a pleasure slave?

Was the answer as simple as that? Did pleasure slaves experience the type of mind-blowing orgasms like she did with Enar?

Probably not.

All right. So her purpose in being captured wasn't to be a pleasure slave. Although pleasuring each other did seem to be part of her new life.

Not that she was complaining about that. Not at all. She enjoyed being with him. A lot.

Lily caught herself as she tripped over, well, nothing, unless one counted a clod of dirt. What if he locked her in his home and never let her out? Never to see Keara again, never to be free, only to be used for his personal pleasure.

The personal pleasure aspect wasn't so bad. The rest of it was a nightmare waiting to happen. And if that was her lot in life, wouldn't he be more controlling? Tie her up and lead her around like an animal?

Most definitely. Since that hadn't happened, she could only deduce the rest of the thought was flawed.

Stick that on the list of things to ward off a panic attack.

All right. He wouldn't lock her up and take away her freedom. But what if he had a wife? What if she was a mistress?

Oh, mercy no. Being someone's mistress while his wife lived around the corner was not on her to-do list. Too much like her parents' relationship.

"Enar! Do you have a wife?"

Enar spun, dropping Jamie's shirt, a look of complete confusion on his face. "What?"

"Do you have a wife?"

"A mate? Goddess's toes, no. Are you jesting?"

Jamie chose that moment to make a dash for it. Where he thought he was going, she didn't know, but he apparently wanted to get there fast.

Enar glanced at Jamie running free. "Flaming swords, woman! Look what you did. Wait here!" Dropping his bags, he dashed after Jamie.

All right. That didn't go so well. She needed a new approach. Maybe if she drank some more water, the new approach would magically fall into her head.

Stranger things had happened. Take dragons for instance.

Lily grabbed her canteen and upended it, pouring the last drop down her throat. Uh-oh. She needed more water, but Enar told her to wait here. He'd also told her to make the canteen last all day. She tilted her head to the sky, noting the sun overhead. Looked back at the empty canteen. So much for it lasting all day.

She could imagine Enar's glower when he returned from chasing Jamie to find her canteen empty. His glaring no longer frightened her. A man who pleasured her the way he did would never hurt her. At least not on purpose. Right?

Right. Great. Now she was answering herself. Was that a sign of lunacy or overheated brain? *Overheated brain.* If she was crazy it wouldn't be bothering her.

The sun beat down on her head, melting away all thoughts but finding more to drink. Amazing how knowing she didn't have water made her thirstier.

Maybe Enar's canteen was in the lump of bags he dropped. Lily walked to the pile of baggage and rummaged through it, looking for Enar's canteen. Food packages, clothes, Keara's herb bag. No canteen. Lily muttered one of Enar's choice words.

Great, now she was starting to curse like him.

Sweat beaded on her forehead, tumbled into her

eyes. She wiped it away with the back of one hand, wishing Enar and Jamie would return so they could find her more water. He could glare and glower all he wanted as long as a filled canteen was the end result.

She heard what sounded like the gurgle of running water and turned to the right, peering through the cluster of trees lining the path. She glanced ahead to where Enar had disappeared after Jamie. Looked back to the trees. If she jogged, she could dip her canteen in the water, fill it and return before he came back with Jamie.

Lily smiled as she headed toward the water.

Chapter 10

"Jamie!" Enar's boots pounded the packed dirt trail, his sword bouncing against his back, his canteen slapping against his hip.

Why had Lily asked if he had a mate? Her question shocked him to the point where he released his grip on Jamie's shirt, letting the boy make a break for it, leading to his current boot-thumping predicament.

Jamie darted into the grass, doubling over as if it would hide him from view. It didn't. But it did slow him enough for Enar to catch up. Stretching his arm out, he grabbed Jamie's upper arm, pulling him to a stop.

"Let me go! I wanna be free!"

"Hush!" Jamie closed his mouth, eyes narrowing as he glared at Enar. "What is your problem?"

Enar started walking toward the path, dragging a resisting Jamie. What was wrong with the boy? Didn't he realize wandering around on his own was not a good idea?

"I need to find Fafnir! I can't stay with you."

"Fafnir is gone. He left. You can't find him."

"He wouldn't leave me."

He did. "Sometimes adults have to take care of things."

Jamie sniffed. "You think he's coming back?"

No. "He might. But he probably went to the

Temple."

Jamie walked beside Enar, shoulders slumped. "I liked Fafnir. He reminded me of my dad." He ran the back of his hand over his eyes.

"And this is a good thing?" If Enar met someone who reminded him of his father, he'd run in the opposite direction.

Jamie nodded and sniffed. Enar glanced at the boy. Was he crying? Loosening his grip, Enar patted Jamie's shoulder.

"You'll see him when we get to Draconia. And until then, you have me."

Jamie's head tilted, looking up at Enar. "But you're a Watcher."

"And your point is?"

"Watchers are cruel."

"You think I'm cruel?"

Jamie's gaze landed on his shoulder, following Enar's hand up his arm until he looked him in the eyes.

"That's only because you insist upon running off. Lack of trust leads to my hand on your shoulder."

Jamie looked at the ground. Three steps, another back-of-the-hand-across-the-eyes and he sighed. "Fine. I'll give you my word I won't run off again, if you promise not to hurt me or Lily."

"Agreed." That had to be the easiest promise he'd ever made. As if he could hurt his woman. Or Jamie, for that matter. "I'll let go of you now and you'll keep your end of the bargain by not running off. If you don't, I'll string a rope around your waist and lead you all the way back to my home."

One side of Jamie's lip curled as if to say, "I'd like to see you try." He nodded. Enar released his grip, holding his breath. Jamie continued to walk beside him. Whew.

They came around a curve in the path and Enar saw his bags lying on the ground. Saw the bags but nothing else. Where was his woman? Where was Lily?

He scanned the grass, looking for any sign of Lily. A breeze blew across the grass, rustling the stems. Taking a deep breath, Enar tried to smell the air, then gave himself a mental smack. As if he could scent Lily. What did he think he was? A dragon? His nose might not work, but his eyes did.

Not that they did him any good. Lily was nowhere in sight. Where had she gone? A hard hammering in his chest caught his breath. Pressing a hand against the pain, he managed to drag in a mouthful of air, planning on bellowing her name.

He never got the chance for a scream reached his ears, terror dripping from every piercing note.

Enar grabbed his dagger out of his boot and sprinted toward the echoes of Lily's scream, the clenching in his chest threatening to cut off his breath.

Time slowed. Things he wouldn't have noticed before passed before his eyes, the color of the blades of grass as they thinned at their tops, the sharp call of birds circling overhead, the crunch of his boots against the ground. Jamie ran behind him as he dashed into the trees lining the path.

Enar ducked under a branch, ripped one free of his shirt. The air felt cooler under the trees and then he came to a stream. A fast moving stream. A fast moving stream his woman had fallen in laden with her bags.

And by the looks of things swimming was not her forte.

Enar ran along the stream bank, stripping the canteen and weapons from his body, keeping an eye on Lily as the current swept her under. He jumped in the icy water, immediately sinking to his chest. Pushing off the rocky bottom, he swam in powerful strokes to Lily. Her head bobbed, the weight of her pack and the strength of the water pulling her under only to push her back up. Her arms flailed, slapping the water, getting nowhere. A wave splashed over her head, she started to cough only to get hit by another wave.

When the wave receded, her face remained in the water. Oh, Goddess, no, no!

Enar swam faster, ignoring the pain in his muscles. One stroke, two and then he reached her. Yanking her head out of the water, he draped an arm across her chest, resting her head against his shoulder. A wave crashed over him and he spit water, coughing it out of his lungs. Kicking hard, he propelled them to the shore.

Jamie stumbled out of the underbrush holding Enar's weapons and dragging the packs Enar dropped in his rush to Lily.

"Is she drowned?" Jamie dropped everything and ran to help Enar pull Lily out of the water.

Ignoring Jamie, Enar yanked the bag from Lily's back, drawing the leather straps down her arms. Laying her on her back, he tilted her head to the side, letting the water accumulated in her nose and mouth drain onto the leaf-covered ground. Then he pinched her nose, tilted her head back, pressed his lips over hers and blew air into her lungs.

One, two, three, four.

Tilting his head, he held his ear over her mouth, praying to the Goddess.

Nothing happened.

Cursing, he started to pinch her nose again, but Lily coughed. Enar turned her to her side and whacked her on the back as she spit up water. Her eyelids fluttered as she drew in a ragged breath. Enar thumped her back again for good measure and was rewarded with another cough.

He heard the metal rasp of a fire-starter, followed by the thick smell of wood smoke filing the air. A quick glance over his shoulder showed the remarkable sight of Jamie starting a fire. Maybe the boy wasn't as big a nuisance as he'd thought.

Tremors vibrated his hand and he saw Lily's body shake. Rolling her into his arms, he stood, carrying her to the fire's warmth.

By the time he walked the few feet to the flames, he shook, tremors racing through his limbs. Must be the icy water. Even a warrior trembled after a plunge into waters that chilly. Lily shook too and his chest pains returned.

Kneeling, he placed her next to the fire on a pallet Jamie made and began to strip her wet clothes from her trembling body. Jamie fetched a blanket and covered her with it, tucking the corners under her. Enar rubbed his chest. Bloody thing wouldn't stop hurting and looking at Lily covered in blankets only made it worse.

He turned to his pack, pulling out a rag to dry his woman's hair. Her gaze was trained on him when he turned to face her.

"Thank you," she wheezed.

Enar looked at her red eyes, red nose and red blotches on her cheeks and his breathing stopped. If he had been farther away from her, if she hadn't screamed, if he had run slower, his exquisite woman would have been lost forever. His grip tightened on the rag.

"What in all things holy were you doing by the stream, woman?" As the words left his mouth, he wondered which of them was more surprised by his bellow.

Lily's eyes narrowed into slits as she pushed herself up on one elbow. "I ran out of water and went to get more. How was I supposed to know the bank would give way under me?"

"If you had stayed where I told you to, none of this would have happened."

"If I had stayed where you told me to, I would have been thirsty."

"But you would have been dry and not half-drowned!" The thin cloth of the rag ripped in two and Enar threw the pieces onto the ground. "You didn't stay where I left you!"

Lily blinked, staring first at the pieces of cloth and then at him as he knelt beside her, gulping in air as if it were a soothing draught. "I'm sorry, Enar. I didn't realize this would happen. If I knew I was going to fall into the stream I wouldn't have done it."

Enar took a deep breath and waged a silent battle to still the rage burning inside. "I know. You just...when I saw you in the water...I thought...well, I'm glad you are all right." He picked up one of the scraps of cloth. "Let me dry your hair."

"Oomph!" Lily said, her voice distorted by the rag covering her head. Her arms pushed weakly against his.

Maybe he was rubbing a bit too briskly.

"Sorry."

But he had to ensure she was all right. What he

needed to do was cover her body with his, sink himself between her thighs and tell her without words how thankful he felt that she lived.

Something told him she would not appreciate it right now.

"Here Lily, I made some tea for you, if you think you can drink it." Jamie held out a cup.

And wasn't the boy helpful all of a sudden. Must be making up for all those times he ran off.

Wonder how long this behavior will last.

Lily took the cup, her hands trembling hard enough to slosh the liquid. Enar covered her hands with his, helping to steady the cup as she drank. He felt the chill of the stream in her bone-white fingers. Despite the blanket, she remained cold. Cold? Try freezing.

As in, if he didn't do something soon, she might catch a lung cold and die.

Which would leave him returning to Draconia minus his exquisite woman.

Enar rubbed the ache that slammed into his chest at the thought.

"Turn around Jamie."

"Why?"

"Because I'm going to undress and get under the blanket to warm up Lily."

Jamie made a face and turned around. Enar made quick work of his clothes and slipped under the blanket, curling around Lily, who placed the cup of tea beside her. She snuggled next to him and he couldn't stop the shiver passing across his skin. Did she even have a pulse?

Yes, yes she did.

He breathed a sigh of relief as his fingers slipped

from the pulse point in her neck.

"Jamie, lay on the other side of her. On top of the blanket."

For once the boy didn't argue, just laid himself next to Lily back against hers, facing the fire.

Enar released a shaky breath as his arms tightened around a shivering Lily. Tucking her head under his chin, he stroked her back, trying to calm her trembling. If only he hadn't left her alone. If only he had run faster. If only, if only. His mind raced with possibilities and he forced himself to focus on the here, the now. All that mattered was the feel of Lily's skin against his, of knowing as long as he touched her, she would come to no harm.

****

Lily snuggled against Enar's warmth, pressed between him and Jamie, trembling despite their body heat.

Would Enar punish her for wandering off, costing them valuable time? It wasn't her fault the bank caved in under her weight. Having the water pull her under, unable to breath, the weight of her clothing and packs dragging her down terrified her. How close she came to dying, closer than anything the town's priests had threatened.

If Enar hadn't noticed her gone when he did, she would have drowned. Fine tremors shook her body, tightening her stomach muscles, curling her into a ball.

Frightened and embarrassed, what a combination. Where was the invisibility blanket when she needed it?

Enar's hands stroked her back until her muscles released, her legs straightening. His muscular arms clasped her against his chest, her legs entwining with his, as if she became part of him. As long as she focused on the now, the heat of his skin, the warmth of his embrace, her limbs stopped trembling. But once she remembered the plunge into the icy water, the currents pulling her under and away from the bank, the certainty death breathed down her neck, the shakes started again.

Lily burrowed her head against Enar's chest, the thought of looking him in the face too daunting. At least he no longer seemed angry.

"Lily, love. Don't. Ever. Scare me like that again." His voice rumbled against her ear.

Lily nodded. Not hard at all to make that promise. Swirling away in water currents to another life would not make her future to-do list.

"Look at me."

She pressed her head against his chest. Why did he have to ask that? Never mind she talked to him only minutes before. At the moment she couldn't stand to give anyone her gaze. They might see the fear in her eyes, know she almost died and pity her for it.

A finger, thick and blunt, reached under her chin, forcing her gaze to his. She stared into blue eyes, and it seemed as if she fell into their depths, took a dive off a cliff and landed in the blue waters of Enar's gaze.

And while she floated on the currents of his emotions, she saw they mirrored her own. His gaze reflected the fear possessing her and it seemed so easy to give him her fear, to hand it over, to forget about its controlling tendrils snaking through her veins.

Enar kissed her forehead, releasing her chin. Lily's limbs relaxed, freed from their burden of tension, and she floated away into sleep, knowing Enar would keep her safe.

Chapter 11

Lily curled onto her side, a stone pressing through the blanket into her hip. Once her limbs stopped trembling she'd move the thing. A breath rasped out of her lungs, caught in her throat and she hacked up more water. Guess that meant time to get moving. Lily opened her eyes, surprised to see dark shadows over the landscape. When she fell asleep sunlight covered the ground. Where did the light go? And where was Enar?

A cough later and she rolled over, her gaze focused on the campfire, its yellow and orange flames licking the air. No Jamie, no Enar, nothing but her and her blanket.

And her packbag. With her wet clothing someone threw over the bushes to dry. How nice. Now she had no dry clothes to wear.

Maybe Enar's bag contained dry clothes. Wrapping the blanket around her naked body, Lily ignored the pressure in her chest and the feeling something was seriously wrong, and walked over to Enar's packs. A wet shirt and pair of wet leathers spread across a bush, drying.

Please tell me he has another spare set in his bag. She knelt and rummaged around until she found a black shirt and leather trousers.

She glanced around. Still no one present. Which meant they'd show up right when she dropped the blanket. Oh well.

But they didn't. Lucky for her, seeing she looked like a child playing dress-up with her parents' clothes.

Enar's shirt hung past her fingers, off her shoulders and halfway down her thighs, long enough to make a dress. But as the night air carried a chill, she pulled the leathers over her bare legs and rolled the hems up. A strand of rope around her waist completed the outfit.

Wasn't she a sight.

The bushes rustled and Lily whirled toward the noise, heart in her chest. What if it was a wild animal? How would she defend herself?

Yanking a smoldering stick from the fire, she faced the noise.

"What are you doing, woman?" Enar's voice boomed from behind her.

Lily let out a squeak, dropped the smoldering stick on her bare toes, jumped back and landed wrong when her feet finally reconnected with the earth. Her arms windmilled as she fell backward.

How graceful could one person be?

Right before she hit the ground in a heap of embarrassment, strong arms grabbed her around the waist, hauling her upright.

"Woman, I swear, you are an accident waiting to happen. What were you thinking, picking up a burning stick?"

She turned to face him, gesturing over her shoulder. "There was a noise in the bushes and I was trying to protect myself."

"That's why I'm here."

"You weren't around."

"I am now." His eyes bored into hers and Lily

shivered. "What are you wearing?" Enar held her at arms length, raking his gaze over her body. One corner of his mouth twitched.

Lily felt her cheeks flame and she doubted it was from the fire. "Mine were all wet. Yours weren't."

The twitch in Enar's mouth gave way to a grin followed by a chuckle. "You look good in those. Maybe I'll just give them to you."

How humiliating.

The feeling washed away on a wave of coughing. No more water came up, but her chest suddenly felt cinched by a tight band of red-hot fire. Enar patted her back. It had no effect, but she appreciated the effort.

"Hurts," she gasped, pointing at her chest before another cough rolled through her.

"Jamie!" Enar bellowed, as he helped lower her to the ground. "Where is that pesky lad? Jamie!"

Lily drew her knees up to her chest and rested her head on top of them, trying to draw in a breath through the pain. What happened? She felt fine when she first got up. Now she felt feverish with a tightness crushing her chest.

She'd gone from well to ill in under a minute.

She might not have Keara's healing abilities, but she knew this was not good.

Twigs snapped as Jamie came running, appearing from behind a bush with a rustle of leaves.

"What's wrong?" He slid to a stop beside Enar, panting like he'd run a great distance.

"Lily can't breathe. Do you know anything to help her?"

"You're the adult."

"You're the apothecary's apprentice."

"Keara never said nothing about what to do when someone almost drowned."

Enar cursed.

Jamie took a step back. "I can try."

"Do it. She has the beginnings of a lung fever."

Enar sat beside her while Jamie rummaged through Keara's herb bag. Lily leaned into Enar, willing him to give her strength, to heal her. It wouldn't happen. She knew it. She felt the illness in the swallowed water spreading through her lungs, choking her breath. She'd never see Keara again. She'd never discover what secret about Draconia Enar withheld from her. She'd never leave these woods.

Wasn't she morbid all of a sudden?

Looking death in the face tended to do that to a person.

She didn't want to die. She wanted to live with Enar. She wanted to see what life could be like away from superstitious priests and hateful townsfolk.

Maybe Jamie knew more about herbs than he thought. Maybe his concoction would help her.

She could only hope.

****

Enar rubbed his chest. Considering how often and hard he'd been rubbing the thing over the past day, he was surprised his shirt didn't have a hole in it. Not to mention the skin under the shirt.

Rubbing didn't help the pains, nor did it do anything to lower the fever coursing through Lily's body.

Sweat beaded on her forehead as she shook from the fever's chills. Jamie's draught the night before had done nothing to help her. Not that he blamed the boy.

An apprentice only knew so much. What she needed was one of the healing priestesses.

Who just so happened to be several days from here.

And judging by the wheezing noises Lily made, she wouldn't make the trip.

Another round of rubbing his chest resulted in nothing happening. The pain remained and Lily still wheezed.

Enar's hand dropped to his side, fingers drumming against his leg as he paced by Lily's pallet. Where was Jamie? The boy had administered a tea to Lily and then wandered off. Maybe wandered was the wrong word. Ran out of the woods was more like it. At any other time he'd be chasing the boy, but right now he had more important things to worry about.

Like that wheezing noise Lily made every time she inhaled.

One minute he paced beside Lily and the next he threw himself across her to shield her from the sudden gust of wind that shook the leaves from the trees. Downburst from dragon's wings.

Enar felt a glimmer of hope.

Jamie's shout echoed in Enar's ears. "Fafnir's here! He came back!"

Enar sat back on his heels as hurried footsteps beat a rhythm in the crack, snap and pop of dry twigs strewn over the ground. One of these days he needed to teach the lad a lesson in walking quietly through the underbrush.

"Fafnir came back! He came back!" Jamie slid to a stop, bouncing on the balls of his feet.

"Good. Maybe he can take Lily to the Temple."

"He said to bring her to him since he can't get

under the trees."

Not a problem. Enar picked up Lily and her blanket and carried her through the trees to where Fafnir sat on the dirt path. Thin light from a just risen moon shone on the dragon's scales, making them gleam even in the dim light. Fafnir glared at Enar with narrowed eyes, his lip pulled into a snarl.

It appeared someone forgot their happy tea this morning.

Watcher. What did you do to the woman?

"Pulled her out of the water. She has a lung fever." *Will you help her?* Those words stuck on his tongue.

Hmm. Fafnir drew in a breath. *She is dying.*

This time the words didn't stick. "Will you help her?"

If she is healed, who is to say you will not injure her again? Perhaps it is better if she journeys to the next world.

Enar opened his mouth to roar, then shut it with a snap. Roar? What did he think he was? A dragon? But everything inside cried out with agony at the thought of losing Lily. His rage-churned grief boiled over, slamming into Fafnir.

The dragon blinked, his eyes widening.

"Will you help her?" Jamie asked, appearing beside Enar. Or maybe he'd been there all along and Enar hadn't noticed.

Did the Watcher hurt the woman?

Jamie shook his head. "Nuh-huh. He wouldn't do that. She fell in the stream and he pulled her out. Now she's sick and I can't fix her."

"Will you help her?" Enar wanted to shake the aide out of Fafnir, wanted to scream and fight until he secured help. But his hands were a little busy holding Lily and something told him in a fight with Fafnir, he might not be the winner.

Watcher. You never cease to astound me. You would not physically harm that woman, would you?

Never. "No, I wouldn't. Are you able to take her to the Temple?"

The Temple cannot help her. She would not last until then. Enar felt the words like a hard punch to the chest, painful and breath-stealing. *But the females in my family were healers and I learned a bit from them. If you will place her on the ground, I'll try to remember my lessons.*

At least his breath returned. Although Fafnir's words didn't install a lot of confidence. What choice did he have?

Enar placed Lily on the ground, straightening the blanket around her. She stirred a little, her eyes fluttering open.

"What?"

"Shh. Fafnir's back. He's going to help you." Enar stroked the hair from her face.

"Hmm." Lily's eyes closed.

Step back, Watcher. Fafnir's breath puffed against Enar's cheek, a touch of fetid air. Had the dragon ever heard of mint leaves?

Not funny Watcher. Cells don't come with tooth-cleaning sticks.

"I didn't say a word."

Enar didn't see well in this light, but he got the impression the dragon was puzzled. It seemed Thoren wasn't the only Draconi to hear Enar's thoughts. He needed to remember that wonderful fact.

No, you didn't, did you? You are an enigma, Watcher, one that I will puzzle over later. Now, step away from Lily.

Enar took a step back, followed by another at the waving of Fafnir's forelimb. A couple of steps later and he stood next to Jamie, watching as Fafnir nuzzled Lily with his snout. Then he took a step back, lifted his foreleg and placed it on Lily's chest.

"Hey!" Enar tried to rush forward, tried to save his woman from being squashed, but Jamie grabbed his arm.

"No! He's not hurting her. See he's barely touching her."

Blinking the anger away, Enar saw Jamie was correct. Fafnir's foot barely touched Lily's chest. But still. If the dragon lost his balance, Lily was done for.

"To heal, you have to touch them, but touching her with his snout didn't work, and since he don't got no hands, he has to use his foot."

"How do you know that?"

"That's what he told me when I asked him to heal Lily. He didn't know if his snout would work. He didn't know if he could heal her at all, but the Temple was too far and he had to try. You know? Hey, look-it! See how his leg's glowing? That means it's working!"

Sure enough, Fafnir's foot and up to the wrist joint of the forelimb throbbed a dim pinkish light that bathed Lily in its glow. Enar released a breath he had no memory of holding. The ache formerly known as his chest eased. It seemed like the bloody pain had a relationship with Lily. An unwelcome thought he refused to process at the moment.

Time passed in a series of breaths, his, Jamie's,

Lily's wheezing ones. Or he should say, no longer wheezing ones. Fafnir removed his foot from Lily's chest and she drew in a soundless deep breath.

Praise the Goddess.

Enar hurried to Lily's side and knelt, running his fingers down her arm. Her eyelids fluttered.

The illness is gone from her lungs. Endeavor to keep her away from bodies of water until she knows how to swim.

"Thank you." Enar touched Lily's arm, watching her take an easy breath, one that went in and out without making a sound.

Lily chose that moment to open her eyes. "Wha—? Where am I?" She tried to push herself up and Enar helped her. Holding her close sounded like a wonderful idea. If he held her, she couldn't do something stupid like fall in a stream and drown.

Enar touched her cheek. "Fafnir healed you. You were sick."

"I can breathe better now." She turned to Fafnir. "Thank you, Fafnir. Whatever you did, I really appreciate it."

Fafnir bobbed his head. *I am glad you're pleased. Where are Thoren and Keara?*

Enar slammed mental barriers around his thoughts. He refused to tell Fafnir what happened.

"She got sick," Jamie said.

"And Thoren flew her to the Temple," Lily finished.

Enar gathered Lily into his arms and stood. When he turned to face Fafnir, he took a step back. Not that he was scared of the dragon. But a male Draconi with steam coming out his ears and mouth was not something you wanted to cozy up to if you liked your arse covered with skin. He took another step back, trying to get out of range of a fire-blast.

Draconi and their overactive sense of caring for their females.

"I'm sure Thoren made it to the Temple with her. The priestesses will care for her."

Steam stopped wisping from Fafnir's mouth, which Enar took as a good sign. So he continued speaking.

"Thoren's fast. He's probably already at the Temple. She's getting the help she needs." He felt the push of Fafnir's thoughts against his own, trying to push through his barriers, trying to determine the truth of his words. He poured more energy into his mental barriers and tried to look like he believed his words.

She appeared to be fine. Perhaps the young Draconi harmed her.

More than you know. A thought best left to himself. "Thoren said she was ill and he would fly her to the Temple." Paraphrase, paraphrase. "We'll see them when we get there."

Fafnir threw back his head, releasing a roar that shook leaves from the trees. Lily clasped her hands over her ears, pressing her face against Enar's chest.

"Fafnir! We'll see them soon. It'll be all right." Jamie ran to Fafnir.

"Jamie! No!" Enar took a step forward, but Jamie had already reached Fafnir. Instead of blasting the boy into oblivion, Fafnir's roar ended on a wisp of steam and a snuffle.

Jamie's arms tried to surround the massive chest and failed. But he managed to calm Fafnir. Point for the boy. A point that came nowhere close to making up for the lack of obeying Jamie had exhibited on this journey.

"You can put me down," Lily whispered. "I'm feeling better."

Enar glanced at Lily. Did his woman actually think he would rather put her on her feet as opposed to holding her? Or was she insinuating he wasn't man enough to hold her for a long time? Either way, she was right where she needed to be.

"What? Think I can't hold you?"

"I might be heavy."

What a jester, his woman. "Woman, sopping wet, you aren't heavy."

She chuckled.

"Jamie, I'm taking Lily back to our bedroll." *Where I will ensure she doesn't want to leave it for some time.* "Think you can stay out of trouble for awhile?"

Jamie harrumphed as he dropped his arms from the dragon's chest and turned to Enar, nose wrinkled. "Grown-ups. Yuck. I'll sleep with Fafnir."

Uh-huh, Fafnir undoubtedly loved that idea.

Jamie is welcome to stay with me.

The glare Fafnir turned on him, spoke volumes: you *are not welcome to sleep near me.*

Likewise. What was it with the Draconi? Enar got along with Draconi better than he did his own race of Watchers, yet Fafnir seemed to have some grudge against him. *Who cares about the grumpy dragon.* For now he held a willing woman in his arms and soon to be in his bedroll.

"Thank you, Fafnir. Try not to let him run off. He's good at it."

Try not to harm the woman. Watchers are good at

it.

This one isn't.

Was that a bit of respect in Fafnir's eyes? In the tilt of his head?

Enar turned, carrying Lily back to their campsite. Fafnir's behavior belonged in the category of thoughts for another day. Did he really care about whether or not his traveling companion disliked him when he had a willing woman in his arms?

A woman it was high time he marked.

And where did that thought come from? He wasn't Draconi, who marked their females with a bite. Clearly he was having an identity crisis brought on by excessive time with the Draconi. As soon as he returned, met up with Thoren and gave his report to the Council, he would take Lily back to his village to show her off. To prove to the Watchers he was every bit as good as they were. To show his father he found the Watchers' ideal woman.

Enar shuddered. And then he'd lose any chance he ever had of Lily caring for him.

But now. Here and now, under the trees, in his bedroll, he could make Lily care for him. He could bind her to him with strands of desire and hope passion kept her there once he returned home.

Chapter 12

Lily watched the determined set of Enar's jaw as he strode through the trees to their campsite. He refused to set her down, insisting upon carrying her. Not a problem. Being carried felt a bit odd, but enjoyable. What woman wouldn't want to be held by a muscular, attractive, and attentive man?

Nothing wrong with her in that regard.

Nothing wrong with her at all. She drew in a deep breath, relieved to feel no pain. No fever either. She didn't remember much of the healing, but she did remember the weight of Fafnir's foot resting upon her chest. And when he removed it, the pressure weighing down her lungs lifted, allowing her to breathe. Before he removed his foot, warmth infused her, bathing her body in drops of peace. It had been years, but that feeling had happened once before. On the day she became friends with Keara.

That day stuck in her memory like honey on fingertips. She remembered the sounds of her parent's store as customers came and went, the feel of the hard wood under her bottom as she sat behind the counter playing with her doll. The blurry shapes of objects, the tinkle of the entrance bell as Keara and her grandmother entered the store. Keara never said what made her notice Lily, if she saw a kindred outcast spirit, if she wanted the doll, if she wanted a friend.

Sitting beside Lily, Keara put a finger over her lips, a warning for a secret, the first of many between the two. Then she placed her hands on either side of Lily's face and poured into her what Lily could only describe as warmth coated with peace. It couldn't have taken long, no one noticed what two girls did as long as the doing didn't interfere with store business, but when the warmth faded, Lily could see.

Shapes, colors, outlines. The grains in the wooden floor. The stitches in her doll. The whiteness of her skin. How Keara's hair shone bright red as she slumped against the wall, unable to move. Lily's eyes popped wide and stayed that way as she stared around her, as she saw her parents clearly for the first time.

The warmth and peace felt the same as when Fafnir healed her. What could Draconi not do? Heal the blind, restore the almost-dead to life, turn from dragons into men. Maybe their abilities also included raising the dead.

Wasn't she a wit?

"You're lost in thought."

"Umm," Lily looked at their campsite and back to Enar. Weren't they on the path? "I guess so."

He placed her on the bedroll, loosened the laces of his shirt and pulled it over his head. "If you're thinking, then I'm not doing a good enough job of distracting you."

Fighting off death and winning—even if she did have help winning—made her realize how much she wanted Enar, how much she needed his touch on her skin, the feel of him inside. Lily let the smile breaking over her lips spread to her face.

Heat pooled in her core, flushed her skin, tightened

her nipples so they brushed against the fabric of her shirt. Not hers, Enar's. And didn't that thought heat her more. Dressed in his clothes, about to be filled by him, but not loved by him.

Love? Why did that word pop into her mind at a time like this? Emotions were fragile things, liable to break in the slightest breeze. She didn't need his love. She needed his caress, his touch, his ability to save her from harm, which was worth a lot more than an emotion.

She pulled his shirt over her head, gasping as chill air brushed her erect nipples. Darkness bathed them, punctuated by the dying breath of firelight dancing across their skin. Even through the darkness she saw Enar's pupils dilate, saw him take a deep breath as his gaze raked her from head to toe.

He cared. She squelched the thrill in her chest and slipped off the rope holding his leathers around her waist, shoving them over her hips. Less clothing made her feel free, unfettered. She stretched against the pallet, raising her hips to him, beckoning him in a wordless language.

Wasn't she the wanton all of a sudden?

And may the Goddess take her where she laid if it didn't feel good.

Enar's leathers dropped to the ground before she took another breath, his body covering hers. He slipped inside, filling her, completing her.

As he moved above her, he crushed her lips to his, kissing her with tongue and teeth, branding her as his. Each stroke, each kiss, drew her deeper into waters only he could save her from. As the waves of pleasure crashed through her, through him, as she cried his name and he echoed with her own, she felt the waters closing over her head and knew that without him, living was worth nothing. He belonged to her and she to him, despite her mind's decree to the contrary.

Did he realize it? Could he feel the bonds tightening around them as surely as if they possessed a physical body?

Enar collapsed on her, his weight pleasant in its own way. He hid things from her, things she needed to know about her place in his society. Not to mention what his society was like. Things that weren't hard at all to say.

Unless it boded ill for her. She shuddered.

"Am I too heavy?" Enar started to move, but Lily grabbed him.

"No. I just thought of something."

"Blast it, woman. Clearly I need work on my technique if you're still thinking."

She shrugged, batting her eyelids. "Show me what else you got."

"You're killing me." His mouth crushed hers, obliterating her reply.

Who needed a reply? Sensations streamed through her, little touches carrying away her thoughts, leaving her drowning in his embrace.

****

Enar woke to the sound of chirping birds and leaves rustling in the wind. Lily slept beside him, her back pressed against his front. Light drifted between branches, dotting the ground with splotches of color. Light?

He sat up straight, trying to get a reading from the sun. Obstinate thing remained hidden behind the trees' canopies. Nothing for it but to leave Lily's side.

Rolling to his feet, Enar grabbed his leathers and pulled them on. After ensuring the blanket stayed wrapped around Lily, he made his way through the trees to the path where Jamie and Fafnir slept.

Only they were nowhere to be seen. Not on the path, not in the grassy field next to the path, not—he squinted up to the sun—flying around. Nowhere.

And it looked like it was mid-morning instead of the dawn with which he meant to start the day.

"Jamie!" He added a mental touch to the bellow, trying to use mind-speak to call the wandering brat, um, boy.

Uh-oh, flickered through his mind before Jamie snapped barriers in place to keep him from hearing more.

Uh-oh was right. "Jamie! Get back here now!"

Enar felt a gust of air, heard the rushing of wind, and Fafnir appeared, landing in front of him, Jamie sitting on the dragon's back. Crossing his arms, he glared at the boy.

"Don't hurt me! I came right back."

"I know. Go pack your bags. We need to leave."

Jamie slid off Fafnir's back and scurried off into the woods. Enar turned to follow.

You hurt him and I'll kill you.

Enar turned and glared at Fafnir. "What is your problem? I've done nothing to you but free you from your cell."

Fafnir returned the glare, eyes narrowed.

Clearly over twenty years in a titanium-lined cell had warped the dragon's mind. Enar had better things to do than posture to a demented dragon. He started to turn back to the campsite.

Maybe I just don't like you.

Maybe I just don't care. Enar continued walking, ignoring Fafnir's huff of mirth or anger, he didn't know which. Fafnir was the first Draconi he'd met who didn't like him on sight.

And it bothered him more than he wanted to admit.

Watchers shouldn't be bothered by such trivialities. They guarded the Draconi, they didn't become friends with them. Except for him. Thoren was his best friend. Thoren's friends were his friends. Before he claimed Lily, Draconi females fascinated him, and he them. Most Watchers, though, remained aloof, apart from the Draconi. Enar spent so much time with the Draconi he now thought like they did.

Not a good place to be in. No wonder he was the laughingstock of the Watcher village. Something that would change when he returned with Lily, when he showed he found the Watcher's ideal woman, when he proved he was every bit as much a warrior as they were.

When he lost her respect.

Enar shook the thoughts away. One must live in the present, not the future.

He burst into the campsite, stalking to where Lily sat, no doubt awakened by his bellowing for Jamie.

"We need to leave. The sun is halfway through the morning and we're still sitting here. Get dressed and let's go."

Twenty minutes later—who knew it took a woman so long to relieve herself, comb her hair and get dressed—they walked out of the trees and started down the path. No surprise to Enar that Fafnir had flown off.

"He left." Jamie searched the sky, more

disappointment written on his face than Enar wanted to see.

"I'm sure he'll return." Lily patted Jamie's arm.

Enar repositioned his pack and continued walking. Fafnir was one odd dragon. Enough said.

Jamie walked by Lily's side, Lily seemed no worse for her near-death experience, the sun was bright, but not hot, the best day of this journey so far. What were the chances of the rest of his journey going as well? Slim or none?

The day passed, bringing them one step closer to Draconia, to home. Fafnir landed right after they set up camp for the night. Two blinks later and Jamie plastered himself against the dragon's side. Surprise, surprise. The dragon actually looked happy to see the boy.

Should he be glad Jamie was happy or wary the demented dragon would somehow cause Jamie to become demented?

Conflicted much?

I have decided to walk back with you. "You" was spat out like a bad piece of meat.

"Did Fafnir just say something?" Lily asked. "It's rather rude to mind-speak when I can't hear it."

My apologies, Lily. I will project my thoughts so you can hear them.

"Thanks."

I said, I will walk with you. This time "you" came out in a cheerful tone.

Fine. Fafnir didn't like him. He was a Watcher. Watchers didn't care about whether or not a Draconi liked them. Enar shook his head. Why did he care?

He didn't. It was just a fleeting thought.

He was such a liar.

"That's great!" Jamie patted the dragon, eyes sparkling. He mustn't have heard Fafnir's thoughts to Enar.

How are you feeling, Lily?

"I feel fine. Better than fine." She glanced at Enar, who tried to stop a goofy grin from escaping and failed. "Thank you for healing me."

Fafnir inclined his head. *I'm glad you're pleased. So, what's for dinner?*

Chapter 13

If she had to walk one more step, she was going to...what exactly? Take another step? Wait for her feet to fall off? Her legs to cramp? Been there, done that. Well, not her feet. Lily's feet remained attached to her legs, although they felt like falling off.

Step after step after step she walked, until the scenery blurred and all she knew was the sun on her skin, the grass rustling against her legs, the strange tension between Fafnir and Enar.

It sure seemed like Fafnir disliked Enar, but the why of it remained a mystery. She liked Enar's company. Especially after dark in the bedroll. Lily blushed and pulled the hood of her cloak tighter around her face. Obviously too much sun beating down on her fair skin.

Or too many thoughts about a gorgeous naked man and his talented tongue. And fingers. And hands.

She tugged the hood further over her face. It did nothing to hide her blush.

Perhaps you would like to walk in my shadow?

Lily turned to Fafnir. Jamie walked beside the dragon, behind her and Enar. They left trees and shade behind that morning to walk through a field, Fafnir's shadow the only shade. Her cloak offered some protection from the relentless sun, but not enough to keep her from burning in spots. Like her nose and hands. As much as she enjoyed walking beside Enar, shade sounded like a cool drink on a hot day.

Speaking of drinks. Lily took a sip from her canteen and let the warm leather-tasting water attempt to soothe her thirst.

"Enar, I'm going to go walk in Fafnir's shadow. I'm burning."

Enar looked at her, a flash of jealousy in his gaze flickering into concern. His eyes widened. Maybe her nose looked worse than it felt. "I thought the cloak hid your skin better. Are you all right?"

"Sun and me don't go well together. Fafnir offered."

"Get on back there. I didn't realize."

"It's not your fault. I have fair skin. Fair skin does this."

"What are you waiting for, woman? Go walk in his shadow. Scoot, now." Enar gestured with his hand toward Fafnir, worry bleeding from his eyes across his face.

Lily stopped walking, waiting for Fafnir and Jamie to catch up with her. Shade, cooling shade, fell across her and her skin breathed a sigh of relief.

She kept the hood on in case a stray ray of light took aim at her again.

How are you?

"A little—"

Do not speak. Think.

—burned. But other than that I'm fine. Thank you for making me well the other night.

Jamie apparently used mind-speak to ask Fafnir a question since Fafnir's head swiveled toward the boy, but Lily couldn't hear him. Only Fafnir possessed the ability to project his thoughts into her mind. Which was a rather interesting way of speaking. It seemed as if everyone on this journey possessed the ability. Everyone but her.

But she had visions, a "gift" none of her traveling companions seemed to possess. If the priests had known about her visions...she shuddered. Would Enar's people be equally as superstitious?

Jamie's shouts as he climbed onto Fafnir's back shook her out of her thoughts. She stared at the boy as his arms thrust into the air.

"Woo-hoo! I'm on top of the world!"

Enar turned, saw Jamie sitting on Fafnir and shook his head. "That's one way to keep him from wandering off."

"Hey, now. I've been good. I've been keeping my end of our bargain."

Enar inclined his head. "That you have. You all right back there, Lily?"

"Perfect! Thank you."

He stared at her for a second, her lover, her man, his look steaming her blood. Even with a sunburned nose and feet that felt like falling off, she wanted him.

As if he read her mind, he grinned, the turn of his lips a reminder of things those lips could do when pressed against her most intimate skin.

And there went the blush again.

Enar winked and resumed walking.

You do not seem to mind the Watcher.

Lily shook her head, glancing at Fafnir.

He saved me. Three times already and I haven't known him long.

So his rescue obscures you from seeing what he

really is?

What is he?

Watchers are guardians of the Draconi. They are known for their fierceness. They are not known for their kind treatment of women.

Her eyes narrowed. *There is nothing wrong with the way he treats me. Maybe you should start seeing him instead of his race.*

She refused to believe Fafnir. Enar treated her well, cared about her wellbeing. Just because he avoided telling her what her life would be like in his village, did not mean he didn't care about her. He cared. She refused to think otherwise.

Fafnir remained silent for so long, Lily thought he dropped the conversation. When he spoke, the words floated like snow flurries across her mind, as if he drifted in memories so deep they disturbed him. *Maybe you are right. A Watcher did me great harm once. But even before then, they were not my friends.*

What happened?

They walked for a good twenty steps before his voice whispered across her mind. *I was betrayed by my Watcher. How do you think I wound up in that cell?*

You were given the same drug Keara was?

Fafnir snorted steam. *My Watcher told the lord of River's Run about titanium and its effects on Draconi.*

What effects?

It renders us unable to perform magic. Makes us useless. They had a titanium sword when they captured me. He shuddered. *I could not fight them with magic. My curse did not kill the bastards, but it did render them not quite sane.*

Lily remembered Lord Simon's father growing

insane, escaping his home to run drooling in the streets, screaming about men turning into large beasts. He finally died, but not before inspiring several of her childhood night terrors.

You did that?

The curse was designed to kill, not render the recipient insane. But seeing how the titanium in the sword was supposed to keep my magic at bay, I suppose I shouldn't complain.

I'm sorry they captured you.

Me too. He shook, a wave-like ripple cascading from head to tail, causing a squeal of delight from Jamie. *Enough of past memories. Isn't the day nice?*

And with those words, their conversation ended.

The next day, Fafnir spoke of trivial things, like the weather and her continuing sunburn despite walking in his shadow. And she had yet to discover what Enar hid from her about his people, but she felt his resolve weakening.

If she said that enough times then it would come true.

She hoped.

"Hey, look up there!" Enar shouted, pointing to a dark blob of—was that trees?—on the horizon. "Draconia borders. We'll be at the Temple tomorrow."

Did Fafnir just stumble? Lily risked sun exposure and glanced up at the dragon. Apparently not, but tension laced his muscles.

"That's Draconia?" Jamie asked. "How exciting! I ain't never been to Draconia, but I've heard all about it. Is it true..."

Lily tuned out his rambling, focusing on the blur of trees in the distance. Her life would change once they crossed that border. But would it be for the better or for the worse?

****

The fire spat and crackled as Lily watched the flames jump into the air. Due to Fafnir taking Jamie for an evening flight, she had the fire to herself. Enar patrolled the perimeter of the campsite, checking for intruders as he did every night of their journey. Which left her mulling over things she wanted to discuss with him, things she learned over the last two days from walking in Fafnir's shadow. Things she thought Enar needed to know.

Maybe then he'd hop onto the sharing wagon and talk to her about her new life.

"You look lost in thought."

Enar's voice broke the rhythm of the crackling flames and Lily jumped. His hand landed on her shoulder as he sat next to her. She patted her chest, trying to get her heart to calm.

"Don't scare me like that!"

He chuckled. "Sorry. So what were you thinking of that you didn't hear my approach?"

"This and that. Things Fafnir told me."

"Ah. Listening to gossip, now?"

"I would hardly describe learning how he got into that cell 'gossip.'"

Enar stilled, his eyes widening. "And?"

"He was captured by Lord Simon's father who had a titanium sword. Fafnir said titanium causes Draconi to loose their powers."

"Titanium is a bane to Draconi. The only thing known to render a Draconi's magic useless. I don't understand how a mere human would know about titanium."

A Watcher betrayed him, sat on the tip of her tongue, but she refused to let it fall off. Fafnir and Enar had a hard enough time getting along without accusatory words being added to the mix. She opted for a shrug.

"I'll have to report it to the Council. They'll need to send someone out to stop the threat. Humans can't run around with titanium swords. Look what happens when they do."

"He doesn't seem too worse for the wear."

Enar raised a brow, looking like he feared her mind had taken an extended holiday.

"What? He seems fine to me."

"Clearly you don't know Draconi. The dragon is crazy."

"Just because he doesn't like you doesn't make him crazy."

"What else did you learn? Anything about Jamie?"

Good avoidance strategy, Enar. "Actually, I did. He watched his family get slaughtered! The poor child."

"What happened?"

"His mother went out to get water and was killed by soldiers, who stormed their house. Jamie's father got him out and told him to hide, but he saw his father killed by the soldiers. He said his father couldn't work magic."

"That's horrible! I bet those humans had titanium. Although how they knew it would work on Draconi is a mystery. Did he say who his father was?"

"He didn't tell me. Fafnir's the one who told me about Jamie."

"So you have been listening to gossip."

Lily shrugged. "Learning about things is not gossip."

"Uh-huh."

"Seriously. See, you can tell me what your home is like and I won't consider it gossip."

Enar's jaw tensed as he turned to face the fire. She watched him draw several breaths, heard the logs do their snap, crackle and pop routine, and thought once again he would deny her knowledge. "Why do you want to know?"

"Why do you think? I need to prepare myself mentally for what my life is going to be like. I want to know. I need to know. What is so horrible that you are hiding it from me?"

He sighed, running a hand through his hair. "All right." He faced her. "In my village, the claims of warriors live in a house, a very large house in the middle of town. The warriors live in surrounding apartments. So you'd live with the other women."

"So I won't live with you?" *What kind of people were these?*

"No."

"Then what about if I want to sleep with you. What would I do to let you know?"

His eyes widened. "You would send a messenger and I would have you brought to my home."

"Then why can't I stay in your apartment? Isn't that easier?"

"It is not the way of things."

"Why not?"

He shrugged. "This way was found to work the best."

"What about wives? Do they still live in the women's house?"

"There are no wives. Only claims."

"So being claimed isn't marriage?" He'd said this before, but that part of her shoving intellect aside in its rush down the road of heartbreak and despair refused to listen the first time around and clearly needed another lesson.

"Right. There is no bonding ceremony. Only the necklace to keep the claim attached to the warrior. Without the necklace she is free to go."

"But it doesn't come off."

"Exactly."

Lily shivered. Although she now knew what to expect, Enar still hid something from her. And she had a sneaking suspicion she wouldn't like whatever it was.

"What if I want to visit Keara?"

"I will go with you. I spend a lot of time with Thoren and his family."

"What about your family?"

A long pause. "I don't want to discuss it."

"Why not?" Wasn't she nosy tonight? Then again, she wasn't about to pass up getting all her questions answered while he was in the mood to share.

"That's it with the questions, woman. I have a better idea of how to spend time with you that doesn't include conversing."

Enar's lips pressed against hers, his tongue stroking the seam of her mouth, encouraging her to open for him. Sinking into the sensations pummeling her body, she forgot her last question, as the invisible strings drawing them together bound tighter. It surprised her to realize desire, need and longing built the road to heartbreak and despair. And as his hands stroked her skin, his gentle touch a power in and of itself, she didn't care. In his arms, surrounded by his strength, nothing mattered but him.

Chapter 14

Lily slept, the moonlight dappling shadows across her face. She looked so peaceful lying there, unaware of what the morning would bring.

By all that was holy, he was a bastard. A gutless bastard. He should have told her the whole truth instead of omitting certain things about her life in a Watcher's village. He wanted to reassure her he would always be there for her.

That much was true.

As was the Claims' House.

But the rest of it. He had no clue how word would get to him that she wanted to couple with him. Wouldn't that be an oddity. No claimed woman ever wanted to sleep with her Watcher. No Watcher wanted to be gentle with his claim.

Capture her, impregnate her, take her child when he was old enough to hold a weapon and then repeat the process. To a Watcher, women were good for only two things.

As if he was going to tell her that. He wasn't a brainless idiot.

And he needed her again. Just to ensure she wasn't leaving, that her eyes held interest not loathing. But he refused to wake her. Instead he curled against her warmth, throwing an arm over her waist, and breathed in her scent.

At long last, his spirit quieted and he slept.

****

A piercing scream sliced through his dreams, yanking him from sleep. Heart racing, Enar gripped the hilt of his sword before his eyes flew open. Lily! Where...oh, she still lay beside him, one arm moving toward her face. If not her screaming, then who?

The fog of sleep lost in the pounding of his heart, Enar rolled to his feet, staying in a crouch as he scanned the perimeter of the camp. Nothing. Even the birds started singing again.

His skin tingled.

"What is it?" Lily sat up, clutching the blanket to her breasts.

"Shh." Enar's ears strained from listening for something other than birdsong. Only one thing he knew made a noise like that, but tree cats were night creatures, fading into their dens before the sun rose. And the sun was clearly rising.

"Where're Jamie and Fafnir?"

Goddess's teeth. More than one thing screamed that way. Enar dropped the sword and yanked on his shirt and leathers. He picked up his dagger, unsheathing it in case he needed it, although he doubted he would.

"Jamie!" he shouted.

The birds went silent at his bellow, which was a good thing as it allowed him to hear a low moan. He cursed.

Enar ran toward the sound, his ears picking up small shuffling noises which grew louder the farther he ran. What he saw gave him pause.

Jamie lay on the ground, a broken doll, limbs at odd angles.

Dear Goddess, why him? Enar cursed, sheathed his dagger and dropped to the ground beside Jamie.

"I wanted to fly." Tears brimmed in Jamie's eyes, escaping as he blinked.

"You did. Need to work on the landing, though."

"I hurt."

"I bet. Let me see."

Enar didn't need to run his hands over the boy to know Jamie had a broken arm and leg. One of the bones of his lower leg jutted through his trousers, opalescent white covered in blood.

He let loose with another round of cursing.

"Oh, my Goddess! What do we do?" Enar jumped as Lily's voice sounded from behind him.

"Willowbark tea. For the pain," Jamie groaned.

"I can make it. I'll return in a few."

As Lily darted back to the campsite, Enar watched her fine arse hustle before Jamie cleared his throat, causing him to focus on what he should be doing.

"Lad, you are more trouble than you're worth." *Where is Fafnir when we need him?*

Gray eyes shot through with a dose of pain turned his way. "My arm hurts too." Jamie tried to move the offending limb and grimaced.

"Don't move." Enar pointed a finger at Jamie and gave the boy his best ferocious stare, the one used to put the fear of the Goddess in others.

Jamie's face paled even more, his eyes widening as he gulped.

Enar gathered two pieces of wood, strong and thin, and carried them back to Jamie.

"When we get to the Temple later this afternoon, the priestesses will heal you. They will set your arm and leg and you'll be up and about in no time. For now, though, I need to splint your arm so the bones don't move."

Silence greeted his statement, punctuated by the rapid blinking of Jamie's lids. Maybe the silence meant the boy took the do-not-move order seriously.

"And you'll need to give up some of your clothing."

Jamie's eyes grew in size. "Huh?"

"To bind the splint to you. You think it just stays there on its own?"

"I've never watched Keara splint a brokened arm before."

"Broken."

"That's what I said."

Enar grunted. Using his dagger, he cut through the leg of Jamie's trousers above the jutting bone, forming long strips of cloth. Picking up the two sticks, he placed one on either side of Jamie's arm, binding them with strips of Jamie's clothing.

One down, one to go.

He gathered more sticks, this time choosing longer, thicker ones. By the time Enar finished foraging and returned to Jamie, Lily sat beside the boy, a steaming cup of hot tea resting between them.

With Lily's help, and despite Jamie's screams, Enar managed to get the bone back under the skin. It wasn't set right, but they would be at the Temple later in the day and the priestesses would fix his clumsy attempts at healing.

Where was Fafnir when they needed him? The dragon knew something about the healing arts and Jamie needed more help than Enar knew how to give.

"Jamie, do you know where Fafnir is?"

"Nuh-uh. That's why I fell."

"Because you didn't know where Fafnir was?" Maybe the boy hit his head hard.

"We had a game. I'd climb a tree and he'd go invisible and then I'd jump and he'd catch me. And there's this bird's nest that belongs to this ginormous bird up there so I climbed and jumped and how was I supposed to know he wasn't around?"

"Why did he let you do that? You could have died!" Lily shook her head.

"I told you Fafnir is crazy."

"He's not crazy!" Jamie glared at Enar. "He was teaching me to fly."

"Obviously not well enough."

"You don't know nothing."

"I know you're hurt and I'll have to carry you to the Temple. I know Keara," *provided she lived*, "will be mad at you for falling out of the tree."

Jamie blinked and looked away. "I'm sorry," he muttered.

"Don't do it again." As if those words would stop him. But at least the next time Jamie took a dive out of a tree, Enar wouldn't have to clean up the mess.

Where had Fafnir gone? Enar focused on the thought pattern Fafnir used to talk to him and tried mind-speaking to call the dragon.

Fafnir!

He waited for Fafnir to respond while Jamie sipped his willowbark tea. Despite calling the dragon several more times during the tea sipping, Fafnir refused to answer.

Maybe he had decided to go to the Temple without

them. Maybe he flew back to River's Run. Maybe the dragon completed his journey to insanity and was stomping about the countryside.

Bloody goat innards. Fafnir clearly was nowhere to be found. Nothing to it but pack up and go. Jamie needed attention sooner rather than later.

"Jamie, are you sure you don't know where Fafnir is?"

"Do you actually think he would have jumped out of the tree if he knew Fafnir wouldn't be there?" Lily raised an eyebrow at him.

He returned the expression.

"He didn't say anything to me."

"It looks as if he's gone." *Again.* "I've tried mind-speaking, but he hasn't answered. We need to get you to the Temple, Jamie. Lily, stay with him. I'll go pack the bags."

Lily thrust Jamie's empty cup into his hands, and he carried it back to their campsite. He stuffed the cup into a bag and wondered what he'd done to deserve this journey.

Who knew a lad could be so much trouble. Had he been this much trouble at Jamie's age? He paused, hand on a bag's drawstrings, and remembered being a child with Thoren. No, they definitely hadn't been as much trouble as Jamie.

They never fell out of trees.

Not only did he have Jamie to contend with, but Fafnir hopped onto their dysfunctional wagon and whipped the metaphorical horses into a frenzy. Something was off with that dragon. Probably due to all the years he spent locked behind titanium bars. Maybe suppressing a Draconi's magic rendered the Draconi insane.

Interesting thought. One he'd investigate later.

And then there was Lily and her questions. He knew she would want to know what her new life would be like. Knew she would ask questions he'd rather not answer.

So why was he so bothered when she did?

Because he stupidly hoped if she never knew then she wouldn't hate him.

And the chances of her continuing to look at him like he was her savior were about to crash into the land of not-very-likely.

The thought of her blue eyes showing fear or hate caused the strange sensation in his chest again. He rubbed at the pain. Think of Lily hurt and he hurt. Why? What happened to him in River's Run that caused this ache? He needed to see one of the priestesses this afternoon and let her diagnosis the problem.

He froze while reaching for a blanket. Why hadn't he thought about the priestesses earlier? Specifically one priestess. Aryana. The High Priestess. His former lover.

Were there rules for introducing one's present lover to one's former lover?

He grabbed the blanket and stuffed it into a pack. Since he found Lily, the memories of all other females faded like a colorless dream. Lily was the one he wanted to live with. The one he wanted to wake beside each morning. He wanted to see her smile and—dare he say it—love in her eyes. None of which would happen once he returned to his village. And not going back was out of the question. He needed to prove once and for all he was ever bit as much of a Watcher as his old man. Maybe then his father would acknowledge him as his son.

Why he bothered after all these years remained a mystery. His father would rather cut off his balls than admit Enar came from his loins. Didn't matter Enar looked like a younger version of the old bastard or that no man dared look at his mother with lust. Never once had he told Enar he was proud of him. No, not his old man.

Enar kicked dirt over the smoldering fire as he remembered being sent to live with Thoren's family as a child. Undoubtedly, his father meant it as punishment, but he saw it as the best thing to ever happen to him. Thoren's family was so, well, normal. Loving. Everything Enar's was not. And therein lay the problem. No other Watcher grew close to his Draconi ward. By his race's standards he was an oddity. His own father, for all intents and purposes, had disowned him, he'd rather spend time living with the Draconi instead of guarding their lands and he had never claimed a woman.

Until now. And what a woman she was. As his people's epitome of beauty, Lily was the perfect female specimen. The whiteness of her skin, the paleness of her eyes. All Watchers wanted a woman with her beauty, but none had found one. No one but him.

With Lily on his arm, the taunts he endured since childhood, the longings of fitting in, would be over. He could start anew. Prove to the Watchers he was a man.

And she would be his way to his father's heart.

Enar slung the packs over his shoulder and walked back to where Lily sat with Jamie.

Enar dropped the packs at her feet. Jamie glanced at the packs and then to him. "How am I going to get to the Temple?"

"I'll carry you. There are leather straps somewhere," he rummaged through the packs until he found the straps. "Ah-ha, here they are. I'll fasten a sling out of these and you'll be nice and not try to jump out. All right?"

Jamie nodded.

"I'll take some of the bags since you're carrying him."

Lily started gathering bags to carry while Enar constructed the sling. He wrapped the straps of leather around Jamie and gave them a tug.

"Ready?"

Jamie squinted his eyes. "Uh-huh."

Lily helped him move Jamie into a sitting position. Back to the lad, Enar fitted his arms through the straps and stood.

Jamie whimpered. And there went the chest ache again. Apparently Lily wasn't the only cause of it.

Lily tied Keara's herb bag around his waist, handed him a pack that he slung across a shoulder, and picked up the rest of their belongings, strapping them across her body and around her waist.

His claim looked like a pack horse.

"You all right?"

"Yes."

"Give me that one," he pointed to the largest.

"You have Jamie."

"You're about to fall over. Give it to me."

With a huff, she ducked her head out of the strap and handed him the bag. Enar threw it over his other shoulder and started walking.

With each step, Jamie whimpered, small involuntary noises that crept out from between his lips like squeaks from a wheel. Lily pulled her cloak over her head, trying to hide from the light that lit her cheeks like a flame.

Enar stared at the sun. The thing couldn't move across the sky fast enough.

Chapter 15

The path widened into a packed dirt road meandering through trees, weaving itself right up to the largest monstrosity Lily had ever seen.

Tall, gray stone jutted from the ground, carved into twisting shapes she couldn't decipher from the distance. A stone wall surrounded the thing and Lily's feet screeched to a halt.

Enar took a couple of steps before turning around. "We're almost there."

Lily's arm pointed at the gray stones in the distance. "What is that?"

"The Temple. Our destination." Enar started walking.

Jamie twisted around, trying to look over Enar's shoulder at his first glimpse of the Temple. "Will Keara be there?"

"I hope she is. But even if she's not, the priestesses will take good care of you." Enar reached behind him and patted Jamie on the head. "You'll feel better once we get you there."

Lily forced her feet to move forward, the gray stones forbidding even from this distance. What would it be like close up? Was the place as scary as it seemed?

Small dots moved around the periphery of the stones, branching out along what appeared to be roads. Lily's chest seized. *So many people!* She clutched her hood tighter around her face.

The dots grew larger the closer they came to the Temple, turning into black-haired beauties. Lily tried not to stare, but the whole lot of them had Thoren's coloring. She tucked wayward pieces of her hair under the folds of her hood. It still covered her aberrant coloring, but she felt the stares as people passed. She took a step closer to Enar.

Who seemed to be thriving with all the attention. Smiling, nodding, he parted right through the mass standing at the gates. Greetings were tossed their way courtesy of a cluster of white-robed women.

Lily felt her stomach roil at the women's greetings and fawning. The whole lot of them must have sand in their eyes from all the blinking they did.

Once through the gates, the smell of flowers assaulted her, overwhelming her senses. The stone walls opened into a green courtyard, filled with shrubs, trees and multi-colored flowers. White-robed women walked through stone-paved paths winding between the trees.

Peaceful. Beautiful. And totally frightening, for as soon as Enar stepped into the courtyard the conversation died as everyone turned toward them, the only sounds the chirping of birds.

Their stares pierced her attempt at disguise, laying her bare for their perusal, but their gazes didn't show hatred. Curiosity gleamed from their eyes as they glanced at Lily, their gazes settling on Enar.

More simpering and fawning. Great. Enar had obviously impressed other women prior to meeting her. The remaining-aloof plan required a sense of not caring, which was rather hard to do with the current seeds of jealousy running through her veins.

Lily stepped out of Enar's shadow and grabbed his arm. He glanced down at her, a smile on his lips, warmth in his eyes. As his arm slid around her shoulders, he pulled off her hood exposing her hair. Gasps rang out, stilling the chirping birds.

Lily felt heat hit her cheeks and she couldn't help dropping her gaze to her feet. What she needed to do was look at the crowd. To look and see fear and hatred in their eyes. To see how, despite Enar's and Fafnir's words, the Draconi would not like her.

Raising her eyes she saw respect and awe. No fear. No hatred. And the women swarmed around them, speaking to Enar, casting smiles and curious glances her way.

It felt...odd. But comforting. Enar told her the truth about the Draconi. They didn't seem to care about her coloring.

She offered the flock of women a tentative smile.

"Where is Aryana or Annaliese? I have an injured Halfling that needs tending to now," Enar asked the fawning flock.

"I will call her," one of the dark-haired beauties said, her eyes closing, a look of concentration crossing her face.

"Who's Aryana or Annaliese?" Lily whispered to Enar.

"Aryana is the High Priestess and Annaliese is the highest ranked Temple healer. They'll be able to help Jamie."

Lily gulped. Despite her earlier confidence these women meant her no harm, a cold ball of fear took up residence in her stomach. What if this High Priestess thought her coloring was an abomination and tried to kill her? What if Enar couldn't protect her? What if everyone here turned against her?

She was so tired of all these what-ifs banging around inside. Lily straightened her shoulders. She had lived through the priests' threats her entire life. She refused to be cowed by some woman she didn't know.

Enar would protect her. Hadn't he proven that already?

Yes, yes he had. There was no reason to fear. Her fear of the unknown was worse than the reality of the situation.

She took a deep breath. She wasn't afraid. Was. Not. Afraid.

If she said those words enough times, they would come true.

She hoped.

Enar's arm clamped around her shoulders, lending her strength, letting her know he stood by her come what may. The sea of women parted and she got her first glimpse of what must be the High Priestess. Lily's breath lodged in her throat, stilling her lungs.

A gold circlet in the shape of a dragon accented the woman's straight black hair. Dragons embroidered in gold played down the front of her green dress and across the hem of the sleeves. Power seeped from the woman, washing into her like a wave.

She knew this woman. Remembered where she'd seen her.

In her dream. Speaking to her. Letting her know she'd see her again.

Lily's dreams didn't speak to her. Ever. They showed her things to come, not carried on conversations with her. But this woman, the High Priestess Aryana, had visited her in a dream.

The cold ball of fear grew tendrils that snaked through her insides, shaking her limbs.

"Lily!" Keara's voice snapped her head around.

Sunlight glinted off red hair as her friend rushed toward her. The ball of cold, writhing snakes froze, banished into darkness by the sight of her friend. Keara seemed alive and well and Lily returned the other woman's hug, tightening her arms around Keara's waist.

Praise the Goddess her friend was all right. That she felt whole and seemed happy.

"Enar, my friend. How are you?" Thoren stepped around Keara and clasped hands with Enar while simultaneously smacking him on the shoulder. Enar returned the male bonding hug, while Keara's brows drew together as she peered around Lily, obviously looking for Jamie.

Before Lily opened her mouth to tell Keara where Jamie was, the boy spoke.

"Keara!"

Keara reached for Jamie, but paused. Steam roiled out her ears. Steam? Since when did her best friend's ears steam? Was that what happened when she came to Draconia? Whatever the reason, her friend looked like she could cheerfully char something.

"What did you do to him?" She hissed at Enar, steam escaping through her teeth.

Thoren placed a hand on her shoulder. "He didn't—"

"I carried him for the past four hours. It wasn't easy. The lad's more trouble than he's worth." Enar shook his head, ignoring the steam wafting across his vision. Removing the sling, he lowered Jamie to the ground.

Lily knelt next to Keara, watching as her friend stared horrified at Jamie.

"What did you do?"

"He fell out of a tree," Lily said. "Broke his arm, sprained an ankle and broke his leg. We didn't know how to set it."

"Can you heal him?" Thoren asked.

The High Priestess stepped closer, the white-robed women moving out of her way.

"Greetings, Enar," Aryana said, peering over Keara's shoulder. "Is this the male Halfling?"

"Male trouble-maker is more like it," Enar said. "Your Highness."

Lily glanced up in time to see Aryana place a hand on Enar's arm, a look of sadness on her face. By the time Lily finished blinking, the moment had passed. In that moment, though, a root of jealousy sprang to life. That woman liked her man. The power seeping from Aryana might scare her, the fact the High Priestess visited her dreams knotted her gut, but the look in the other woman's eyes just made her want to kill.

So much for intellectual knowledge trumping emotions.

"His arm and leg are broken. I need to get him to the infirmary," Keara said.

Aryana knelt at Jamie's feet. "My apologies for not noticing earlier, young one. Hang on and I'll send you to the infirmary where Keara and our priestesses will help you."

Jamie's eyes bugged at the High Priestess, but the

speechless performance didn't last.

"You're the High Priestess? You don't look old enough. My daddy said you were old."

"Who has my herb bag?" Keara looked at the sacks hanging from Enar's belt, obviously embarrassed by Jamie's outburst.

Lily poked the boy's good arm, hoping he stopped embarrassing her friend. Not to mention herself.

"I'm older than I look. When you feel better you'll have to tell me all about your father." Aryana touched Jamie's shoulder.

The air around Jamie warped, shimmering like the reflection off water on a hot day. He started to disappear right when Enar spoke. By the Goddess, what was happening?

"Catch." Enar pulled the herb bag from around his waist, tossing it to Keara.

Lily watched Keara's hand grasp the bag and then she felt every small particle in her body rip apart. She opened her mouth on a silent scream, which made sense seeing how she no longer possessed a mouth to make words. The pain crashed over her, streaking through her limbs as she disappeared. Her awareness centered on dark blurs of objects streaking past her vision, until they stopped moving, coalescing into a bed and four walls.

A scream pierced her ears, bouncing off the stone walls, crashing through her. It took her a moment to realize the noise came from her mouth. Not that the realization made her lips close.

Keara elbowed her in the ribs and the pain snapped the scream out of her throat. "Lily! Stop that! You'll wake the dead!"

Lily took a deep breath and pursed her lips

together. If they pressed together, they couldn't allow loud noises to escape. Looking around, she saw Jamie lying on a bed, a smile evening out the pain lines etched on his face.

Jamie's eyes gleamed as he looked at Keara. "Can we do that again?"

"Sweet Goddess, I hope not. What happened?" Lily's hand fluttered at her chest, as if the hand could make her heart stop its frantic beating. How did she get from the Courtyard of the Temple into this room? Where were they?

"It's how the Draconi move about. Takes awhile to get used to it. But once you do it's amazing."

Lily watched Keara rummage through her herb bag, looking for Goddess only knew what. Her racing heartbeat calmed, but continued to thud like she had walked a long distance straight uphill. The Draconi traveled by splitting their body into dust and flying across the sky. Where was her list of unusual items? It needed another entry.

Keara spoke some to Jamie, then began cutting off the leg of his trousers, her face lost in thought as she examined his injuries.

"Lily? Would you mind setting the pot of water to boil?"

"Of course not. Where's the pot?"

Keara gestured to the stack of pots against the wall. Grabbing the top one, Lily looked around the room for a pump, finding it in the corner.

Several pumps later she had the pot full and resting on the grill of a brazier, being warmed by red-hot rocks that produced heat without being aflame. She stared at the rocks, mentally adding them to her unusual items list while Jamie told Keara his story of the ginormous bird and falling out of the tree.

How did the rocks produce heat if they had no fire? What kind of land was this?

The rocks held no answers, just continued to emit heat. She turned away. Her face held enough heat from the sun without adding fire-less rocks to the mix.

She went and sat next to Jamie, turning her attention to Keara's movements as her friend prepared an herbal mixture for the boy. Keara gave Jamie a lecture about the herbs she would use to treat him and what he could expect from the bone-setting.

Pain, pain and more pain. And a dose of possible death to round out the brew. Lily shivered. She should have watched Jamie better. Should have ensured the boy stayed feet-down upon the ground. Then perhaps the poor boy wouldn't be suffering so now.

"Try not to kill me," Jamie's voice remained strong, but she saw fear in his eyes.

Lily patted his good arm. "Don't worry. I'm sure Keara knows what she's doing. She's done this before, you know."

She sat beside the boy in silence while Keara finished his potion. What could she say to ease his mind? To ease her own? She settled for more of the arm patting, the silent movements expressing her concern.

"Bottom's up."

Jamie made a face, but drank the cup dry. Soon his eyes closed and he drifted to sleep.

"What do you need me to do?" Lily sat on the opposite side of the narrow bed from Keara, watching her friend as she gathered up splints and strips of cloth.

"Stabilize his arm. I'll pull and adjust the bones,

but I need you to hold it like so," she demonstrated for Lily, "and not let go. Can you do that?"

Lily nodded. How hard could holding an arm be? Keara grabbed Jamie's arm, one hand at the wrist, the other at his elbow and tugged, applying steady pressure. Lily's muscles strained, shaking as she struggled to maintain her hold.

To make matters worse, little spots of lights flickered at the edges of her vision. Flickered in such a way she knew one of her dreaded visions was about to make an appearance.

Why now? Keara needed her help. *Do not pass out, Lily. Do not pass out.* She muttered one of Enar's curses under her breath and squeezed her hands around Jamie's arm, hoping the pain would ward off the vision. Beneath her fingers, she felt the bones in Jamie's arm slip into place, saw the bulge straightening out, and then the flickering lights coalesced into a bright flash and she crumpled to the floor.

Chants and the low rumble of drumbeats sounded in the darkness. Lily looked around, trying to find the source of the chanting, seeing nothing but a whole lot of dark air. She blinked. And again. And one more time for good measure. Darkness remained. Darkness and chanting and drumbeats. Since when did she only hear a vision and not see it? After all, that was why they were called visions and not hearings.

As if realizing a mistake was made, light cut through the darkness, blinding her, the area of the light's focus lit up like the brilliance from a thousand suns.

Keara stood in a circle, the circumference composed of silver runes etched into the stone of the floor. Fafnir stood in the circle with her. Or at least Lily assumed it was Fafnir. It looked like the dragon, but as he and Thoren were the only dragons she'd ever seen, she could be mistaken. Her gut, though, told her it was Fafnir.

"Are you ready for the ritual?" Keara asked.

As ready as I'm going to be, Fafnir responded.

Keara took a long knife, placed the tip upon the silver runes and drew a circle with the knife over the runes. Lily saw the circle spring to life, enclosing Keara and Fafnir in its grasp.

A pressure at her waist caused her to look down. It felt like someone grabbed her around the waist. She looked back at Keara, only to see her friend grow smaller, distant, as if Lily ran backward away from the circle. The pressure at her waist increased as Keara disappeared from view.

What was happening to her?

The pressure on her waist disappeared. Where was she?

White walls surrounded her. White floors, white walls, white fuzzy mist. From out of the mist stepped the raven-haired woman who came to her before in a dream. Aryana. The Draconi High Priestess.

Lily took a step back. As if that would help. If Aryana wanted to obliterate her, Lily wouldn't have a chance. Forcing her feet to stop their backward flight, she squared her shoulders, looking Aryana in the face.

"Greetings, Enar's claim. I apologize for taking you from your vision, but I wanted to ask you a question."

"Why didn't you just come to me in person?"

"Because this way is much more interesting. I

needed to see your vision to make sure you had them."

"Why?" *And how for that matter.*

"Our Seer died many years ago and we haven't found another one as promising as you. Even if you are human."

Lily's eyes narrowed of their own volition. She made an effort to look calm and composed instead of bristly and insulted.

Aryana laughed, the sound like the tinkling of broken glass. "My, my. For a human you have a temper. Now, now, don't be insulted. I'm not meaning to insult you. I want to ask you to stay here at the Temple and become our Seer. You might be human, but you have a gift and we'd like your help."

She must have hit her head hard when she fell in the healing room, because this had to be a dream. A really odd, totally weird dream, but a dream nonetheless. Lily closed her eyes. *When I open my eyes, I'll be in the healing room.*

Aryana remained standing in front of her.

She tried again. *When I open my eyes, I'll be in the healing room.*

Aryana occupied her view. So much for the dream theory. It appeared the real Aryana wanted her to use her cursed visions to help the Draconi. Maybe the High Priestess suffered from a knock on the head too.

"I can't control the visions. I can't help the people who I see in my visions. I can't do anything but watch scenes unfold. It's a cursed gift. I wouldn't even call it a gift. Why do you want it?"

"We can teach you how to use it. How to focus it. It is not cursed. It is only untrained. When you learn to use it correctly, you will not mind the possession of such a gift."

"I am Enar's claim. I wish to stay with him."

Aryana nodded once. "As you wish. But my offer remains open. If you find you would rather work here with us, you are welcome to return herein."

"All right. I thank you for your," *really bizarre*, "offer. If I change my mind, I will let you know."

"Until we meet again, Lily."

Aryana touched Lily's cheek, her fingers cool, and everything vanished in a wave of darkness. Lily opened her mouth to scream, but the wave swept the sound away, leaving her floating in the depths of unconsciousness.

Chapter 16

Enar popped a slice of apple into his mouth and stared at Thoren, who sat across the table from him in the Temple's dining room. Ari had invited him to partake of the meal, and he didn't need to be asked twice. Thoren's brows met his hairline and decided to hang out with the follicles upon Ari's invite. Apparently Thoren's mind was trying to catch up with his sight and drawing a picture his friend didn't want to see. A picture of Enar and Aryana. Together.

Previous history. The only reason it crept into the present was due to him being here at the Temple. Once he left with Lily, the whole romantic interlude would disappear back where it belonged: in the past.

He looked forward to that moment.

For now, he needed to pull Thoren's brows back to their normal resting spot. Needed to convince his friend he saw nothing out of the ordinary. Thoren wouldn't turn him in to be sentenced to death for bedding the High Priestess, but he didn't want to see anger in his friend's eyes when Thoren realized what happened.

It was bad enough he hid the affair from Lily. He didn't need to add Thoren to the hiding-and-lying list.

"Jamie is more trouble than he's worth. Climbing trees, disappearing, reappearing in places he's not supposed to be, falling out of trees." He stuck another slice of apple in and proceeded to show good manners by speaking around the bite of fruit. Hunger beat out manners any day. "Surely we weren't that much trouble as boys."

After all, they never broke bones falling out of trees.

Thoren grinned. "Of course not. We never got in trouble."

"That's what I thought. But I did learn how he came to be in River's Run."

"You did? How?"

"Well, it was really Lily who learned it from Fafnir, who Jamie confided in..."

"Listening to gossip, now?"

Enar shook his head and proceeded to tell Thoren about how Jamie's parents died, including his suspicions that the soldiers possessed a titanium sword.

What else could it have been? Somehow, humans discovered the bane of the Draconi, the one thing guaranteed to drop a dragon. The words "security threat" didn't begin to describe the matter. One Draconi had already suffered, how many more would follow?

How did humans discover our poison? The words drifted into Enar's mind. At least Thoren's puzzlement focused on things other than illicit affairs.

"I don't know, but it seems odd Fafnir was in a titanium cell. Especially when combined with Jamie's father being killed by titanium-wielding soldiers."

"Why did the soldiers come to his house?"

"He heard them say something about 'the boy,' who he assumed to be himself. It seems like the soldiers were after Jamie. If the rogue Draconi worked with the lord in River's Run, then maybe they tried to get Jamie first and settled on Keara when Jamie escaped."

"We need to report this to the Council." Thoren's face twisted as he slammed his hands over his ears.

Since Enar didn't have a splitting headache, he could only assume Keara called Thoren using mind-speak.

"I need to go. Keara needs me. I'll come back and find you."

With those words, Thoren disappeared. Well, that was one way to distract his friend. Lily remained with Keara and apparently Thoren was joining their happy little party in the healing room.

He remained stuck in a dining room with a horde of fawning acolytes and no Lily and too much time to think. His thoughts bounced like leather balls. First on Lily, then to his father, then back to Lily.

The Council would call Thoren and him soon for the report on their mission. By the time the thirteen males who comprised the Council finished pulling details out of the two, the day would be over, which meant it would be too late to journey to his village. Therefore he and Lily would leave on the morrow.

Tomorrow he'd present Lily to his father, prove to all the Watchers he was a real man by bringing a claim—and their ideal one at that—and gain his father's acceptance.

Why did he bother? Being around his father caused his lip to relocate to his cheekbone in a permanent snarl and he swore smoke boiled in the back of his throat. Thinking of the man elicited almost the same reaction. The echoes of Viktor's taunts still rang in his mind. Taunts he wasn't good enough. Taunts he would never live up to his father's expectations.

"Sir?" An acolyte stood before him, holding a plate

of meat. "Would you care for the noon meal of venison?"

Enar inhaled, drawing the rich aroma of roasted venison into his lungs. "I would. Thank you."

With a blush and a smile she placed the plate in front of him and scurried off, leaving him alone with his meal.

And his thoughts. Can't forget about those.

He stabbed a piece of meat with his knife and popped it into his mouth. The juices cascaded over his tongue, the taste an explosion of flavor. Much better than the direction his mind traveled.

His father might be a lost cause, but he wanted to give the man one more chance. And Lily was his opportunity.

Of course, by taking Lily home and introducing her to life in the Watcher's village, he risked losing her forever. Risked alienating her. Risked the kindness in her voice turning to shards of ice.

He could stay at the Temple with Thoren. Didn't know what he would do, but he could stay. Lily wouldn't hate him then, but the Watchers wouldn't see his perfect woman. None would know that he, Enar, the one they laughed at, found the epitome of perfection. Through Lily he would be vindicated.

Her happiness for his father's approval. A chill snuck down his spine and he shook the guilt off.

Taking her home was a necessary risk.

Perhaps Lily would like living there.

Stranger things had happened.

He munched his meal in silence, while listening to bird song drift through the open windows. Good meal. If only he possessed the birds' attitude of happy and carefree instead of brooding and morose.

Enar gestured to one of the acolytes to take his plate. She scurried over like he held a catch of glittering stones, right in time to see him clasp both hands over his ears as pain ripped through his skull.

"Sir? Sir? Are you all right?"

Not unless she considered all right to include having one's brains shattered from the Council's call. It felt like the top of his skull would explode. And as soon as it came, the pain left.

"Sir?" The acolyte had the shoulder-patting routine going on.

He waved her hand away. "I'm fine. It's the Council's call."

"Ah. Why do they call in such a way to generate pain?"

Now wasn't that the question of the day? "I have no idea. Thank you for the meal. I must attend to their call." *Before round two of the brain splitting occurs.*

He strode out of the Temple, wanting to do anything but stand in front of the thirteen who comprised the Council. Anything. Maybe his feelings had something to do with his father sitting on the Council. Or maybe they had to do with the way the males called, with the pain that split through his mind.

Or maybe he just wanted to spend his day with Lily before she started hating him.

He strode down the path, which led from the Temple to the circular stone building housing the Council, his long legs leaving eddies of dirt in their wake. By the time he arrived at the Council's Chamber, his fists were cranked into tight balls and the tasty venison served at the noon meal turned sour in his stomach.

Viktor sat behind those twenty-foot-tall wooden doors. Sat on his arse in his carved wooden chair and snarled at Enar. Sat and did nothing but jeer at his only son.

If only Lily stood beside him. Then Viktor would cease his jeers, his taunts, and show some respect.

For now, Enar must walk through those doors and endure the angry rhetoric. The sooner he finished with this meeting, the sooner he could return to Lily.

Enar shoved open the heavy doors and glared at the thirteen males sitting on carved wooden chairs in a semi-circle and felt an unwanted and unwarrior-like chill slide down his spine. The priestesses might hold the true power of the Goddess, but these males possessed a bone-chilling amount of magic.

Thirteen males sat on the Council, six Draconi and six Watchers led by Alviss, the oldest and most powerful male Draconi. Another chill crept toward his feet. What kind of Watcher was he to get chills?

A poor excuse for a warrior, that's what.

Grabbing a door in each hand, he slammed them shut behind him.

"Instead of summoning me, why not just kill me? It's bound to hurt less." Enar stalked into the room, nodding to Thoren who stood in front of the males.

"You still live, Aylasson? Thought you would be dead by now." The man two chairs to the left of center grasped the arms of his chair, knuckles white, as he stared at Enar, his dislike a palpable throb in the stone chamber.

And so it starts.

Enar snarled at his father's insult of calling him by

his mother's name, insinuating he wasn't Viktor's son. "It's nice to see you too, Father. Give my regards to the demon that set you free for today's meeting." Enar stood feet shoulder-width apart, arms crossed, hoping the position stopped him from doing something stupid. Like putting his hands around his father's throat and squeezing.

Why had he even thought his father would see Lily and be proud of him? After all these years, why did he even care?

Hope lives eternal despite evidence showing otherwise.

Viktor pointed a finger at Enar. "You ungrateful whelp! I-"

"Silence!" The male seated in the middle of the semi-circle spoke, his words echoing off the high stone ceiling, before settling like a shroud across the assembly.

Enar shuddered as the spell slammed into him. Alviss was the most powerful Draconi who sat on the Council. And the oldest. His white hair hung in long locks over his shoulders, his face a map of lines. He walked with a cane, from all appearances a frail, withered man. Despite the frail appearance, his magic ran strong, through his veins and the veins of his only surviving child Annaliese, the primary Temple Healer.

And the spell had the benefit of knocking his angry attitude away while thrusting him into mission-reporting mode.

"We are gathered today to hear the reports of Thoren and Enar, not to bicker with them," Alviss spoke quietly; even so, the words reverberated throughout the room, creeping under Enar's skin. "Did you locate the Halfling we sent you to find?"

"Yes sir. Along with others," Thoren said.

Of course, the Council wouldn't have been told about Thoren's arrival days past. He forgot that despite the close proximity of The High Chamber of the Council to the Temple of the Goddess, Ari refused to discuss most of the happenings of the Temple to the Council members. Some disagreement years ago sparked tension between Aryana and Alviss and she refused to discuss certain things with the Council's leader.

As a result, despite Thoren's being back for several days, the Council would not have known about it until Enar's return. Both members of a spy pair were required to return in order to alert the Council.

Quizzical looks greeted Thoren's news.

"Others?" Alviss white-knuckled the chair arm.

"There was a mature Halfling female and a captured male Draconi locked in dragon form."

Before he finished drawing a breath, the room erupted into shouts.

"A Halfling female!"

"What's the dragon's name?"

"Where is the boy Halfling now?"

Questions flew faster than Thoren and Enar could answer, rendering both silent as a defense. Given enough time, Alviss would call for order to let them finish their report. And he didn't disappoint. His cane thumped against the marble floors as he shouted above the ruckus.

"Silence!" *Thud, thud, thud.* Voices died, vanishing into the room's dark shadows.

"First things first. How did you find the boy

Halfling?" Alviss pointed the tip of his cane at them.

"When he wandered out of Thoren's containment spell. He's been wandering ever since." Enar fought to contain the weariness in his voice and gave up. Thinking about Jamie's escapades made him want to pull up a mattress and dive between the sheets.

A bushy white eyebrow popped up as Alviss stared at Thoren. "You are two of our best reconnaissance specialists. How could you not ward an area to contain a Halfling?"

Thoren shifted his weight. "We didn't realize what he was."

"Pardon? Are your eyes giving you trouble?"

"No sir. The boy does not have the typical Halfling coloring. He has brown hair and gray eyes."

Another round of murmuring followed by a thumping cane.

"We knew Bjorn had a Halfling boy, but we did not know about this."

Bjorn was Jamie's father? Bjorn and Thoren had been close as children, which meant he had been one of Enar's closest friends too. At least while they were younger. As the years strode onward, the three grew apart, Enar and Thoren becoming reconnaissance specialists and Bjorn moving onto things Enar knew nothing about. Last he'd heard, Bjorn disappeared several months ago.

Having Bjorn for a father would explain Jamie's mischievous behavior.

"Does he use magic?" Alviss asked.

"None that I saw. What about you?" Thoren turned to Enar.

"Not unless you consider a penchant for climbing

trees and falling out of them magic." *And disobeying orders. Along with other imp-like actions.*

"Maybe you didn't give him the right incentive. We'll question him ourselves."

"He's injured—"

"Falling out of a tree. He thought he could fly," Enar added.

"He broke his leg and arm and is being tended by the Halfling female we found."

"And my claim." Enar stood a little taller. *Take that Father.*

The Watchers' gazes landed on Enar and Viktor snarled. He felt their shock like cold water thrown over his skin. Wait until they saw Lily. They'd regret everything they ever said. All the teasing. All the jokes.

With Lily by his side, he could prove once and for all he was every bit as much of a warrior as they. Even better since he found the perfect woman.

Alviss's questioning continued, rolling right over their words.

"Draconi heal fast. We'll speak with him tomorrow or the next day. Tell us about the female. How did we not hear of a mature Halfling?"

"I don't know the answer to that. But the town we found them in is full of superstitious people who convinced her magic was evil and she was too. Don't worry, I've convinced her otherwise. Her name is Keara and she was…is…an apothecary. Annaliese has taken her on as an apprentice."

"You've been here long enough for her to meet Annaliese?"

"I returned with Keara several days ago. I went through the Change while on the mission and gave her a crash course on helping me, but she absorbed the magic and went into a coma."

As one, the Draconi wore horrified expressions, while puzzlement settled over the Watcher's faces. Enar and the other Watchers didn't know what was so bad about absorbing magic, but he remembered Thoren's face in the wooded clearing and Keara's still form. Clearly absorbing magic was not on a Draconi's pleasure list.

"She lived despite absorbing magic?" Alviss's coloring matched his hair.

"She did. I turned and flew her back. Figured it was an extenuating circumstance."

"Of course, of course. Are you sure she absorbed your energy?"

"Both she, the High Priestess, and Annaliese said that's what she did. She's tending Jamie, the boy Halfling."

"We need to speak with her too. Now about the dragon." Alviss made a circular motion with his hand.

"We found him in a dungeon—"

"What were you doing in a dungeon?"

"Rescuing Keara. She'd been captured. Oh, speaking of which," Thoren shook his head as if trying to get his thoughts in line. "One of her captors was a Draconi."

"A Draconi?" Alviss gripped his chair's arms in a white-knuckled grasp. "Who? Did you see this male?"

"I did not. Keara said she recognized him by his mark."

"She was also drugged up but good," Enar pointed out.

"So it's possible she did not really see a Draconi?"

Alviss asked.

"I suppose," Thoren said. "But she was insistent on that fact and she remembered everything that happened to her. The drug didn't affect her memory. She said the Draconi wanted to use her for revenge."

"We will question her about that. It's very disturbing. Continue with the dragon."

"As I said, we were in a dungeon and there he was. Apparently, he'd been captured many years ago while in human form and he Changed while in the dungeon," as one, the Draconi shuddered, eyes wide, "and is now stuck in dragon form. He arrived at the Temple earlier today."

Viktor glared at Enar, as if it was his fault Fafnir spent the last however many years in captivity.

"Why did he not come back with you?"

Thoren shrugged and looked to Enar.

Enar mirrored the shrug and ignored Viktor. "I don't know why, but he came with me, not Thoren." *But it probably had to do with the fact the bloody beast was crazier than a drunk dragon growling at the moon.*

"He'll also be questioned. How was he captured?"

Thoren shrugged. "I don't know, but the bars of the cell were made out of titanium."

"Titanium? How can a mere human know titanium renders a Draconi's powers useless?"

"I don't know. Oh, Enar discovered Jamie's father is dead."

Enar glanced at Thoren. What was up with his friend being forgetful? Thoren usually nailed these mission wrap-ups, not forgot half the items he should be speaking on. The image of a red-haired Halfling popped into his mind. Oh yes, Keara. No wonder his friend was forgetful. Mated males made lovesick fools look intelligent.

Alviss's eyes widened, his mouth tightening. "How?"

Enar related what he knew about Bjorn's death and his speculations regarding the rogue Draconi trying to capture Jamie before he tried capturing Keara.

"That is a major security threat. We cannot have humans working with Draconi to capture Halflings. We will send a team tomorrow to eradicate the problem. Do you know anything else about this dragon?"

"Sir, I discovered how the dragon was captured," Enar said. Save the best for last, thanks to Lily and the gossip-vine.

"Well, we're waiting." Alviss leaned forward.

"He was visiting River's Run and ran afoul of one of the nobles there who somehow knew of titanium's effect on Draconi. I'm not sure why the noble captured him, but Fafnir cast a spell on the noble before he was thrown in the cell and the man went crazy."

"Serves the human right. Do you know more than that?"

"No sir. I didn't discover more about his story."

"Very well. We'll question all involved and find out the answers ourselves. First we'll talk to the female, you said her name was Keara?" Thoren nodded. "We'll try to discover who her father was. Please bring her to us."

A few seconds later and Keara stood beside Thoren, her face pale. But she straightened her shoulders, staring Alviss in the eyes. As Alviss began her interview, Enar's focus drifted to Lily, despite the stare and glare Viktor turned his direction.

Where was his woman now? Still in the infirmary? Taking a tour of the Temple grounds? Waiting in a room half-naked for his arrival? That image made Viktor's glare vanish like snow in the sun.

And then Lily's image disappeared as Thoren snarled at Alviss. What just happened? Why was he so busy daydreaming he missed the trigger setting off Thoren's rage?

Enar took in the scene. Thoren held an unmoving Keara around the waist, his lip peeled into a snarl. Alviss's eyes stood at attention, white brows faded into his hairline. Balthor, Thoren's father, paused halfway out of his chair. Whatever just happened, Thoren reacted like the mated male he was, primed and ready to rip apart whatever threatened his mate. Even if said threat was the most powerful Draconi around.

Not very bright, but then newly mated males weren't exactly known for their intelligence.

"Hey, now. That was rather exciting, eh?" Enar slapped a palm against Thoren's shoulder and stepped between Thoren and Alviss, using mind-speak to project his voice into Thoren's head. *Goddess's teeth, Thoren, what do you think you're doing? You can't fight Alviss. Do you have a bloody death wish?*

Thoren blinked, steam curling around his ears. He glanced at Keara as she pressed a hand against his chest and took a deep breath. The steam circling his head dissipated and Enar breathed a sigh of relief. His friend managed to pull it together before he was turned into charred dragon shish-kabob.

"I apologize. I'm not sure what came over me."

He thumped Thoren on the shoulder and went to stand where he had been before Thoren started the mated male dragon posturing. Which he then proceeded to lie to the Council about.

Clearly his friend had issues.

He was a fine one to be talking about issues. He had a claim who liked him but wouldn't tomorrow, a father who despised him, and all he wanted to do was remain in a Draconi village.

Put into perspective, Thoren's refusal to acknowledge Keara as his mate seemed rather trivial.

Alviss continued to ask Keara if she wanted to discover her ancestry. Apparently Thoren's dragon posturing had something to do with Alviss discovering Keara's family. Like the rest of the Council, Enar stood with his mouth hanging open as Alviss announced he was Keara's grandfather.

And then the two transported out of the Chamber, leaving Thoren and Enar alone before the remaining Council members for further questioning.

After that little revelation, the Council members' questions came in starts and stops, before fluttering out, their astonishment overwhelming their curiosity.

The words, "You are dismissed," had to be the happiest ones in his life.

Ignoring Viktor—perhaps that snarl of his froze into a permanent fixture—he yanked open the doors and stepped out into the late afternoon light where the air no longer suffocated him. Freedom.

Thoren stepped beside him, looking from side to side. "Where do you think they went?"

"When do you think you'll tell her she's your mate?"

"You know, when someone asks you a question, it's polite to respond with the answer and not another question."

Enar grinned, spotting Keara and Alviss behind Thoren, tiny spots on a bench at the edge of the property. "You should tell her, you know."

Thoren ran a hand through his hair. "It means I can no longer do my job. I like being a reconnaissance specialist."

"The rule makes sense. We do have some danger each time we go into the field. No one wants the responsibility of telling a male's mate he was killed in action."

"I know. It's just, what will I do?"

"You'll figure something out. You can't live without her and you need to let her know."

"What about you?"

"I'm taking Lily back to my village tomorrow."

"When will you be back?"

"Not long. By the way, your mate is that way." Enar pointed to where Keara sat.

Thoren turned his head, running a hand through his hair. "You're right. I'll let her know." He started walking in the direction of Keara, waving over his shoulder at Enar.

Thoren and Keara made a good match. Just like Lily made him a good match.

The thought sucker punched him in the gut. She belonged to him. His to cherish. His to l...He choked on the word.

He wasn't Draconi. He was a Watcher. Watchers did not bond with their claims. Therefore, the almost slip of the "L" word meant nothing.

Liar. And dragons didn't know how to use magic.

He needed to find Lily. To find her and tell her

what he felt. Maybe then her sparkling blue eyes wouldn't shine hatred when he returned her to his village.

It never hurt to hope.

Chapter 17

Lily rested her chin on her knees, arms wrapped around her legs. Jamie slept in the other bed, his breathing even from the potion Keara gave him before she set his broken bones. Right when she opened her mouth to tell her friend about her vision and ask what it meant, Keara's eyes grew distant. With a "Gotta go, Thoren needs me," Keara disappeared, leaving Lily alone with an unconscious ten-year-old.

Lily lost track of how long she sat on the bed, her thoughts spinning through her mind like eddies in a stream. Did the High Priestess really come to her in the dream and offer a position at the Temple? No matter what the future held with Enar, it had to be better than seeing visions all day.

She shivered. Could the priestesses really teach her to control what she saw? To force a vision to come? What kind of people were the Draconi?

Maybe if she took a tour of this place, she'd meet a priestess to ask. She glanced at Jamie, who still slept the sleep of the drugged, and walked to the door. Would the priestesses mind if she left the healing room?

Only one way to find out.

Lily pulled open the door and stepped out into the hall. A quick glance left and right showed no one standing around, willing to answer her questions. And that was why she had feet—to transport her where she needed to go.

If only she knew where that was.

Picking a direction, Lily headed to the right down polished stone floors. Brass knobs in the shape of dragon heads dotted the doors, gleaming gold against the wooden panels. Light emanated from globes hanging next to the line of doors, casting a gentle glow over the corridor.

When she arrived at the end of the hall, she picked right to head. This corridor was short and ended in a large foyer lit by the evening sun shining through a wall of windows. A cozy circle of cushioned chairs clustered around an unlit fireplace. Huge, intricately carved doors took up the wall opposite the windows. Lily tilted her head back and took in the sweeping expanse of a ceiling. Something was painted up there, but the angle of the light shining through the windows prevented her from seeing the painting. What a perfect room to paint in and thanks to Enar she had her brushes. Maybe someone would loan her paints, canvas and an easel.

Someone. Anyone.

Where was everyone? Shouldn't a priestess be around to talk to her? She looked from one end of the space to the other, gave up finding a priestess and headed to the chairs.

Her bottom had no sooner touched the chair when the doors opened, Enar stalking inside.

"Enar!"

He paused, turning toward her, squinting in the sun.

"Lily?"

"Hi! There's room here for another." She gestured toward the chairs and watched as he walked to where she sat.

Muscles flexed under leather as he strode across the floor, the soles of his boots whispering against the stone tiles, killer quiet. Lethal. Why hadn't she noticed during the past week, he was built like a killer?

Probably because she was too busy sighing over pleasure-filled nights.

"What are you doing here? Aren't you supposed to be in the healing rooms?"

"Keara left. Jamie was unconscious. I couldn't find a priestess and I got tired of waiting around. So I took a walk."

"Where are the priestesses?"

"Do I look like I know?"

He grinned. "I guess not. Would you like to walk around?"

"I was hoping for a bath and change of clothes. Where are all our bags anyway?"

"In one of the rooms."

"Really? Do you happen to know which one? Does it have a bathing room?"

"Hold on." Enar's eyes grew distant, much like Keara's had seconds before she disappeared. But instead of disappearing, he remained where he stood and a priestess popped in next to him.

Lily bit back a scream. Next up on the to-do list: get used to Draconi suddenly appearing in front of her.

"How may I assist, Enar?" The black-haired priestess clasped her hands in front of her waist, but Lily could tell the woman would rather have placed them on Enar.

Was that growl coming from her throat?

Both Enar and the priestess looked at her and Lily

took a deep breath. If she got busy breathing in, then nothing could come out. Right? *Right.* She forced a smile. The priestess turned back to Enar, her face full of hopeful expectation.

Lily clasped her hands together until the knuckles turned white. What was wrong with her today? Why did she have this desire to smash the smile off the priestess's face for talking to Enar?

Perhaps she hit her head when she fell earlier. Although that didn't explain the growling noises escaping her throat or the overwhelming urge to commit murder.

"Which room has our bags?"

"Ah. Right this way. Please follow me." The priestess started down the hall, tracing the path Lily took earlier.

Instead of turning down the corridor to the healing room, the priestess continued straight until she reached one of the many doors set in the wall. With a shove, she opened the door and took a step back.

"Here you go! The bathing room is to the right and the relief room is to the left. Enjoy your stay." A brief nod of her head and she disappeared, vanishing in a wisp of smoke, taking with her Lily's insane urge to kill.

"I really need to get used to people popping in and out like that." Lily blinked at the empty spot formerly containing the priestess.

"It shouldn't take long." Enar walked to the bed and began to disarm, shrugging out of the holder for his broadsword.

Lily headed to the bathing room. Clean skin coming up. Maybe they had a clean set of clothing, since Goddess only knew hers needed a good scouring.

"And just where do you think you're going, woman?"

"To take a bath. You'll like me better afterward."

"I like you fine right now." His teeth gleamed a predator's white as he loosened the tie holding his hair. The blond waves fell around his shoulders as he stalked toward her.

So much for the bath. Not that she was complaining.

His lips captured hers, his arms banding around her waist. Her hands stroked through his hair, holding him close. One of his hands skimmed from her back to the underside of her breast, his thumb flicking against the peaked nipple.

She moaned into his mouth.

"Like that?" His lips slid to her ear, clasping gently on the lobe, sending chills racing around her limbs.

"Mmm. Keep it up and you'll find out."

He chuckled, a dark knowledge in the sound. "As you wish, love."

Love. His fingers drew sensations from her she didn't realize she possessed. Was that love? Had the emotion snuck past her aloof decree and embedded itself into her heart? Did he love her? Or was love just a word bandied about with no thought?

Too much thinking on her part. In the moment was where she needed to be, not all up in her head.

Lily drew his lips to hers as his hand slid across her stomach, stroking lower, each inch taken making her core weep, tantalizing her with the remembrance of his fingers' past talents and tempting her with future ones. Right when she feared the anticipation would drive her crazy, he cupped her mound. Even through her trousers, Lily felt the heat of his palm, searing her, branding her his.

His. She, who had never belonged to anyone, belonged to Enar. And because of it, she would do anything for him.

She stroked her tongue against his, feeling the wet heat of his mouth, hands fisted into his shirt. He lifted her, pressing her back against the stone wall, his arousal pushing against her stomach. The chill of the stones seeped through her tunic, clashing with the heat of her body against Enar's.

Hot and cold. Strength and gentleness. Enar took her out of the cold and showered her with warmth. Her hands slipped beneath his shirt, feeling the hard planes of his stomach. Slipping lower, she untied the laces of his leathers, pushing them over his hips.

"What—"

Lily pressed a finger to his lips, silencing his question. Heat burned in his eyes as she dropped to her knees, one hand sliding along the length of his shaft until she reached the sensitive head. She dropped her eyes to what she held, taking a deep breath. She could do this, take him into her mouth, give back to him a taste of the pleasure he gave her.

Her lips kissed along his shaft, tracing the contours with her tongue, while one hand cupped his sack, kneading gently.

Enar moaned, his hands clutching her hair, pushing her tighter against him.

Opening her lips, she welcomed him in, all the while her tongue flicked around the head of his shaft, finding the spot that elicited another moan. Wrapping her lips around him, she took more of him into her mouth, trying not to gag when he hit the back of her throat.

"Goddess, woman, that feels good," Enar's words rasped on an exhale of breath.

Lily smiled to herself as she slowly pulled him out until only the head remained. Circling her tongue around once, twice and then she took him back in only to repeat the process, until she tasted the salt of his essence. As she swallowed, he pulled out.

"If you keep that up any longer I'm going to explode in your mouth and I want to be in you when I come."

Lily looked at Enar as her eyes shuttered in pleasure.

"I'm waiting." She ran a finger along the hardness of his shaft, watching as a pearl of liquid beaded on the tip.

Enar's hands lifted her, pulling her tunic off, pushing her trousers down. He picked her up, hands under the curves of her bottom, and carried her to the bed.

She landed with a muffled screech on the mattress, Enar dropping on top of her.

"Ah, Lily, love." One of his hands came between them, flicking across the bud that gave her so much pleasure. His lips played with the lobe of her ear while his fingers stroked her. When he spoke, his voice was a whisper that sent shivers scuttling across her skin.

"What did I ever do without you?" The head of his shaft pressed against her wet opening before forging inside.

He pulled out, until he caught against her opening

and then pushed back into her depths, stroking over her inner sweet spot. As if they moved of their own volition, her legs wrapped around his waist, drawing him deeper into her.

In and out, pushing and pulling until Lily didn't know where he stopped and she started. All she knew was the pleasure his lips, tongue and shaft brought her. The crest of pleasure started in her core, working its way through her body until she screamed his name as the wave crashed over her, over him, until nothing mattered but the heat of his skin molded to hers.

So this is what love feels like.

She squelched that little thought. Just because Enar managed to break through the barriers of her heart did not mean she needed to pull out the big "L" word.

"What about that bath?" Enar raised up on one elbow, staring down at her.

"You coming?"

He cocked a grin. "Wild dragons couldn't keep me from it."

She returned the grin and pushed herself up. Lying around with him sounded good, but a warm bath sounded wonderful.

Beating Enar to the bathing room entrance, she pushed open the door and stepped into a tiled room with a step-down pool in the middle of it. Large enough to hold two, the stone tiles lining the pool gleamed white in the glow of the flameless torches set in iron sconces that dotted the walls. Steam floated above the water of the pool, heating the room. White fluffy towels sat in neat rows on wooden planks surrounding the pool.

Enar popped her on the bottom and she jumped. "Woman, are you going to stand around staring all night, or get in the water?"

Lily took in the wall of rippling muscle as Enar walked to the pool, stepping into the water. He had a point. Why was she standing around staring when she could be getting a bath? With Enar?

Several strides later and she stepped into the warm water. Ah, bliss. Hot water, good-looking man, what more could she want?

Soap.

"Looking for this?" Enar waded through the water toward her, his hands containing bubbles. The man must be a mind reader.

"Where did you find it?"

"Little indentions in the tile." He ran his bubble-filled hands down her arms.

A thrill of excitement strummed through her core. Desire and lust warred with another emotion that slid into the depths of his gaze. His lips claimed hers as his soapy hands stroked over her breasts, down her sides.

And just like that, she wanted him again. Wanted him to fill her, to—dare she say the word—love her. Her brain spit out the word she'd been trying to hide in the inner recesses of her mind. Spit it out and left it standing there like a brand, searing her, refusing to leave.

She gave a mental curse.

Enar pulled away from her lips, his brows pulling together. "What's wr—"

His words cut short as he doubled over as if in pain, hands clasped against his ears.

"Enar! What's wrong? Are you all right?"

She shook his shoulder, her stomach in knots. What was wrong? With a moan he straightened, white lines storming around his lips.

"Bloody Council. What do they think they're doing, calling me twice in one day?" He stomped out of the pool, dripping water on the stones as he reached for a towel.

"Council?"

"Bloody, buggering group of males poking their noses into business best left alone." His muttered words continued in a hot rush as he marched out of the bathing room.

Lily sucked in a breath as the cold air hit her wet body. Like Enar, she grabbed a towel, wrapped it around her waist and followed him into the bedroom.

"Twice in one day. It's unheard of."

"Twice?"

Enar fastened the laces on his leathers, his lip crawling up as he glanced at her. "Don't go anywhere. I'll be back as soon as I can."

"What do you mean 'twice'?"

"The Council called Thoren and me to report on our mission. It's normal when a spy pair returns to Draconia."

"Do you always go out in pairs?"

He yanked his shirt over his head, his voice muffled by the cloth. "Yes. It's a rule." His head poked out of the neck-hole. "We have a mission, come back and report and then go our own way. We don't get called back again." He sat on the bed and reached for his boots. "Twice is unheard of."

Lily leaned against the door frame and watched as Enar dressed. What she would give to have him back in the bath. "How do they call?"

"Didn't you notice my head-pains?"

"Well, yes, but didn't realize that's what it was. You had me worried."

His eyes widened and crinkled at her words. "They use mind-speak to tell you they request the honor of your presence in their Chamber and Goddess help you if you don't show up immediately."

Boots on, he strode to her, wrapping his arms around her waist. "As I said, don't go anywhere." His lips crushed hers, a brief statement of possession that sent a thrill straight to her core. "I'll be back."

One of her fingers touched her lips as Enar walked to the door. He stopped and winked at her before pulling the door shut behind him. The click of the latch engaging freed her limbs and she rested her head against the wall.

So much for more sexy fun in the bath. She wiped dripping suds from her breast as she walked back to the bathing room. No sense in ignoring the bath. The hot water felt soothing as it embraced her in its heat, as she soaked in its slippery depths.

Resting on a conveniently located stone shelf that allowed most of her body to remain submerged, Lily floated her legs in front of her. If the rest of Draconia was as nice as this pool, she would enjoy living here.

But something told her Enar's village would be different. How different? What was he hiding from her?

Despite the warmth of the water, a chill shook through her body and her eyes squinted closed. Before the vision struck, she pulled her upper body out of the water, pressing her cheek against the cold of the stone tile. The scene slammed through her mind like a knife through skin, the pain curling her fingers as she clawed at the unyielding stone.

A wail slammed through the room, echoing off the walls, rattling her bones.

Her cry as her heart felt ripped into jagged shards. Dear Goddess, no!

Chapter 18

Enar stormed out of the Temple, crossing the Courtyard to the back gate in record time. As if his back sprouted wings and flew him. He wished he had wings. Then he could fly away someplace with Lily.

If dreams were gold pieces, he'd be rich.

The gate leading out of the Temple Courtyard squeaked open only to slam shut, the wood shuddering as Enar's hand released it. Gravel crunched under his boots, his shadow elongated from the glowing orbs of light lining the path. Darkness crept to the edge of the light circles, rustling insects' wings into a cascading symphony in the deepening twilight.

Twice in a day. What was the Council thinking to call him back into their presence? He'd rather have a cold enema.

Not only did his head hurt, but they interrupted his lovemaking with Lily. He needed to convince her she couldn't live without him, despite his returning with her to his village. What would he do without her?

Goddess, but he loved that woman.

Enar froze at the thought. Just up and stopped moving. Love? His brain must be addled by the Council's call. Yes, that was it. Love was a sappy emotion demonstrated by the average Draconi male. Like Thoren. Watchers didn't possess anything resembling love.

But he couldn't stop his chest from clenching as he thought about Lily, as he remembered the beauty in her face, her laugh, her smile.

She belonged to him. His.

Clearly he'd been around the Draconi too long as evidenced by these thoughts of l...He coughed. Not using that word again.

His feet got with the walking program and continued on their way to the Council.

Enar marched to the heavy wooden doors barring entrance to the Chamber of the Council, slapped his hands against them and shoved. The doors flew open with a bang, ricocheting off the stone walls. Enar caught them on the rebound, adding to their momentum so they slammed shut, the noise echoing in the round, stone chamber.

Thoren stood arms crossed in front of the half circle of men, his lips twisting into a grin at Enar's approach.

Bloody, blithering bastards. Why had they called both him and Thoren?

His gaze ran over the faces of the thirteen, landing on his father's snarl. And in an instant, his anger went from simmering to blown out rage.

Enar stalked past Thoren, stopping directly in front of Viktor.

"Twice in one day? I have a life outside of this Council."

"Not by my wishes, you don't," Enar's father hissed at him.

"Silence!" Alviss's voice boomed throughout the room as he gestured for a snarling Enar to stand beside Thoren.

"You have been called here because intruders have been spotted on Draconi territory. We thought you would like to handle it." Alviss's eyes sparkled as he looked at them.

"Why us?" Thoren asked.

Good question. Usually reconnaissance specialists did not fight off intruders. On the rare occasion an intruder crossed into Draconia, the Council used their special set of Watchers and Draconi trained to handle that type of thing. And he and Thoren did not belong to that special set.

Not that he'd mind knocking around some heads at the moment. Starting with his father.

"Because of whom we suspect the intruders are." Alviss waved his hand, causing a ball with flickering images to hover mid-air. He beckoned Thoren and Enar to peer into the depths.

White mist swirled in the seeing ball, coalescing into clouds that separated in half, forming a vision. Enar squinted at the flickering images. Son of a goat. How had they crossed the Draconian ward lines?

Simon from River's Run and a figure wearing a cloak that hid his face sat around a campfire surrounded by a contingent of soldiers. Enar's hands tingled at the thought of fighting the pompous lord from Lily's village. Those men had kidnapped and drugged Keara, causing harm to a Draconi female.

For that alone they needed to die. Enar glanced at Thoren, taking in his best friend's snarl as steam escaped his ears, whipping around his face.

One mad, mated male Draconi and his equally infuriated Watcher coming right up. Blood Seeker vibrated against his back as the sword shook in anticipation of drinking blood.

The thing was thirsty.

And he was more than happy to feed it. It had been a long time since the sword fed.

"Where are they?" Thoren growled.

"So they are the ones that captured Keara?" Alviss asked.

Thoren swallowed and the steam circling his head disappeared, the snarl crossing his lip remaining etched. "Yes."

"Is the mission capture or destroy?" Enar fingered the hilt of Blood Seeker.

"Destroy," Thoren said, his stare daring Alviss to refuse him.

Alviss's wrinkles convulsed into a smile. "Destroy. These are the ones that harmed my granddaughter." He peered closer, his eyes blinking. "Is the one in the cloak a Draconi?"

"According to Keara he is." Thoren's jaw ticked.

"Then you must capture him and bring him to us for questioning. Then you may kill him after we speak to him."

"It will be my pleasure."

"They are right inside Draconi territory. The wards must be weakened for them to have crossed the border or that rogue Draconi has more power than he should. After you have secured the territory, see if you can determine the strength of the wards so we can send someone out to restore them. May the Goddess bless your mission and may the ones that considered defiling my granddaughter die in pain."

Thoren grabbed Enar's arm and transported him to the woods where the soon-to-be-dead men camped.

Five fires burned brightly in a small clearing in the woods. Six men sat around each fire. If Simon and the rogue Draconi had prepared well, several men would be patrolling the perimeter of the camp. No more than forty men to their two. Not a problem.

Blood Seeker started to hum as it scented fresh blood, vibrating through its sheath, through the cloth of Enar's shirt. The hum cycled into a higher pitch as Enar pulled the sword from its sheath, the vibrations traveling up the metal into the flesh of his hands. Power ran alongside the vibrations, power that slammed through his veins, infusing him with its magic, its strength. Enough power to defeat all the intruders, but Enar knew better than to kill Simon or the hooded Draconi. Thoren wanted that privilege.

Thoren crouched in the shadows, staring across the campfires into the darkness of the trees, obviously locating his target. Those who sat out in the open, defiling Draconi lands by their mere presence.

"Blood Seeker is thirsty. Are you going to sit on your arse all night or do we get to have some fun?" Enar stroked the runes on Blood Seeker's blade, readying the sword to drink.

"Simon and the Draconi are mine."

Just as he planned. Enar inclined his head. "May the Goddess go with you."

"And also with you."

Enar crept away from Thoren, leaving his best friend to his own devices. Once out of Thoren's listening range, Enar touched Blood Seeker's blade again, this time whispering words to turn the sword into a conduit. Each blow dealt, each life taken, each drop of blood spilled onto the cold metal blade infused Enar with powerful magic, rendering him virtually invincible to anything non-magical.

The runes pulsed beneath his fingers, a wordless communication. Enar said a brief prayer to the Goddess and then let out a war cry as he ran into the clearing.

The soldiers scrambled for their weapons, tripping over their feet, turning the clearing into a frantic jumble of bodies. Enar swung at his first victim, Blood Seeker severing a head of a slow moving soldier. He tilted the sword's tip toward the canopy of leaves, crimson rivulets streaking across the runes etched into the blade. Blood Seeker hummed as it absorbed the blood's power, sending a jolt of energy through Enar's hands, supercharging the blood running through his veins. Strength, power, invincibility.

Time slowed, soldiers running toward him as if stuck in mud, their movements slow, cumbersome. A thrust through the heart, turn, parry, block. Another fell, rid of his spirit, his life's blood fueling the fight.

This part of a battle thrilled him, the hum of too much power coursing through his veins, the knowledge of invincibility. One against thirty, more like twenty-eight, make that twenty-seven now. Soldiers from the other campfires joined the fight, trying to circle around Enar. He heard their footsteps crackling in leaves, the pop of a log settling in the fire, the brilliance of sounds loud with his hyped-up senses. He looked the soldier in front of him directly in the eye, and bared his teeth.

"Don't move."

The Adam's apple of the soldier bobbed, the mouth opening in horror as Enar rammed his sword into the man's belly.

The power of persuasion was a real killer.

A whish of air heralded the movement of a weapon from behind him. Enar jumped to the side and spun, Blood Seeker slicing through the neck of a narrow-eyed soldier. Twenty-five left.

He might be the laughingstock of his village, but no one, not even his father, could refute his fighting skills. Speed and agility followed him in a fight, making him the fastest Watcher with a blooded magical sword. He won all practice fights against men stronger than himself.

But speed and agility only slowed the taunts.

Thoughts like those didn't belong on a battlefield. Wiping everything but what stood before him from his mind, Enar swung at the soldier standing in front of him. Another speed-impaired man fell. The quicker he dispatched the soldiers, the quicker he could return to Lily's side. He picked up his pace.

His last fight had been so long ago he had forgotten the rate at which time slowed. How quick his movements became in relation to his opponents. The heightened senses. The more Blood Seeker drank, the faster Enar moved. The faster Enar moved, the more soldiers died.

And thanks to the magic passed to him through his mother, he could suggest a man stand still and let Enar kill him. It might not be the most sporting thing to do, but it had its advantages. Like now.

Enar spun in a circle, shouting, "Stop!"

The soldiers attempting to engage him froze while Enar darted out of the circle, jogging around the ring of men until he stood at their backs.

"Go," he muttered, swinging his sword through a belly.

Gasps sounded as the men looked around, trying to determine where he went. He hacked through the mass, the soldiers stunned motionless by his reappearance. Not sporting, but it definitely sped things along. Twenty left.

Several of the little weasels tried to run off, obviously frightened by his disappearing act, but were stopped dead by the Draconi wards. At least the exit wards still worked even if the entrance ones had lost power.

Curious thing, that. One he didn't have time to ponder as another wave of soldiers brandishing swords advanced.

Metal screeched against metal as swords locked, battling for dominance. Enar pulled his blade free and kicked backward, striking the man sneaking up behind him. The man fell on his arse with a grunt. The soldier in front of him swung his sword with the speed of a slug. Enar stepped to the side and stabbed the soldier, blood spraying as he yanked the blade out of the man's chest.

Enar barely registered the surprise on the now-dead soldier's face before whirling to counter the man he kicked. That one went down with a parry and thrust, more bluster than fighting skill.

Two more took flight directly into the Draconi wards, either not seeing their dead brethren or not caring in their race to escape Blood Seeker.

A dozen ringed him, fear in their eyes, their swords trembling. Enar laughed, the sound bouncing off the trees, echoing like frightened fire in the reflections of the soldiers' gazes. He swore a couple even wet their pants.

He darted toward one, Blood Seeker raised, feeling the movements of the others as they stepped closer, trying to find an opening in his defenses. But Blood Seeker drank well in the battle, the invincible power spilling into Enar. His motions became a blur as he swung his sword in a circle, severing heads, cleaving guts, until nothing remained but the crackle of logs, the smell of death. Enar knelt beside the last soldier killed and drove Blood Seeker to the hilt in the ground, discharging the remaining energy into the Goddess's keeping.

He said a quick prayer for the souls of the slain soldiers. They were scum, but even scum deserved a prayer for the afterlife. Most of them died with honor.

Thoren should have found and killed Simon and the rogue Draconi by now. Enar glanced around the clearing, seeing only the bodies of the slain soldiers. No Thoren.

And then his eyes fastened on movement across the clearing. Simon held a sword, shadows dancing down the blade. Thoren raised his hands as if to blast the goat-sucker into oblivion, but nothing happened.

Thoren glanced at his hands, his face hidden in shadows, nonetheless radiating surprise. What happened to his friend's magic? The only thing able to stop a Draconi in his tracks was titanium. Like the bars that held Fafnir captive in Simon's cellar. Clearly, Fafnir spoke the truth when he claimed Simon's father possessed a titanium sword.

Enar's breath hitched as Simon thrust his sword through Thoren's belly, pulling the sword free with a kick to Thoren's hip. Thoren clasped his hands over his stomach and fell to the ground. His friend's fall freed the air stuck in his lungs and he wheezed in a gasp, his blood pounding in his ears.

"No!" Enar jumped to his feet and ran, Blood Seeker pointed at Simon as if the sword wanted its own vengeance.

He felt the pulsing of Thoren's blood in his heart, felt Thoren's pain as if it was his own. Knew his friend would die without immediate help. Red clouded his vision as he rushed forward to save Thoren. He made it halfway across the clearing before he saw a movement in the trees a ways from where Thoren lay dying. A shadow stepped from the trees, a shadow with a hood thrown over its face.

The Draconi threw a blast of energy, striking Enar with enough force to throw him backward into the trees. He landed with a thud, feeling the hard ground, smelling the blood pooling around him and not able to move. Blood Seeker screamed, a high pitched noise audible only to him, a noise he never thought to hear. A Watcher's sword only screamed when the Watcher died.

Lily. He should have said the "L" word to her.

His thoughts floated away as the dark canopy of branches faded from sight.

****

Lily watched the elongated shadows dance over the walls of the room. Night-cooled air from the open window drifted across her bare skin. Insects chirped outside the window, announcing the arrival of darkness. The scent of cooked grain wafted from the door where it had popped into the room, transported, she assumed, by one of the priestesses.

She remained curled into a ball on the bed,

watching the door, hoping Enar would walk through. Her vision still caused her to shake and the cool breeze on her naked skin did nothing to help the matter.

And Aryana wanted her to go through this in order to see the future?

Crazy priestess.

Why would she want this? This pain of knowing what was to happen and being unable to stop it? As soon as she could move after the vision, she had raced down the hall, ignoring the fact she forgot her clothes, rushing to find Enar. She had found a priestess instead who assured her Enar was in the Council's Chamber and Lily needed to return to her room. Nothing Lily said convinced the priestess she needed to talk to Enar right then.

So she remained in her room, the vision replaying through her mind like a spinning top, circling round until she thought she might go crazy. What would she do if her vision came true? What would she do if Enar never walked through the door? If he never returned?

She drew in a breath, trying to make it stop shaking. She lived with priests trying to kill her throughout her entire life, she would get through this.

But she'd rather have Enar by her side.

So much for the remaining-aloof plan. Right when she decided to give love a chance, her vision struck, crushing her feeble hopes as if they were reeds in a fast moving stream.

The necklace moved as she shifted. Moved. The shaky breath she drew froze. Her necklace had moved. It never moved. Blood rushed from her head, pooling in her chest, making her heart skip a beat. She touched the round beads and the necklace fell into her hand.

No! Enar's words echoed through her mind, *The necklace can't be removed unless I die.* Sitting up, she stared at the beads in her hand, watched as they became blurry. Her vision came true. She swiped under her eyes. If only that bloody priestess had taken her to Enar, this wouldn't have happened.

Who was she fooling? Her visions always came true. Always. She had never stopped a vision from happening, never, despite her efforts.

Maybe Enar hadn't spoken the truth about the necklace falling off with his death. Maybe the energy blast she saw hit him hadn't killed him. It had just knocked him out. Maybe the necklace had somehow come loose. Something might have happened to the clasp.

Keara would know. And if she didn't, her friend would be able to offer comfort.

Holding the necklace like a beloved pet, Lily made it halfway to the door, stopping in the middle of the room. No, she couldn't go out nude. Again.

Where were her clothes?

There. Her tunic rested by the window, her trousers by the bed. She hurried to the tunic and yanked it over her head, then pulled her trousers on and dashed out the door. Halfway down the hall, she stopped, trying to remember where the healing rooms were. Left or right? Right. So why was she running to the left?

An about-face later and Lily sprinted to the right, taking another right where the healing room wing dead-ended into the hall she was on. Which room was Jamie in? Nothing to it, but to push open doors until she found him.

On the third try, she stumbled into the room Jamie

lay in. A tall, dark-haired priestess whose features resembled Keara's sat by Jamie's bed, her green eyes widening as Lily burst into the room.

"Where's Keara?"

"Who are you?"

"Her friend. Where's Keara?"

The woman rose, walking closer to Lily. "How do you know Keara?"

She didn't have time for a query session. "We're from the same town. Jamie can tell you. I need to see her." She needed to pull her voice back to a non-ear-shattering pitch.

"Jamie is sleeping. Why do you need Keara?"

Taking a breath, Lily clutched the strand of beads tight. "Are you going to tell me where she is or not? I need to speak with her."

What felt like a brush of wings fluttered against her mind, gentle, light. Lily swatted at her ear and ran a hand under her eyes for good measure.

"Oh my. You're the one Aryana mentioned."

"What?" Wasn't she a barrel of intelligence?

"You are Enar's claim."

"You know Enar?"

The woman's lips turned. "I'm Annaliese, the primary Temple healer. You must be Lily."

"How did you know that?"

"Aryana told me."

"But you acted like you didn't know me."

"Why do you need Keara? She has...gone to take care of some things."

"Do you know when she'll be back?"

"I do not. Would you like to tell me what troubles you?"

Something about the woman soothed Lily's emotions, calming them to a more manageable level of panic. Lily wanted to trust Annaliese, wanted to tell her everything. Why? What about this woman made Lily want to share her problems? What if Annaliese was offended by her skin color? She did after all work in the Temple. What if she was like the priests in River's Run?

"Do not be afraid. I mean you no harm. You are severely worried. I am a healer. I would like to help, if you'll let me."

The feelings of panic subsided, replaced by feelings of warmth. She needed to tell Annaliese her worries. Needed to unburden her soul.

Before she knew what happened, her mouth opened and words spilled out. "I saw Enar dying. In the woods."

"Did you see Thoren?"

"No. But my necklace fell off." The words ended on a sob, her eyes closing as she thrust the strand of beads at Annaliese.

A soft touch pressed against her outstretched hand and Lily's lids flew open. Annaliese cradled Lily's hand in both of hers.

"Perhaps the clasp broke."

"I saw him die. The necklace only comes off when he dies." She sniffed.

Annaliese glanced over her shoulder at Jamie. "Come. Show me where you're staying."

The healer wrapped an arm around Lily's shoulders, leading her down the hall until they reached Lily's room. Opening the door, Annaliese glanced at the food tray and bent to shove it out of their way.

"Now, Lily. Why don't you lie down? When you wake, I'll come back to see you. All right?"

Lily wanted to lie down. Lying down sounded like a good idea.

"I want to put the necklace on first." In case her vision was wrong and Enar came back. He shouldn't know the necklace fell off.

"All right."

Lily tucked a leg under her as she sat on the mattress. When the ends of the necklace touched, they stuck together, held in place by an invisible force. But unlike when Enar placed the string of beads around her neck, the clasp released at the slightest touch. She fastened and released it, fastened and released, fastened...who was she kidding? It no longer stayed permanently clasped. A heavy weight settled in her chest. He couldn't be dead. He couldn't.

If she could just put the necklace back on, he would come back. He had to. What would happen to her if he didn't?

Confident she knew how the necklace clasped, she touched the ends together behind her neck. It stayed in place, even when she tugged on it. *See, it stays on, just like it used to. That means he's alive, right?*

"All right, you have it on. Why don't you lie back now?" Annaliese gestured to the bed, one hand on Lily's shoulder.

Leaning back, she touched the stone beads. *Please Goddess, let Enar return alive and well.*

Annaliese placed a hand on Lily's forehead. "Sleep well until tomorrow, Lily."

A wave of exhaustion crashed into her, through her, chasing the panic and fear into the far recesses of her being.

What did Annaliese do to her?

The thought vanished as sleep washed over her, her eyes closing as the darkness claimed her.

Chapter 19

Enar woke with a gasp. Where was he? Insects chirped a melody while the scent of decaying leaves filled his nose. The forest. What was he doing in the forest? Like a dam breaking, memories tumbled free of their confines. Thoren dealt a death blow, falling into the detritus of leaves. An energy blast throwing him across the clearing. An energy blast designed to kill.

Why was he alive?

He pulled in a deep breath, his eyes popping wide. Definitely alive. As far as he knew, spirits didn't breathe.

Keara leaned over him, her pale skin a contrast to the darkness of the forest. The magic emanating from her possessed its own smell, dark and damp, the taste clogging his throat.

The scent of death.

He swallowed, the knowledge of what she had done, what she could do, caught the breath in his lungs. He had died. Dead. Gone. How many people could raise the dead? Was that reality instead of myth? Obviously, seeing how he continued to suck in air. How did Keara possess a mythological ability?

He grabbed her wrist, checking to see if she existed. She felt like flesh and bone.

"You're hurting me," she hissed and he dropped his grip.

"What are you, female?" Her death-raising ability might have cured him of a lack of heartbeat, but it did nothing to stop the crackle in his voice.

She shivered, staring at a point in the darkness. "I am me."

And he was a Draconi.

But if she wanted to act like nothing happened, he'd play the game of pretend. If she could restore him to life, then she could do the same for Thoren. If needed. Enar shuddered. His friend. What happened to Thoren? Was he dead? Nothing to it, but to find him. And if he was dead, well, the cure for that sat beside him in the leaves.

Enar raised his head, checking to see where the energy blast seared into his chest. Healed. The shirt was ruined, but the gaping burn no longer existed. He ran a hand across the skin. Smooth as a newborn's.

He narrowed his gaze on Keara, who squirmed under the scrutiny.

"You are special. I owe you my life, it seems. Last I saw, Thoren was this way and he was in trouble."

Thoren must be dead by now, too much time had elapsed for him to still live. The ache he associated with Lily smacked him in the chest, snagging his breath. Rubbing a hand across his chest, he rolled to his feet. Bloody, aching chest. He grabbed Blood Seeker and took off through the forest.

Keara was his friend's only hope for survival, provided she made it to Thoren's side. She looked half-dead herself. Pale skin glowed in the strands of flickering firelight. Her footsteps stumbled behind him as he led the way through the woods, skirting the perimeter of the clearing.

The last time he saw his friend, Thoren lay a short distance from where he and Keara stood. Enar stopped, pulling Keara down behind a bush. Goddess help him, but she would have to rescue Thoren on her own. Only she could transport them back to the Temple infirmary. He needed to find Simon and the hooded Draconi and hope his second chance at killing the bastards succeeded.

"It looks clear, but I last saw Simon and the Draconi here. Thoren was over there," he pointed to where he last saw his friend, "and he'd been stabbed."

"Stabbed?" Keara's voice came out in a high-pitched squeak instead of a whisper. He placed a finger across his lips, hoping she'd get the message.

"That's the way it looked, although how he let Simon stab him is a mystery." Unless one gave serious thought to Simon understanding the effects of his father's titanium sword. A thought best left to himself for now. "Your job is to heal Thoren and get him out of here."

"Can you transport him? Because I just learned how to transport myself. I've never tried taking anyone with me."

"Best learn. Heal him up well enough and he'll transport himself. Now go, but be careful."

"Where are you going?"

"To make sure we're alone."

"How will I find you?"

"Don't worry, I'll find you."

Enar touched her shoulder as he disappeared into the trees, letting the shadows claim him.

A titanium sword. Could it be? If it was the same one used to capture Fafnir, could he find it? It beat thinking of Thoren dead. Thinking of how he failed his friend. He needed that sword. Chances were good it was here in the clearing. Why else would Thoren's powers not have worked against Simon? And the blast that killed him came from yards away from Simon and the sword he'd stabbed Thoren with.

Hiding behind a tree, Enar observed the scene. Dead men surrounded the campfire, several piled up yards away at the Draconia ward lines. Perhaps they had been too scared to venture far into Draconia, preferring instead to be close to the border in case they needed a quick way out.

Bad idea.

Their reasons didn't matter. What mattered now was finding that sword. He knew it had to be here, knew it was what prohibited Thoren from blasting Simon into oblivion.

He was a reconnaissance specialist. How hard could it be to find a titanium sword?

And the answer? Not as hard as he thought.

Simon walked out of the woods carrying the thing, shaking his head as he looked at the carnage. Enar shrunk into the shadows, trying to merge with the tree trunk. Simon placed the sword on the ground and walked back to where he'd come from, disappearing from view.

Enar watched the shadows, waiting for Simon to pop into view again, but the scum remained hidden. Nothing moved but insects and the fire. All the better for sword retrieval. Walking as quiet as possible through the leaf-strewn ground, he snuck toward the sword. Once there, he knelt on the ground, checking for Simon.

Nothing. He saw Keara kneeling by Thoren, her body swaying. Was Thoren de—? His brain stuttered on the word, refusing to let it out. Keara was beside his friend. She would heal Thoren.

He prayed.

No use thinking about it. Shoving his feelings into a dark corner of his soul, he grabbed the sword and stuck it through his belt as he began to circle the perimeter of the clearing back the way he came.

His palm still tingled from where it grasped the hilt of the sword. If titanium affected him, he could only imagine what it must feel like to a Draconi.

A movement in the trees where Keara tended Thoren caught his attention. Where was Keara? His heart jumped, fluttering as he sucked in a breath. There. By Thoren. Why was she laying facedown?

Two shadows walked out of the trees, converging on where Keara and Thoren lay unmoving on the ground. Had she died? What happened to her?

No time to think about her, when Simon and the rogue Draconi hovered over Thoren. Simon, who had captured Keara and threatened a female Draconi's life, who had driven a sword through his friend. Simon, who was about to breathe his last.

Simon and the Draconi gestured to Thoren, arguing about something. He stepped closer, not bothering to mask the crunch of leaves under his boots. So engrossed in their conversation, they didn't even hear his approach. His loud, noisy approach.

Stupid bastards.

Keara lay by Thoren, toppled onto the bed of leaves like she slept. Thoren lay on his side, facing Enar, his brow furrowed. Alive!

The thought no sooner crossed his mind than he squelched the emotion. No time for emotions, he needed to kill the two who threatened his friend.

The hooded Draconi faced Enar, standing opposite Simon.

"Stop arguing and kill him." Magic layered the words. Magic spoken by the bloody Draconi. Affected by the magical tone, Simon raised his sword.

Which was the last thing the bastard did.

Double-handing Blood Seeker, Enar swung, the blade slicing into Simon's neck, blood spurting over Thoren.

Clearly blood had gotten into his eyes too. He blinked a blurry vision at Thoren, who sat, blinking at him. Both males swiped a hand across their eyes. He wasn't crying. Watchers didn't do such feminine things.

Especially when an enemy still remained.

The Draconi clapped, the slap of his palms stilling the insect chatter. "Thank you. He was getting annoying."

Enar peered into the folds of the cowl, trying to see the Draconi's face, meeting up with a whole lot of darkness. Not a trait to describe him.

Between one breath and the next, Thoren jumped to his feet, tackling the Draconi around the waist, slamming them both into the ground. The Draconi flipped Thoren onto his back, one hand posed for an energy blast.

Not happening. Enar kicked the Draconi in the shoulder, flipping him off Thoren and pointed the tip of the titanium sword at the bastard's heart. With one smooth roll, the Draconi crouched staring at the two, surprise rolling out of the dark recesses of his cowl.

What he wouldn't give to disobey the Council and kill the bastard where he crouched on the ground. Unfortunately, he had to return the goat sucker for interrogation.

"Titanium is a bitch, eh?"

The Draconi's head wavered as he took in Enar's stance and then looked at Thoren.

"Bid your aunt greetings from me." Jumping to his feet, he spun and ran, his cloak disappearing into the shadows.

Enar pounded after him, refusing to let his prey run off. Deeper into the forest they dashed, until he no longer saw the Draconi. Pulling to a halt, Enar looked around. Nothing. Whispering branches and the ragged gasps of his breathing echoed off the trunks.

No Draconi.

Goddess's teeth. Had the Draconi managed to transport despite the titanium sword?

Tilting his head back, he took in the branches. No Draconi hiding up a tree. No Draconi on the ground. And without a torch, he couldn't track the bastard's trail.

He cursed.

No use standing around the trees staring at shadows. He ran back to Thoren and Keara, his boots slapping against the carpet of leaves, his breath heaving through his lips. Darting around a tree, he dashed to where Thoren knelt before Keara.

"Lost him," Enar gasped, dropping both swords as he bent over, hands on his knees, his breath ragged. Definitely needed running practice.

"She won't wake." Anguish laced Thoren's voice. "I need to get her back to the Temple but that sword is prohibiting it. I don't know what's wrong with her!"

"It might have...something to do with her...raising both of us...from the dead." He gasped like an overweight dragon on a dash for gold.

"We died?"

Enar wiped Blood Seeker's blade on Simon's tunic, trying to get his wheezing breaths under control. "Being stabbed generally does that to a person." He sheathed Blood Seeker and knelt by Thoren. "I need running practice."

"Or bigger lungs."

"Thank you." Thoren clasped Enar on the shoulder.

The bloody ache started again in his chest and Thoren's face blurred. Enar blinked, shrugging.

"What do we do with the titanium sword?"

"The Draconi mentioned a safe distance of thirty paces. If you hide it, can you remember where it is?"

"Do I look like a dumb goat?"

Thoren stared at him, one eyebrow cocked at an angle.

"Thanks. It's nice to see you again too. I'll go hide the sword. Don't leave without me."

He strode across the clearing, counting his steps, wondering what else the Draconi said while standing next to Thoren. Why did the bastard come for Thoren? Or had they come for Keara? Why, why, why?

He sounded like a toddler.

Taking extra steps for good measure, he placed the sword below a tree root and buried it under a pile of leaves. Keeping to the shadows, he circled around to where Thoren held Keara in his arms.

"It's done. Is it far enough for you to get us out of here?" Enar placed a hand on his friend's shoulder.

Thoren formed an energy ball in his palm. Guess that was a yes. "Hold on."

Thoren transported them to the Temple Courtyard and ran, carrying Keara, into the Temple, Enar dashing behind. Clearly his friend was rattled by either Keara's condition or being raised from the dead. Why else would he land them in the Courtyard instead of in the infirmary?

As they ran, Thoren used mind-speak to call Annaliese, his voice slamming through Enar's mind like a burst of energy. The air swirled in front of them and with a muted pop Annaliese appeared.

"What...By the Goddess! Bring her in here!" She shoved open a door and Thoren rushed inside, laying Keara on the bed.

"What happened? She left to tell Father about a vision she saw of you injured. Are you well?"

"Well enough. She won't wake. Can you help her?"

Annaliese placed a hand on Keara's brow and closed her eyes. Her eyes flew open, wide and frightened.

"She raised you!"

How did she know that? He'd been taught Draconi considered it rude to forge into another's mind without permission. But Draconi also blocked out other's probing thoughts, allowing them privacy. Perhaps the priestesses thought themselves above societal rules and read minds at will.

He shoved extra barriers around his thoughts.

"Don't say that out loud." Thoren hissed, crossing his arms. "Do you know what others will do if they discover her gift?"

"I'm sorry. It's just...not even my mother had the ability to raise the dead. I've never seen it done before."

"How did you know what she did?"

"I need Aryana. Only she has the ability to heal Keara. I'll return." The air shimmered as she disappeared.

"You get the feeling she doesn't want to speak on how she knew Keara was a death raiser?" Enar slumped against the door, arms folded.

Speaking as he moved, Thoren grabbed a chair and placed it by Keara's side. "Just because we can mind-speak doesn't mean we can invade another's mind. Unless we project them to another, our thoughts belong to us."

"You sure about that?"

Thoren stared at Keara, lost in thought. Or maybe he was just ignoring Enar.

"Thoren?"

"I don't know."

"She'll live. Ari will work her magic—"

"Ari? You're on a pet name basis with my aunt?"

And between one breath and the next his comforting words ran against a wall of anger. Enar gave a silent curse. He did not need to go in the direction this conversation headed. He did not need a reminder of a past indiscretion. Of how he skirted the laws and danced with death. Watchers weren't supposed to touch Draconi females. Thoren looked the other way as did most Draconi his age. Females should have a right to choose who they slept with and not be bound by ancient societal rules.

But Ari?

Any male besides a Draconi who touched the High

Priestess did so on punishment of death.

And he hadn't needed to use his magic to convince her to lay with him. He hadn't convinced her of anything. She started and ended the entire relationship for reasons he never knew. Never cared to know. Over and done now. He had Lily. Why bring out old affairs?

But red suffused Thoren's face and Enar doubted he'd get out of this conversation unscathed.

Son of a bloody goat.

"You didn't."

Enar shrugged, answering with the only thing that mattered. "I have Lily now."

"She's my aunt!"

"You didn't have a problem with it when it was a female in some village."

"But Ari is not a female in some village. She's my aunt!"

"It's over. We ended it."

"You ended it? You mean it was more than once?"

"Do you really want to hear this now?" Enar gestured to Keara. "What's done is done. In the past. Over."

Thoren shoved a hand through his hair, his hand cranked into a fist. The air crackled with tension and Enar shifted, tightening his fists. He might deserve Thoren's punch, but it didn't mean he'd roll over and take more than one hit.

Pop! Pop!

Aryana and Annaliese appeared in front of them, both females hurrying to Keara's side. Ari stopped, though, and looked from Thoren to Enar and back again, her eyes narrowing. One finger pointed at Thoren.

"We'll discuss your discussion later."

He swallowed at the implication. Clearly, the priestesses jumped at will into minds despite barriers erected to keep them out. And he had never even felt Ari brush against his mind.

A chill snuck down his spine and he shivered it gone.

"Move away from the bed." Aryana motioned Thoren back and he scooted the chair against the wall.

Enar took the steps necessary to stand in front of Thoren. Keara's condition eclipsed what lay festering between them like a rotten carcass. Thoren needed his support.

Or not.

Thoren slugged him on the shoulder and walked to the bed. Enar swallowed. His friend would get over his anger. With Thoren, anger was like a spark from a fire-starter, hot and bright and if you did nothing to stoke it, it faded into ash.

Aryana rested her hand against Keara's brow, eyes closed, her face relaxed.

When she spoke, her gaze fixed on Thoren. "She is drained of energy. Annaliese told me what Keara did. I'm sorry, but it will have to be reported to Alviss."

"I know. I just don't want everyone knowing. Can you heal her?"

"I can try. No guarantees."

Annaliese placed both hands over Keara's heart and Aryana placed hers on top of Annaliese's. Chills broke out over Enar's skin as Aryana chanted in a language he'd never heard. The sing-song words rose and fell, filling the room with a spell as old as the Draconi race, a spell of powerful magic. Aryana's hands started to glow, the light spilling into Annaliese's.

A current shot through the room, ricocheting off the stone walls, bathing them in a blue glow. Enar felt the magic push against his skin, wanting his power, his strength.

Unlike his conscious, the small drop of magic he'd inherited from his mother knew what spell Ari cast and shrank in fear. He needed to hide that part, hide the magic festering inside, the magic Aryana's spell sought. No one, with the possible exception of his parents, knew what resided inside him. His inner magic that he swore caused Viktor to hate him, to degrade him. He refused for anyone else to know his inner secret.

What would Thoren think? What if his best friend saw his magic and rejected him?

Instead of being all up inside his mind, he needed to focus on the problem at hand and set up barriers to ensure Ari's spell didn't touch him.

Who was he fooling? He was dealing with a Draconi spell. Resistance was futile.

Whatever spell Ari weaved resonated deep within, drawing forth his magic, pulling it out to help Keara.

Just because it went to a good cause didn't mean he had to like it.

Enar fought against the spell, unwilling for anyone, not even his best friend, to know he possessed a bit of magic. But the current in the room pounded against his skin, crashing through the meager barriers he tried to erect, seeking his magic. He let loose with a yell as the blue current blasted into him, sucking on his energy, drawing out a small portion of it to hover over the priestess's joined hands.

Great jumping dragons, what was in that spell? He felt as if pieces of his innards had been yanked out through his nose. Pain he could live with. It was Thoren's reaction he worried about.

Clearly for no reason. Thoren only had eyes for Keara. He didn't notice what happened to Enar.

Praise the Goddess.

More energy filled the room, blue light pouring through the windows, the cracks in the door, the walls. Small magical portions from who-knew-how-many formed a ball of blue energy that hovered above Aryana's hands, growing larger with each stream of light that entered it. The priestesses exchanged a look, a silent communication, and removed their hands from Keara's chest. The ball slammed into Keara, bowing her off the bed as it covered her with its glow. Keara gasped in air, her body slamming into the mattress as the blue glow intensified.

"What did you do?" Thoren rushed to Keara's side, one hand hovering as if to touch her.

"Don't touch her! The spell might target you instead." Annaliese grabbed Thoren's arm.

"I gave her more energy," Aryana said. "She'd drained hers raising both of you. Do I even want to know how the finest reconnaissance specialists ever managed to get themselves killed?"

"They had a titanium sword," Enar said. Good for him. He could still speak after the blast of blue light.

"Titanium?" Annaliese gasped.

"How did they discover the effect titanium has on a Draconi?" Aryana's eyes popped wide.

Good question. Thoren shrugged. "I don't know, but the Draconi—"

"A Draconi?"

"He was working with one of the lords from Keara's town. He said he wanted revenge. He seemed to recognize me, though, because he referred to me as the 'bitch's nephew' and told me to give my aunt his regards. I'm assuming he meant you."

Aryana stopped breathing as she exchanged a look with Annaliese. "What did he look like?" Her voice shook and despite their past history, Enar felt an urge to wrap his arm around her shoulders.

"I don't know. He wore a cloak that concealed his face."

"He ran fast," Enar added. "I lost him and I don't normally lose my prey."

"Maybe that had something to do with you gasping like an old dragon."

"You try running after being killed with an energy ball and then rising from the dead. See how fast you go."

"Enough!" Aryana sliced a hand through the air. "You need to report these findings to the Council."

"Report away. I'm needed here with Keara." Thoren crossed his arms in an I'm-not-going-anywhere stance.

Annaliese placed a hand on Thoren's arm, her face a mask of healer's kindness. "Keara is going nowhere nor is she waking until the energy is released into her body. See how it's still visible? She'll wake when the blue disappears, which won't be for some time. Go make your report and return."

Thoren snarled and Enar yanked him back. "Relax, Thoren. She's right."

Not that he blamed Thoren. If Lily was lying in the

bed instead of Keara, he would be performing the same act.

Shaking off Enar's hand, Thoren turned to Aryana. "We need to talk."

"No, we do not. My body is mine to give as I will and you will not report it either."

"What's to stop me?"

"I know something you don't want told and you know something I'd like to keep secret. We are at an impasse, are we not?"

Well, that was one way to stop Thoren's righteous anger. Blackmail. Enar tried to keep his lips from turning in mirth. His secret would remain a secret.

Thoren ran a hand through his hair and glanced at Keara, clearly trying to decide why he was upset. His thoughts reached Enar, thoughts of his sense of right and wrong. Once they got through this, Enar never wanted to upset Thoren like this again. He hid the affair on the advice of Ari, never realizing it would affect Thoren this way.

He should have known better.

Which did nothing for the current situation. They would get through this. He refused to lose his best friend.

"Deal." Thoren cleared his throat. "You have my word I will not mention your...indiscretion if you do not mention Keara's ability."

"I'm glad you see things my way. Now go and report. Return by morning and Keara will be as you left her."

Thoren clapped a hand against Enar's back and transported them to the Council's Chamber. Instead of sitting in their chairs, the thirteen males clustered around the seeing ball.

"How is my granddaughter? I cannot see her in the ball," Alviss shoved his way out of the pack of males and shuffled toward them.

"Aryana performed a spell to replenish her energy." Thoren said. "So you saw everything?"

"Not everything. Enough to know what Keara can do. Enough to see my best reconnaissance specialists get their arses kicked into the grave. We've been discussing Keara since then and missed the rest. Where's the rogue?"

"He got away." Enar glared at the males.

"You lost him. No whelp of mine—" Viktor snarled, his face red.

As if it moved of its own volition, Enar's lip pulled into a snarl.

Alviss pointed his cane at Viktor. "Quiet! I'm tired of your squabbles." He turned back to Enar as Viktor continued to snarl. "How did the Draconi escape?"

Enar shrugged, lowering his lip. He held no quarrel with Alviss. "He ran, I chased. He disappeared. I looked around and nothing. Keara was injured so I returned. The titanium sword is hidden for your retrieval."

"And do you know who the Draconi is?"

"No sir."

"He apparently knew Aryana. Said I was the 'bitch's nephew' and to give my aunt his regards," Thoren said. "May I go now? I need to see Keara."

Alviss shook his head. "We'll bring Aryana to us. You will stay to hear this."

Two blinks and a popping noise later and Aryana stood beside Thoren. Her face pale, her eyes snapped wide, she stared at Alviss. Taking a deep breath, she exhaled through her nose.

"Alviss. How nice of you to bring me here without warning."

"Aryana. Thoren tells me the rogue Draconi who attacked him seemed to know you. Do you know who he is?"

Aryana cut a quick glance to Thoren before returning her glare to Alviss. "My nephew did not describe the male, only that he wore a hood. Not even I can definitely determine who someone is without a description."

"Give us your best guess."

"I have banished a couple of Draconi during my service to the Goddess. The most recent banishment occurred four months ago. My guess would be Fasolt."

Alviss's eyes narrowed. "You banished someone without my knowledge?"

"It is not required for me to inform you of those who are banished. In case you forgot, I am the High Priestess. Part of the duties involves banishing those that need it. And Fasolt needed it," she snarled.

"Why did you banish him?"

Aryana's fists clenched. "He assaulted one of my priestesses, claiming it was her fault he did not see the Goddess during his session with her. She almost died. His face was...damaged in the struggle to subdue him. He swore revenge upon me. It sounds like him, but again, I was not there to see."

"Did either of you know Fasolt?" Alviss turned to Thoren and Enar.

As one, the two shook their heads.

"No, sir," Thoren answered for the two of them.

"This presents further issues for us to discuss. You can go now," Alviss waved his hand and Aryana disappeared. "You may go too, Thoren. No, Enar, you stay. We need to know how to recover that titanium sword."

Enar nodded at Thoren. Thoren slapped a hand on Enar's arm.

I'm sorry for overreacting.

It's all right. Get back to your female. Wish I could see my woman now.

You will soon.

Yes, but not soon enough.

With a nod and a quick turn of his lips, Thoren disappeared, leaving him alone to face the Council.

Chapter 20

Several hours later, Enar trod down the hall to his room. To where Lily awaited him. He couldn't stop the grin from turning his lips. Wait until she heard about his adventures tonight.

Who would have thought Alviss hid a wooden chest that blocked the effects of titanium on the Draconi? And that none of the Council members realized such a chest sat in a dark recess of the Council's Chamber? A spell must have been placed on the chest to hide its location since as soon as he left the Chamber, he could no longer remember the location of the recess that housed the chest.

No matter. The important thing was the chest now contained the titanium sword, thanks to a little rescue mission by him and Balthor. What a shame Balthor couldn't have been his father.

All in the past. Once he showed Lily to his father, things would improve. Hope reigns eternal.

He shoved the door open to his room and as he thought, Lily sprawled in their bed. Small streams of morning light filtered through the shutters over the window and he stifled a yawn. He had all day to sleep. For now, he needed the touch of his woman, the feel of her skin on his. Proof she wouldn't loathe him when he returned her to his village.

He needed to convince her she belonged to him.

That she could never leave him. That no matter what happened in his village, he cared for her.

And what about the word that crossed his mind before he died? The "L" word that slapped him like a conviction? He dropped his weapons on the floor by his side of the bed, keeping them close in case they became needed. Clothes followed, soft drops against the wooden floor. He slid between the covers, running a finger up Lily's arm, feeling the smoothness of her skin.

Watchers were warriors who lived in the moment, who fought to their last breath. They didn't have such trivialities as the Draconi male's sappy emotions. His brain clearly hadn't spit out the "L" word as a real scenario. It had been dying. As a Watcher he didn't need that word. He only needed the woman lying beside him.

"Lily, love. I'm back."

****

Lily woke to the feel of Enar's fingers stroking her arm. A dream. It had to be a dream. A memory. He died. Her visions never lied. But this felt so real. Like he lay in bed with her. Her eyes fluttered open.

He was in bed with her. She closed her eyes. Had to be a dream. Opened her eyes. Enar still lay in front of her, his fingers touching her skin. He felt real. He looked real.

"Enar?"

"Who else would it be?" His lips followed the trail of his fingers over the skin of her arm. Definitely felt real.

"I thought you died."

He froze. "Why do you say that?"

"I saw you. After you left. You died from an energy blast. My visions never lie."

"You have visions?"

"Sometimes. I don't like them." She refused to mention Aryana's offer for her to live at the Temple and become the Temple Seer. No use in mentioning things that would never occur.

"You saw me die?"

"Yes. You need to be careful! I thought it happened last night, but it will happen soon."

Enar rolled onto his back, one muscular arm thrown over his eyes. "It already happened."

"What?" How could he say he died when he was beside her?

"Did you know Keara had certain abilities?"

Like making the blind see and healing the sick? "Like what?"

"Promise you won't mention it? She doesn't want others to know."

"Promise." Keara was her best friend. Didn't she know everything about her?

"Keara has the ability to raise the dead." All right, clearly she didn't know everything about her best friend. "Thoren and I were killed on our mission to capture Simon and the rogue Draconi. You knew they kidnapped Keara in River's Run and tonight they entered Draconi territory."

Lily listened to Enar recount how they had been killed, how Keara raised them, how she now lay in a coma in the healing ward, all about Lord Simon's death and the rogue Draconi escaping, and how the titanium sword was hidden in a wooden chest, which rendered its power over Draconi magic null. Her heart tripped an uneven rhythm.

"Will Keara be all right?"

"Aryana and Annaliese say she will."

"And you? Are you all right?"

"Of course. It takes a lot to keep me down."

Lily tried out a small smile and found it did nothing to calm the beat of her pulse. She almost lost him in the night. If not for Keara she would have. And now Keara lay in a coma.

"I'm glad you're alive."

Enar turned to face her. "Are you?"

"Of course. How can you think otherwise? I was so panicked when I saw you die that Annaliese had to spell me into sleep."

His eyes widened. "You...enjoy my company?"

"Didn't I just say that?"

His face broke into a smile, happiness slipping out to surround him like a cloak. "Woman, you make me happy."

Her pulse still beat its erratic rhythm, but now for a whole different reason.

He reached for her, drawing her against him. She felt the hard planes of his chest, the steel bands he called arms, the erection pressed against her stomach. All warm and living, not the cold of death as her vision showed, as she had feared when the necklace slipped off her neck. Good thing she managed to repair the clasp on the beads. Enar would never know his death broke the clasp. And since the necklace stayed around her neck all night and Enar remained alive, perhaps it meant the magic holding the necklace on had returned.

What did it matter? He was with her now, warm and living. What difference did it make if the necklace broke earlier? As long as Enar didn't find out about it, who cared?

Definitely not her. All she cared about this moment was the touch of his skin against hers, the press of his lips as they trailed from her ear to her breast.

Her hands wrapped around his neck, pulling him closer, holding him to her as his tongue circled her nipple. Her vision narrowed, focusing on him, her world. Goddess, if Keara hadn't raised him...

Settling his hips between her legs, Enar met her gaze and held it as he thrust himself into her. Lily gasped at the pleasant invasion, amazed how much she wanted him, needed him. One hand reached to stroke his cheek, the only way she knew how to tell him what he meant to her.

"Goddess, woman." A slow slide out. "I missed you." He slammed back into her, starting the whole process over.

"And I missed you. Oh, that feels good."

His teeth flashed white. "Hmm. You like this—" he stroked into her, angling his hips to rub against the sensitive spot inside "—huh?"

"Oh, Goddess, yes!"

"Mmm. Good." Lips nuzzled against her neck, causing chillbumps to run down her arm. She was almost there. If he would just stroke...one...more...time...yes!

She felt her body shatter, drowning in waves of pleasure crashing over her. One minute she floated alone in her bliss and the next Enar joined her, calling out her name with his release.

Tightening her hold on his shoulders, she pulled him closer to her, not minding that his powerful body threatened to suffocate her as it pressed her deeper into the mattress. Death by Enar. Not a bad way to go.

He rolled to the side, her body grasping his as he slipped out, his arms wrapping her against him. Security. Strength. Love.

She loved him.

The thought both scared and invigorated her. Invigorated, because that was what love did. Scared, because he would never return her feelings. And what would happen if she spent the rest of her life loving someone who did not return the feeling? She'd become like her mother, bitter, bickering, the way she swore she'd never be. So much for erecting a wall around her heart. Enar managed to shatter that barrier, chipping away at it brick by brick until he rescued her heart from its confinement. Now she would live with loving him and not having him return the emotion.

Sadness tainted her joy at his return.

What would happen when she went to his village?

Her heart skipped a beat. Not much time left until she'd meet his family. Did he have a family living? She tried to remember and came up with nothing. Either way, family or not, the whole thought of going to his village gave her chills. Odd that. She didn't normally get chills thinking of a place. Maybe it was because she was nervous and he wouldn't answer her questions.

Yes, that had to be it. Nothing else made sense.

"Enar. About going to your village."

He stiffened, his entire body going ridgid. "Woman. I don't want to talk about it. There're better things to do with my lips than speak words. Let me show you."

He did and she forgot the question.

Chapter 21

Lily stared at the squat white building set in the middle of the town and swallowed. Unlike the pristine temple of the Draconi, crumbling corners in desperate need of repair bled into the street. The white rock gleamed in the sun like teeth on a wolf. She tried to swallow, but it stuck in her throat.

Last night they attended Keara and Thoren's wedding. Keara looked beautiful, no trace remaining of her brush with death. Her friend was happy with her mate, happy and glowing. Lily glowed too, but her gleam had more to do with the sun and less to do with Enar, who had been acting strange all morning.

Not once since they left the Temple grounds did he speak to her. Not to answer her questions. Not to reassure her. Where her caring lover went, she didn't know.

But she really wanted him back.

Enar strode forward as if he couldn't wait to drop her off at this squat house.

"What is that house?"

"That is the Claims' House." Not the best conversation, but at least he spoke. It beat the rest of the morning.

"All the claims live here?" What kind of place was this?

"Yes. You'll meet my mother."

"Your mother lives here?"

He nodded. Lily scampered to keep up with his long strides.

"Please don't leave me here. I can stay with you."

"No, you can't. Claims stay here."

"But—"

"No buts, woman. This is how it is."

Lily's jaw ached. If she clenched her teeth any tighter her face muscles might spasm and freeze in place. She wanted to speak back and she probably would have if they hadn't turned down a street filled with blond male Watchers. All of whom were staring at her white hair and skin.

And why were they staring? Maybe it had to do with Enar insisting she leave her hood back, allowing all to see her unusual coloring. She felt their eyes on her like a brand, searing her to her soul and she shivered.

"Come, woman," Enar gestured her forward until she stood beside him in front of the solid oak door barring entrance to the crumbling building.

The door was locked from the outside.

The outside.

Chills shook her body despite the heat of the sun. A glance at Enar showed a tense jaw, the muscles bunching under his skin. If she wasn't so nervous, she'd make him think twice about leaving her to his mother's whims.

Enar pushed the bolt back on the door, the metal bar sliding along the wood with a groan. She heard him draw a deep breath before shoving the door open. Scurrying, as if from a hoard of rats, sounded as flashes of white darted into the shadows, out of the way of the light streaming in. Rats? No, not rats, women. Lily blinked in the dimness and looked around, hoping the action would still the pounding of her heart.

No such luck.

Couches crowded the small antechamber they stood in, basking in the dim light filtering through high windows. That were barred. Her heart flopped like a beached fish.

"Ayla!" Enar bellowed as he shut the door behind him.

The entire house grew silent before the scurrying noises started. Even over the noise, Lily heard a distinct set of footsteps drawing closer. The scurrying stopped as the steps grew nearer.

A tall, thin woman with strawberry blonde hair shot liberally with gray stepped into the room. An aura of power surrounded her, similar to what Lily felt with the priestesses in the Temple. Similar to Keara's. But much weaker. Still, the woman's aura crept across her skin, its path raising chills.

But the woman's power was not what made Lily gasp and take a step closer to Enar. It was her face.

Small beads had been placed in geometric designs across her cheeks, beautiful, and yet frightening. What did the designs mean? Why would someone decorate their face that way? If she had to venture a guess, she would think the designs a warning, some sort of beacon broadcasting this woman's power. The designs met at the bridge of her nose, a nose that had been broken judging by the lump on it. Lines bracketed her eyes. Laugh lines or lines of pain?

Maybe pain seeing how her arm hung at an odd angle as if it had been broken and not healed properly. A twin to Lily's necklace hung about her neck and she was clothed in a white sleeveless dress.

The woman took one look at Enar and let loose with an exhale that drifted into the shadows of the room.

"Mother, I'd like you to meet my claim, Lily." One hand gestured to Lily, his voice flat. "Lily, this is my mother, Ayla."

Mother? Lily looked from Enar to the woman, forcing her mouth to close. Wonderful. His mother was more frightening than she thought. Would the woman kick her out?

His mother took another step into the room, cocking her head to the side as she peered at Lily.

"So you became like your father after all." The word "father" was spat out like "dung heap" despite her voice sounding like bird song.

Clearly no love lost between the two of them.

Enar stiffened at her words, gritting his teeth as he spoke. "I am nothing like him."

"And yet," her hand waved toward Lily, "here is your claim. Did you take pleasure in her injuries? Did you give her a choice?" She advanced closer as she spoke. "Of course not. She is here, is she not? Depart from my presence. You have done what you came here to do. Go reap your reward."

One hand grasped Lily's upper arm, tugging her away from Enar and behind the woman before Lily could move or voice her displeasure. Clearly tall and thin did not equal weak.

Lily turned to stare at Enar, hoping he understood her silent plea not to leave her here with his mother, his powerful, obviously a little off, mother. But he either didn't understand or didn't care. Anger and hurt flashed in his eyes before he schooled his face into a blank mask. Not her lover, no longer the man she knew, he nodded once to his mother and turned to the door.

No! He couldn't mean to leave her here. Surely not!

"Enar—"

He turned and faced her, cold blue eyes staring like ice, slicing her heart into shreds. Where was the Enar she knew and thought she loved? Where had he gone?

"You'll see me again, Lily."

With that he shut the door behind him, shutting her into the dimness, the slam of the bolt like a stake in her heart.

"Come, Lily. We will tend to your injuries."

"Injuries?" Lily hated to tell Ayla nothing could be done for her hair and skin color. But who knew, maybe the woman could change the color.

Ayla placed a gentle hand on Lily's arm, the touch feather-light. "Surely you are hurt. Watchers are not known for their gentle care of claims."

"What?" Had she missed something? "I'm sorry, what do you mean?"

Ayla sighed, stroking Lily's arm slightly with her fingers, the effect soothing. "Didn't Enar hurt you when he claimed you?"

"What?" Great. Enar left her with a crazy woman and departed to places unknown. What in the name of the Goddess was Ayla talking about?

The older woman stopped walking and crossed her arms, one eyebrow raised. Lily felt like a bug caught in a net. Like she had when the priests at home stared at her, knowing she must have done something wrong but not knowing what that something was.

"Enar never hurt me. He saved me from death several times. Why would you think he'd ever hurt me?" She mirrored Ayla's position, arms crossed, one foot turned outward.

The woman's eyes rounded, surprise and pleasure filling them. "He didn't?"

"Why would he?"

"Ah, yes. That is the question we all ask. Why do the Watchers treat us so badly?"

"What do you mean?" Lily felt her left eyebrow rise.

Ayla's head cocked to the side as she sucked in her lip. "Hmm, maybe something I said got through his thick skull after all. The Goddess only knows he spent enough time with me. If he truly has not hurt you, then he is the only one. Watchers derive pleasure from watching those weaker than themselves writhe in pain." Ayla's eyes grew distant, her jaw tensing.

The soothing effect given when Ayla's fingers had rested on her arm disappeared like a puff of smoke. Lily stared at the older woman's arm, remembered its stiffness and a hollowness formed in her stomach. "Is that what happened to your arm?"

Sharp eyes focused on Lily. "And my nose." Ayla touched the bridge of her nose. "He liked to make me scream when he took me. At the time, none of the other women were healers and the arm didn't set right. I tried to set it, but I couldn't get it to slide into place. It healed wrong."

Lily shivered, the hollowness in her stomach growing into nausea. She swallowed a couple of times, trying to banish the image of what the poor woman went through. "Why didn't you call for a Draconi priestess?"

"Are you crazy?" She spat and Lily jumped. "The Draconi don't care about us. They turn a blind eye to our suffering. As long as their precious Watchers guard them, they don't care what the men do on their own time. And don't even get me started on why powerful sorcerers need a bunch of violent warmongering men to guard them. Why—"

"Maybe they don't know what goes on here." Ayla had asked to not get her started on a rant and Lily was only too happy to oblige. Lily didn't know the Draconi well, but she couldn't imagine the priestesses allowing such atrocities to happen to other women.

"Oh, they know. How could they not? They see everything, don't you know? They don't care." She threw her hand out in a slicing motion.

"I'm not so sure about that—"

"Well, that's because you just arrived. Live awhile here and you'll see what goes on. Then you'll know how little sorcerers care about those who aren't Draconi. As a matter of fact, they'd kill me on sight, just because I have some magical abilities. They eradicate those who have magic."

"I know for a fact that's not true. They brought back Jamie and my friend Keara. Both of them are Halflings."

"How do you know they aren't killing your friends now? You don't." Ayla shook her head, rolling over Lily's protests. "I'm telling you, they don't like other magical beings."

"What makes you say that?" This she had to hear as she knew the Draconi weren't a thing like Ayla described. She knew quite well nothing bad was happening to Keara and Jamie. Keara was happily mated and would soon adopt Jamie as her own.

Where was help when she needed it? Someone needed to rescue her from this insanity.

Ayla's eyes grew distant, haunted. "Because they'd come to my village when I was a child and take those who possessed magical abilities. My parents forbid me from practicing my magic in public when they realized what I could do." Her voice lowered, shame tinting the words. "I'm the reason why the Watchers raided my village. They were supposed to bring me back to the Draconi, but The Bastard claimed me instead." Her gaze focused on Lily's feet. "He told the Draconi I died in the raid so they wouldn't look for me."

"And you believed him?"

"I'm still here aren't I?" Ayla's head jerked up, eyes blazing, her voice the hiss of snakes. "If they wanted me they would have come and found me. Further evidence they just don't care. Anyway, why are we discussing Draconi? You are a Watcher's claim now and need to meet the other women and hear what it's like to live in this grand place."

With that, she turned on her heel and started down the hallway, leaving Lily blinking in shock. She had not expected that conversation. Ayla was a fountain of information if Lily could get past the waters of bitterness.

Drawing in a breath, hoping to calm her racing heart, Lily followed Ayla down a short hallway, into a huge open area. Sunlight streamed through a glass window in the ceiling, reflecting off the water flowing from a fountain set in the middle of the courtyard. Palm trees waved from around the perimeter, their fronds offering shade from the light pouring through the huge skylight. Women in identical white dresses sat or lay on colorful pillows strewn about the tan stones of the courtyard.

They all turned to her, a rainbow of skin and hair colors. Many were in various states of pregnancy. Most had colorful bruises on their faces. Lily swallowed the bile rising in her throat.

"Ladies, I'd like you to meet Lily. She's a new claim. Lily, these are the Watchers' claims." Ayla gestured to the women.

All eyes swiveled to her, a mixture of sympathy, curiosity and disinterest, but no outright hate. Maybe they would accept her.

Ayla touched her arm. "Come. I'll show you where things are and then bring you back to this room. Most of the women stay in this area throughout the day and you can meet them later." She started walking down a long hallway, white walls sparkling in the light of a torch stationed midway down the length. Their footsteps echoed as they drew farther away from the fountain room, a slow beat of doom.

So this was how one became claustrophobic.

Breathing a sigh of relief when they reached the end of the hall, Lily looked around what was obviously a kitchen. Aromas of herbs and meat assaulted her nose and her stomach growled. Yum. By the smell of things dinner would taste wonderful.

As they stepped into the kitchen, a wave of heat smacked Lily in the face like an invisible brick wall. She looked up at the ceiling, at the fans circling a slow dance, at the small barred windows. How the cooks managed to work in this heat without fainting was beyond her understanding. Someone should insist on larger windows.

Oh, but then the women would all escape. Bad idea.

Several white-clad women chopped vegetables, their hair pulled back into scarves, faces red from exertion and heat. Their eyes flicked toward Lily and Ayla and then focused back on their chopping boards, the slap of their knives against the wood a primal beat. A huge brick fireplace—the obvious source of the heat—took up half the wall facing the door. Large enough for a person to stand in, it contained a fire and two iron pots hung over the flames. A brown-haired woman, her back toward them, added a dash of some herb to the liquid, stirring with a long-handled spoon.

"Greetings, Marshene. I have a new claim here that I'm showing around." Ayla walked toward the cook.

Not bothering to turn around, the woman took a sip from the spoon, nodding her head. Spoon in hand, she turned to face Ayla.

Her face broke into a smile until she saw Lily.

"What have you done bringing a cursed one into my kitchen?" She screamed, making the sign against evil to Lily. "Get her away before she poisons the food!"

As one, the workers stopped chopping, turning to stare at the new arrivals. The breath caught in Lily's throat, surprise and shame warring for dominance. Shame won out and she pulled the hood of her cloak over her head. Who would have thought Marshene—a name Lily had almost, but not quite, forgotten—would be here? The woman had disappeared when Lily was a child, thought to be a victim of a wild animal attack.

Not much older than Lily, Marshene had been her main enemy, taunting her, calling the priests when Lily went into public, wishing her dead. Lily felt like throwing a party the day Marshene disappeared. Which didn't reflect well on her, she knew, but it was still one of her favorite memories. And now that snide bitch was back in her life.

The day just kept getting worse.

Now that Ayla knew Lily was cursed, what would she do? Ayla couldn't kick Lily out, but would she banish her to her room, provided she was even given a room? And what was wrong with Enar for dropping her off in this place? They should have stayed with the Draconi.

Ayla paused, gaping at Marshene. "What is wrong with you, woman? She is a claim. Same as you, same as me, same—"

"She is not the same as me!" Marshene shook the spoon at Lily, her face red, her hands shaking. "She is cursed, I'm telling you. Cursed!"

"You superstitious fool! What is it about her that makes her cursed? You should be cursed for your superstitions, for not welcoming her. We are a band of sisters. Your superstitions are making us weak when we need to be strong."

Lily saw smoke coming from Ayla's hands. Marshene obviously saw it too as her eyes grew wide and she took a step back. Her glance traveled from Ayla to Lily and back again and she swallowed.

"Apologize now," Ayla hissed.

Lily ventured a glance upward to Ayla's face. Fury laced the older woman's features, causing the illusion of a wave of smoke passing over her face. Or maybe it wasn't an illusion, fire consumed her hands.

Lily gasped. How did Ayla catch her hands on fire when she stood across the room from any source of flame? Water, where was water? The only liquid Lily saw was in the pot boiling over the fire. That wouldn't do. A rag caught her eye. Maybe she could beat the flames out. Why wasn't anyone else helping?

Marshene dropped to the ground, forehead pressed against the stone. Lily stopped mid-reach. Was the woman addled?

"Forgive me, Ayla. I knew her as a child. She was one the priests warned against."

Well, son of a goat. There went any chance of Ayla liking her.

"That is how I know she is cursed, but if you want me to welcome her I will. Please forgive me."

Lily watched the fire fade from Ayla's hands. Pink, unburned flesh covered her hands. Normal flesh. It wasn't polite to stare, but Lily couldn't help it. She couldn't stop her eyes from focusing on Ayla's unburned, previously flaming, hands. How could her hands not be burned?

"Then welcome her properly," Ayla said, her voice forced through her clenched jaw.

Marshene raised her head, looking at Lily, her eyes glaring hatred. Her voice, though, floated through the air smooth as still water. "Welcome, Lily. Please forgive me my outburst."

Lily straightened her shoulders, pushing her hood off her head. Marshene's lip curled in a snarl at Lily's movements. Gulping, Lily nodded.

"Forgiven. Nice to see you again, Marshene. We thought you'd been killed by a wild animal." She deserved a reward for keeping the sarcasm almost out of her voice.

Marshene turned her gaze, now contrite, back to Ayla and rose slowly. "I must finish cooking if dinner is to be served on time."

Ayla waved her hand, dismissing Marshene.

"Come, Lily. Let me show you the rest of the building." Turning on her heel as if nothing happened, she walked out of the kitchen, the wide eyes of the workers following her every step.

Lily glanced at Marshene—who made the sign against evil and snarled—before hurrying after Ayla. Hopefully Marshene wouldn't poison her dinner. Or follow her out and stab her in the back with a knife. Lily glanced over her shoulder. Whew. Marshene once again stood by the fire, her spoon slapping circles around the pot, her concentration on the boiling water, not Lily.

Maybe Marshene would stay in the kitchen.

Lily jogged to catch up to Ayla, the older woman's long legs carrying her quickly away from the overheated room. What would Ayla do to her now? What had she done to make Enar leave her in this place? Would he ever come back and take her away from here or was Marshene to be an everyday staple in her life?

Goddess's toes, I hope not.

And now she had to deal with Ayla knowing what she was.

Lily swallowed, the words thick from a bad case of dry mouth. "Do you want me to stay hidden so as not to offend?"

"What in the name of the Goddess are you talking

about, child?" Ayla stopped mid-stride and stared at Lily.

"I—"

One hand waved in the air. "Don't let the ramblings of that superstitious fool bother you. I don't know what got into her. She's not normally like that."

"I grew up with her." Lily lowered her eyes. "According to my town's priests, I'm offensive to the gods."

Ayla snorted. "What a load of rubbish. Everyone is made in the Goddess's image, we are all Her children. Some people are just superstitious fools. Don't let Marshene bother you. If you have any trouble with her, come to me, you hear?"

Lily blinked at her. Did she hear Ayla right? Ayla didn't mind her cursed state? Just like the priestesses at the Temple. Her shoulders relaxed.

"Don't look so surprised. Everyone in this house is equal, no matter where or from what station in life we came from. Once here, equal. Understand?" The wave of heat shimmered around the older woman. Smoke curled from her hands.

"Your hands." Lily took a step back and pointed to the flames now licking Ayla's fingertips.

Glancing down, Ayla shook her hands and took a deep breath. The smoke and fire disappeared. Lily shook her head. Was she seeing things?

"Haven't you seen a firestarter before?" Ayla's head tilted as she peered at Lily as a snake would a bird. "No, I guess you haven't. Marshene hadn't seen one either and if you're from the same village...well, that's what I am. A firestarter."

"So you can start fires? With your hands?" *Good*

job stating the obvious, Lily.

"Yes. Where I come from firestarters are highly prized and must remain hidden from the Draconi because they will capture and kill those of us with magic."

Again, Ayla's version of the Draconi didn't match what Lily knew of them. "Are you sure they killed them?"

"The tales state the firestarters disappeared and never returned. What else would've happened to them? When my parents realized what I was, they forbid me from showing my powers in the open, but unfortunately I had trouble controlling my powers when I got angry and word got back to the Draconi who sent the Watchers and you know the rest of the story."

"I'm sorry."

"Me too."

"Did anyone else in your family have the firestarting ability?" A ghost of a thought brushed her mind before vanishing. She tried to grab it, to remember, but it slipped away.

"My grandmother had much more of an ability than I do. Smoke would come out her ears and sometimes things would fly around. I don't remember much as she died when I was young. My mother's hands just smoked, no fire. I suspect Enar has some ability, but he's never said and I'm not going to ask."

"I don't think he can start fires. Or at least I've never seen his hands catch on fire. He might be able to do other things. I'll ask him."

"Are you daft? You don't ask a Watcher anything. I like you and don't want to see you hurt."

Lily couldn't stop the eye roll. "Enar would never

hurt me." Unless dropping her off at the Claims' House counted as hurting. Next time he stopped by he was getting an earful.

Ayla paused, brows gathering. "You've said that before."

"And I'll say it again. With the exception of dropping me off here, he has been nothing but kind to me. He took me out of a horrible situation, saved me from drowning, and I...I..." she took a deep breath, refusing to say the words. "He's a good man."

Eyes blinking rapidly, Ayla stared at Lily. If the woman's jaw widened any further Lily would be able to see all the way to her toes.

Lily smelled the scent of oil burning in the torch, heard the flicker of flame mixed with several moments of the inhale and exhale of breath rustling through an open mouth.

She defended Enar to Ayla, but a part of her wanted to rail against him. How dare he drop her off at this place? And with her archenemy inside. Most definitely, the next time he showed his face around here, she'd let him have it. She might not possess the ability to shoot fire out her hands, but she remained a force to be reckoned with all the same.

Chapter 22

Enar opened the door to his barrack room and took a deep breath, expecting to smell the musty scent of mildew. Instead, the room smelled fresh, like someone had lived here recently. The cover on the bed looked clean, not the dusty mess he expected to see. Striding to the window, he pushed open the shutters, allowing light to flood the small room.

A bed, chair and night-table stood against one wall. The opposite wall held a small fireplace. With fresh ashes. Enar knelt and ran his finger through the remains of wood. Then he walked to the door and peered out, looking at the number tacked onto the wood paneling.

Yes, he was in the right place. So why did it look lived in instead of abandoned?

He kicked shut the door and fell into the chair. Legs stretched out in front, arms resting behind his head, he tilted the chair back so it balanced on two legs.

A mystery. Good. It gave him something else to think about besides his reaction to his mother and Lily's panic-stricken face as he'd left her with Ayla. He'd almost turned into a sap like Thoren, but despite the ache in his chest—bloody idiot, he'd forgotten to ask a priestess about those pains—he'd managed to leave Lily behind.

As a claim, she should reside in the Claims' House. Not with him. No matter what he wanted. What kind of a Watcher would he be if he stayed with his woman? All the teasing he received as a child would seem like nothing compared to what would happen if he took Lily away from the Claims' House to live with him.

No, it was better she stayed put. He'd learn to deal with missing her curves snuggled against him, her smile in the morning, the way she touched him like she cared for him.

And his mother. Their relationship was tense, to put it mildly. He wished he could take her away, take her back to her own people, but Viktor's claiming necklace hung around her neck, prohibiting her from leaving. At least his father had stopped visiting her, had stopped hitting her years ago. Viktor's hate toward Ayla filtered down to her son.

Putting those not-so-happy memories out of the way, Enar focused on the door.

And waited.

Before long he heard light steps followed by the rustle of a lock being picked. The door cracked open and a small body snuck inside, looking up and down the alley before shutting the door.

Enar sat forward, the weight shift causing the chair legs to hit the floor with a loud crack. The boy jumped, spinning around, flinching when his back pressed against the wooden door, his breath hitching in his throat.

· "Have you been keeping care of my place for me?"

The boy gulped and one hand tried to crawl upward to the doorknob.

"Stop. Sit." Enar pointed to the bed.

Face pale, the lad inched to the bed and sat upright, his gaze dropping to the floor.

"I'm sorry, sir. I didn't take anything. I just wanted a place to stay."

"A lad like yourself should be with your father." Enar pulled the chair so it faced the bed and sat, watching the minute movements of the boy, the way his breath caught, his upright posture.

The boy's knuckles whitened. "Yessir."

Enar reached forward to lay his hand on the boy's shoulder, his fingers encountering wetness as they touched his back. The lad jumped, his already pale face taking on the complexion of the recently dead and Enar saw the flutter of his shirt as his heart thudded in his chest.

Poor lad. A sudden memory surfaced, one of himself as a boy, hiding from his father in another Watcher's empty room, breath shallow from the pain clawing at him.

Enar dropped his hand and sat back. "What's your name, lad?"

"Galvin, sir."

"Well, Galvin, why are you not at training?"

"I finished early." Galvin's gaze skittered across Enar's face before resting on the fireplace.

Enar waited, not moving, knowing a lie when he heard one.

The boy sighed. "He said I was worthless and should leave his presence. He'll forget about it by tomorrow and never tells my father so I do as he says and come here."

Nice to know his internal lie detector still worked. "And you go home when training is over and your father is none the wiser?"

Galvin swallowed. "Sometimes. Sometimes I stay

here. Like tonight. But I can't now that you're here. I'll just be going." He tried to stand, but Enar placed a hand on his arm.

"Not so fast." Enar took a deep breath, remembering his own childhood until his father banished him to live with Thoren. "You may still stay here if you'd like. Unless I have Li—my claim here, then you must stay away. Agreed?"

"But what do you get out of the deal?"

Enar shrugged one shoulder. "Doesn't matter."

Galvin's lips turned up in a ghost of a smile. "Thank you. I won't be no trouble. I promise."

"I know, now take off your shirt and let's see to those stripes."

The boy's mouth fell open. "How'd you know that?"

"Observation. Go on. I'll get this salve the Draconi priestesses gave me for healing wounds."

"Draconi?"

Enar heard the sound of the boy's shirt dropping onto the floor as he rummaged in his pack looking for the salve.

"Yes. Here it is." He showed the jar to Galvin as he sat next to the boy on the bed. "Go on and lay down and I'll put this on."

Galvin stretched out on his stomach, his face to Enar. "So you like the Draconi?"

Pausing with his fingers halfway dipped into the jar, Enar stared at the lad. "What kind of a half-brained, silly question is that? Of course I like the Draconi, I protect them. That's what we're supposed to do, what Watchers are bred for. What are they teaching you children nowadays to have to ask that?"

Galvin blushed, but didn't turn away. "Some think Watchers should stop caring for Draconi. Why do they need us anyway? They're powerful sorcerers and don't need guardians."

"That's just crazy talk." But he wondered the same thing. Why did a race of sorcerers who had the ability to blow a person into pieces with a word even need warriors to guard them? Not that he would mention those thoughts to Galvin.

A half-shrug flitted across Galvin's frame. "Some say we are more powerful. That Draconi have lost the ability to become sorcerers."

Enar snorted and rubbed the cream against the welts on Galvin's upper back. The boy flinched but plodded along.

"Well, some think that. No one ever sees Draconi work magic. You say you've seen a priestess, but no one else has. They sit on the Council with our elders, but the elders do not talk about Council activities or about if Draconi still work magic. Some say that's because the Draconi no longer practice magic, that they aren't as powerful as we are and that we should overthrow their oppressive regime."

Enar stopped spreading the cream, too shocked to move. Of all the crazy things he'd heard in his time, this one had to be the most insane. How could anyone think Draconi didn't work magic? Worse was the overthrowing part of Galvin's statement. "Are you saying Watchers are planning to kill Draconi?"

Galvin nodded.

"And when is this killing supposed to start?"

"I don't know. Father won't tell me. He doesn't like me."

"And what do you think about the Draconi?"

"I've only met the one who is supposed to be my assignment once. He didn't talk much."

"So you agree with your father?"

"I dunno. I mean, it doesn't really make a lot of sense, does it? For us to be guarding them if they're so powerful?"

He'd wondered the same thing, but it didn't mean he wanted to overthrow the Draconi. As if he could. If the Watchers continued on this path, they would be slaughtered and if the Draconi got angry enough, the village of Watchers would be razed. A chill passed through him, shaking his fingers as he spread the salve across Galvin's back. Although he had been teased without ceasing as a child, and to some extent remained shunned, it didn't mean he wanted to see his people destroyed.

"Draconi are more powerful than you can imagine. Your father and his cronies should know better. Don't they guard their assignments?"

"They do, but they've never seen one work magic. No one Father has met has seen a Draconi work magic."

"He hasn't met the right people. The Council members see magic worked. I've seen it worked and let me tell you, you don't want to be on the receiving end of an angry Draconi."

"If you say so."

Enar wondered who he should tell about this. His father? Maybe not his father. He didn't plan on speaking to his old man until he had Lily on his arm.

But someone needed to be told and quick.

Thoren? Thoren sat on the Council now. The next

time he returned to their stone chamber was one minute too soon. But who better to counter a threat?

He cursed. He'd need to report to the Council one more time. Just when he thought he'd never had to see those thirteen carved chairs anytime soon, a threat occurred.

A thought struck him, curving his lips. He could take Lily. Spend some time with her. Erase the memory of him leaving her with his mother. Good idea. He would take Lily to see Keara and Thoren would know what to do about the Watchers' insane plan.

But first he needed to show Lily to his father if the old man was in the village. Prove to him Enar was worthy of being a Watcher. See what he said when Enar showed up with the Watchers' ideal claim.

And then, after he shocked his father into acceptance, he could take Lily to the Temple and tell Alviss what half-brained plans the Watchers had percolating in their spare time.

In order to leave, though, he'd have to ensure Galvin didn't get suspicious and return home to his father. Tomorrow would be best as Enar doubted the Watchers would attack tonight.

He finished smoothing the cream on Galvin's back, remembering being caned for not paying attention in class. Another thing he liked about living with Thoren as a boy, no canes.

"Well, son, you're all patched up and ready for action."

Galvin pushed up to a sitting position. "Thanks. It feels much better."

"It should. The priestesses are great healers."

"You keep talking about them. What are they

like?"

Since he asked, Enar decided to give a lecture of his own. One on the benefits of working for the Draconi.

****

"Lily!"

The bellow thundered through the fountain room like an enraged boar, rattling the white-robed women sitting on colorful pillows. Eyes wide, the women shrunk into themselves, scared despite the bellowing boar not being their Watcher.

Lily smiled. Enar had come for her.

She ignored the aghast looks as she leapt from her colored floor pillow and raced to the antechamber where Enar waited.

Once they were alone he'd get an earful about leaving her here, but for now excitement at seeing him reigned.

The air expelled from Enar's lungs in a loud oomph as Lily smacked into him, wrapping her arms about his waist as tight as she could. His arms tightened about her ribs in return, clasping her against his chest. She refused to release her grip. Under no circumstance was he leaving without her.

"Enar! Thank goodness you came back. You have to get me out of here. They—"

"Enar! You're back so soon." Ayla walked into the room, her steps so quiet, Lily missed hearing their sound.

Then again, seeing Enar occupied her thoughts to the exclusion of all else.

She felt the subtle switch in Enar, the tenseness in his muscles as he turned to Ayla. She refused to look and see the coldness she knew had crept into his eyes. Why did he act this way around his mother?

"Greetings, Mother. Please gather Lily's clothing and put them in this bag." Enar tossed a brown knapsack to Ayla. "We're going on a journey and she can't wear the white dress."

Thank the Goddess. Lily hated the white dress almost as much as she hated staying in this house with haunted women and Marshene's evil whispers. If Enar wanted her to go live in the woods and eat ants, it beat staying in this place. As long as she remained with him, he could go wherever he wanted.

"A journey?" The knapsack dangled from Ayla's hand as she stared at Enar.

"I have business with the Draconi."

Lily pressed her ear tighter to Enar's chest, the steady thump-thump of his heart a balm for her nerves. Ayla continued to stare at him like he had sprouted another head.

Enar cleared his throat. "And I wanted to take Lily along. And she needs to be logged in."

"You didn't take her yesterday before you dropped her off?"

"What?" Lily looked from Ayla to Enar. Yet another custom in this place she didn't understand.

"I wanted to wait until today."

Pity flickered across Ayla's face. "As you wish, but it won't help. You must accept that. I will have this," she shook the knapsack, "ready when you return." Nodding to Lily, Ayla turned on her heel and marched out of the room.

"What do you mean logged in?" Lily asked as Enar escorted her through the door.

Lifting the iron bar on the outside of the door, he spoke with a grunt. "All claims must be presented and logged in."

The bar fell into its metal brackets with a clang and she felt the reverberations in her bones. Who was he presenting her to? What would they do when they saw her coloring? Lily swallowed. Why had she eaten so much for breakfast? One more swallow and she managed to look Enar in the eye when he grabbed her hand.

Emotions flashed through his eyes, almost too fast to read, a mixture of nervousness, excitement and fear. Fear? Since when did Enar, her fearless savior, show fear?

"Listen to me, woman. In this town, you are nothing but mine. You will walk behind me, you will keep your eyes down. Do not speak to anyone, no matter what they say. Do you understand?"

"Yes, but why?"

"I will explain later. Please, follow the rules."

He looked so serious, so fearful she might not follow his rules that her breakfast turned into a leaden weight. She gulped at the bile sticking in her throat and tried to get her panting back into a normal breathing pattern. What would happen if she didn't do what he said? Although she knew Enar would never lay a hand on her, she saw the bruises left on the other women. Her time in his village showed her a side of humanity she wished she'd never seen. Living here frightened her more than life in her village with fanatical priests.

At least then she knew the rules. Here, she didn't understand why women were kept sequestered, why they were abused, why Enar left her in a house with other claims instead of keeping her with him. Why did the other Watchers need to see her? A chill darted down her spine and lodged in her gut, adding more threat to her tenuous hold on breakfast.

Taking a deep breath and wiping her hands on her washed-so-much-by-its-previous-owner-it-was-now-almost-see-through white dress, she followed behind Enar, eyes focused on the beat of his boots against the packed dirt. If only she had her cloak to pull the hood over her head. What if the men here found her as appalling as the priests in her own village had?

Despite Ayla's introductions, Marshene's views spread around the house of women like a foul odor on a hot day. So far only Ayla had talked with her.

If women in the same predicament as she wanted nothing to do with her, what would the men do?

In through your mouth, out through your nose, Lily.

Self-talk didn't help much when her breakfast wanted to reappear and her body shook despite the warmth of the sun.

Get ahold of yourself.

Enar walked with her. He might leave her in a house full of women who hated her, she doubted he knew their feelings, but he would never let anyone harm her. Time and again he'd proven that.

She had nothing to fear with him by her side.

Despite the knowledge, the fear remained, weaving a path through her marrow, charging her heart until it pounded an erratic rhythm. Buildings passed by as they marched along the dirt road and she managed to venture little glimpses, daring to raise her eyes. Nothing exploded, no one yelled at her, nobody came running to reprimand her for those stolen glances.

Maybe Enar was being overly cautious when he told her to keep her eyes on the ground.

They entered a courtyard ringed by white stones similar to those of the women's building, but standing only a man's height. Men sat in front of the stones. Cold men, with eyes frozen and unrest flowing out of their pores like blood from a wound.

After one brief glimpse, her gaze dropped to the ground. Maybe a hole would suddenly appear in the dirt and she could dive in. What were the chances of that happening? Slim to none. No escape for her. She'd rather face Marshene's villainous stories than stand before these men.

How dare Enar bring her here. Couldn't he have left her where she was and logged her in by himself? What was wrong with the man? He brought her into the midst of a bunch of misogynists.

Despite her lowered gaze, the nape of her neck tingled from the stares of the Watchers. Questions like stones flew at them as the Watchers shifted to ogle her.

"Hey, Enar. You have a claim?"

"Never thought I'd see that."

"She's the perfect claim. Are you sure she's yours?"

"Of course she's mine. You think she'd be following me around if she wasn't?" Enar came to a halt in the middle of the courtyard, Lily stepping as close to him as she could.

If she melted against him, no one could see her.

One hand reached for her, pulling her to stand beside him, dashing her plan of hiding. He ran a hand through her hair, caressing her spine, his hand resting on her low back. The gesture should have felt comforting, instead she felt like a slave on display.

"This is Lily, my claim." Pride laced Enar's voice as some of the men stood to peer closer at her, like she was an animal for sale. Please Goddess, let her not be for sale.

Lust like a palatable wave smacked into her. Enar must have felt it too judging by the way his hand stiffened on her back. Lily raised her eyes enough to note the men shifting toward her. What would keep them from killing Enar and taking her?

Now why did she have to go and think that lovely thought? As if being brought to stand in front of these men wasn't scary enough, she had to go and add to the fright.

"Where did you find her?"

"Cautasia." Caution replaced the pride in Enar's voice.

"Any more like her there?"

"We've never seen one like her before, only heard about them." Yet another voice.

Some of the tension eased out of Enar as his hand relaxed. At least one of them felt better. "Only saw her."

"Maybe we should go check it out."

"Check it out yourself, I already have a claim." This new voice received laughter, although Lily didn't understand the humor.

Banter she didn't follow ensued. Her attention focused on Enar, who stood to her left and back a step. Although she couldn't see him, she felt his emotions as if they were her own. He was at ease in this group, but something seemed wrong about his demeanor. She darted a lower-lidded glance at him. Instead of looking at the men gathered around them exchanging talk that would have made her ears burn if she had been paying attention, Enar scanned the periphery of the courtyard.

Wonder who he looked for. Whoever it was didn't show and she felt Enar's body sag on an exhale.

Maybe now he'd get a move on and take her away from this courtyard. If her heart pounded any louder the men would hear the thumping.

Take me away, take me away.

And miracle of miracles, Enar heard her thoughts.

"Now that you've seen my claim, I'm going to take her back to where she belongs."

One hand grasped her by the neck and guided her, keeping her in front of his body, sheltering her from all the ogling. She blocked out the ribald jests and focused on the entrance to the courtyard.

Five steps, four, three, two, one and now they were through the entrance.

Praise the Goddess, she lived.

She turned around, side-stepping so she faced Enar. "What—"

"Quiet. Eyes lowered. Walk fast."

All right. She'd give him an earful later. Probably better that way too.

Lily wiped her sweaty hands on the thin fabric of her dress and walked as fast as she could to keep up with Enar's long strides.

The trip back to the Claims' House didn't take as long as the journey to the courtyard, thank goodness. Enar yanked the iron bar out of its brackets, shoved her through the door and followed behind her, slumping against the wall.

"That was fun, eh?" He grinned at her, his eyes not believing the words.

"Fun? Are you crazy?"

"Ah, you have returned. Here is your bag." Ayla walked into the room holding the knapsack. Ayla's glance ran from Lily's head to her feet, clearly checking her for injuries.

Enar grabbed the bag, hoisting it over his shoulder. "Thank you. We'll return eventually."

Not if she had anything to do with it.

Lily walked over to Ayla and gave her a hug. "Thank you for your kindness."

Ayla held her a little longer than necessary. "Take care. We'll be here when you return." As she pulled away, Ayla ran her hands down Lily's arms, grasping her hands.

Lily looked down to their clasped hands and noticed something she should have seen yesterday: a big black smudge on Ayla's forearm.

"What's that?" Lily nodded in the direction of the mark.

Ayla released Lily's hands, one hand covering the mark, a finger rubbing the stain. "It's nothing but a birthmark."

"What?" Enar stormed over, removed Ayla's hand and stared at the mark. He looked at his arm and then back to Ayla's.

Lily followed his gaze. Unlike Ayla, Enar only had a small black circle on his forearm, barely noticeable. And here she thought she'd covered every inch of his body with her tongue. Obviously covering it with her tongue didn't mean looking at it with her eyes.

Enar cursed and dropped Ayla's arm. He stepped

back, his face red, his eyes wide, looking like he couldn't decide on anger or shock as a dominant emotion. "Why didn't you show this to me before?" It looked like anger won.

Ayla's hands started to smoke and her mouth opened, then shut as she clearly tried to break her own rule about not speaking back to a Watcher for fear of repercussions. Lily took a step back. Getting in the middle of a family argument was not her idea of a smart move.

"Oh? So I'm supposed to show you all my marks? I have one on my bum, you want to see that one?"

Lily took another step back until she pressed against the wall. Smoke poured off Ayla's hands as flames brushed her fingernails.

"Don't be ridiculous, Mother. This mark," he pointed to the one on Ayla's forearm, "is the only one of concern."

"Well, maybe if you paid more attention to me you'd have seen it earlier!" Flames licked up Ayla's palms, turning her hands into balls of fire.

"Stop it!" Enar yelled and Lily felt the words repeat in her mind, freezing her muscles.

The balls of fire that were Ayla's hands withered to puffs of smoke as the woman froze in place.

Lily tried to move and got nowhere. The echo of his words died from the room, but still reverberated inside her, controlling her. She couldn't breathe, couldn't hear her heart beating, couldn't feel the pulse of life coursing through her veins.

"Son of a goat! Breathe!" Enar hollered, but the command was a weak cousin of what he just yelled.

A small breath entered her lungs, not enough to

fully inflate them, but enough to stop her from dying. And once she took one breath, more followed in gasps. She dropped to her hands and knees, sucking back air like a starving man ate food. Lily saw Ayla in the same position and then Enar knelt in front of her, eyes wide, face white.

"Lily! Breathe!" He shook her. She slapped weakly at his arm.

"Stop it! You'll break...my neck. Ayla?"

Enar gathered her into his arms and pivoted on his knees to where Ayla struggled to sit back on her heels. One hand rested against her throat and she stared bug-eyed at Enar.

"I don't know what happened, what I did. I've never...I would never hurt you...either of you. Nothing like that has happened to me before."

Ayla coughed and swallowed and blinked, but the fear remained in her eyes. "The command was inside me."

"Me too," Lily chimed in.

"Only Draconi...Son of a goat. Why didn't you tell me?"

"Tell you what?"

"That you have Draconi blood."

Lily counted her heart beats, and made it to five, before Ayla moved. The older woman burst out laughing, doubling over.

"Oh, oh, oh. You're hilarious."

"I'm serious. You carry the mark of the Draconi. You belong with them."

The laughter vanished from Ayla, although tears still trekked down her cheeks. "What? The Draconi sent your father's band of Watchers to my village to kill me for possessing magic. They want nothing to do with me."

"What? Father knew you were Draconi and still claimed you?"

"Of course he knew I had magic! He decided to claim me and told them I died in the fight so they wouldn't try to kill me themselves. Sometimes I wish he'd let them have me."

"Right you should because they didn't want you dead, they wanted you alive. They want all Halflings alive. That's why a band of Watchers came for you."

"Quit spinning tales, Enar. All in my village knew that if a child was born with magic, the Draconi would come to take them away and kill them. It's why I was supposed to be hidden."

"I can't leave you here. Draconi females are supposed to be protected."

"I...am...NOT...Draconi! And leaving me here never bothered you or anyone else before. Don't change on account you noticed my birthmark." She rose to her feet, weaving a bit. One arm extended, pointing to the door. "Go. Take your woman and leave. Stop spinning tales and telling lies."

Taking a deep breath, Ayla walked through the beaded curtain into the hall, leaving Lily alone with Enar.

Leaving sounded good. Leaving this place, this people, those scary-eyed men. Great idea. Best one she'd heard all day. Using Enar's shoulders to heave herself to her feet, Lily headed toward the door. Enar still knelt, watching where Ayla had disappeared. A whisper of a thought crossed her mind, he wanted to chase Ayla down and take her with them.

"Then take her."

Enar whipped around, eyes wide. "If I could I would."

"What's stopping you?"

"Her necklace. If she leaves without Father, then she will die. It's part of the magic."

"What kind of messed up magic is that?" One hand touched her necklace and for once she was glad the thing was broken.

"I don't know. It keeps the woman here or with her Watcher. I never questioned it." He rose to his feet and grabbed her arm. With his other hand, he slung the knapsack containing her clothes over one shoulder and pushed open the door. "We need to pick up my things and then we need to go to the Temple."

"Why?"

"Quiet." Enar dropped the metal bar into its resting place, locking in the claims. "Eyes down, remember. I'll explain later."

Lily's head spun as she followed Enar to his room. What else had he not told her? How many more revelations could she take in a day?

"Stand here."

Lily raised her eyes, only to see a row of wooden doors. Enar opened one of them and motioned for her to stand in the doorway while he grabbed his packs off the floor. The bare room with its bed, chair and stone floor exuded loneliness despite the bright sunlight drifting through the window.

And he'd rather stay in this room by himself than with her?

"Come. The sooner we leave here the better."

At least they agreed on something.

Playing the meek-mannered claim, Lily slung her bag over her shoulder and followed Enar through the town gates, trying to decide what she felt more: anger, fear or surprise. Enar must have been dealing with his own issues as he remained quiet, setting a quick pace once they left the confines of the village walls.

Not so quick a pace she couldn't pepper him with questions. "Why did you leave me there?"

"I told you. That's where claims stay."

"Well, I didn't appreciate being left in that house."

"I didn't have a choice."

"You always have a choice."

"All right. I choose to walk faster and make it to the Temple sooner." His stride left her almost jogging to keep up.

If she jogged, she couldn't talk. And standing in the middle of the road yelling at his retreating back didn't do anything except give her a sore throat.

Men.

The sun beat down from its apex and still Enar remained silent, marching along like a soldier on a mission. When the stone walls of the Temple appeared on the horizon, he slowed his stride. Good thing too seeing as her legs ached from the effort to keep his pace. If he thought distance made her questions disappear, he had another thing coming.

"Hey!"

Enar turned, one brow cocked. "What?"

"Why get so upset Ayla is part Draconi? Shouldn't you have gotten upset over the way she was treated, which had nothing to do with whether or not she's a Draconi?"

He looked at her for a moment, his gaze turning

into ice-blue rocks. Lily shivered.

"As a Watcher, we are trained to revere Draconi females. Not to the extent a Draconi male would, but enough to value her. Draconi females possess a lot of magic and it's said the Goddess dwells in them. For my Father to claim one is despicable. It's not done."

"So it's all right for other women to be abused like so many of the claims are? How could you let those women live like that?"

His jaw tensed. "I never said I liked it. You of all people know I don't agree with it. But it's the way of things. I can't take any of them out of there. I can't even free my mother. What do you expect me to do about it?" Fists clenched, he stopped to face her.

Lily took a step back. "I don't know! But something needs to be done. They can't live like that!"

"I'm doing something now! We're getting my mother out of there. She's Draconi, they'll take care of her. As for the rest, I don't know."

With a glare, he turned on his heel and strode down the road. Four steps later he stopped and whirled back around. "Taking a claim is part of being a Watcher. And if I hadn't claimed you, you'd be back in your village. So you should be glad Watchers take claims."

Lily watched him stride off. After four strides, she jogged to catch up. "You would have taken me anyway. Even if you had a claim."

"You're the perfect embodiment of a claim. White hair, white skin, light eyes. You're right. I had to take you. And I had to show you off. Show everyone that I," he whacked his chest, pride infusing his words, "I claimed you. So yes, you'd still be here even if I had another claim."

Something snapped inside her. "So you took me because I looked perfect? It had nothing to do with me?"

"Woman, I just said it had everything to do with you. Do you not listen?"

"Me not listen? I've heard every word you said, every lie you told me!"

"I've never lied to you. What's wrong with you? You're...upset."

"Upset? Upset? Why wouldn't I be upset?" Anger pulsed inside her, a snake coiling in her veins. Her normal even-temperament welcomed the rarely used emotion.

The one person she trusted, who she loved, betrayed her. So, yes, the description fit.

"I said we're going to do something about my mother. And maybe the Draconi can do something about the other women too."

"Great! I'm sure they'll all be happy to know the only reason anyone is doing anything is because one of them was a Draconi."

"But you're still upset."

"Of course I'm upset! How can you think I'd be otherwise?"

"I said I'd ask the Draconi to do something about the claims."

"This has nothing to do with them! Why can't you understand?"

If his teeth got any closer together they'd fuse. "I'm trying. You're not making sense."

She knew anger consumed her, knew to continue speaking would only hurt matters, but really, how much worse could they get? And some part, granted a very small, and yet loud spoken part, wanted to make him hurt like she did.

It embarrassed her to know the small part won.

"That's because you're not listening! You don't care! You've never cared!" Even through her temper, she knew that wasn't true, but she was on a roll. "I thought I meant something to you, but you lied to me about everything. About being a claim, about where I'd stay, about your mother, your father and everything else about you. And you don't understand that I'm upset?"

Birds squawked and flew out of the trees at Lily's escalating voice. Enar blinked, all other parts frozen as he stared at her.

"Lily..."

Thank the Goddess the Temple was directly ahead because she could barely see for the tears pooling in her eyes. If she could only make it to the Temple then she wouldn't have to see him again.

She ran, the stupid white dress she didn't bother to change out of catching between her legs. Yanking it above her knees she ran faster and darted into the Temple Courtyard, Enar so close behind her she felt his breath on her neck.

He grabbed her arm. "Lily. You belong to me. You wear my necklace. You will always be mine."

"Oh you think? Well, you died and the necklace fell off." She pulled hard and the shoddy repair work snapped. Pitching the necklace on the ground she pulled a hand across her eyes. "There, have your bloody necklace. I don't belong to you anymore."

With a sob she ran through the Temple doors, calling for the High Priestess, Aryana.

Chapter 23

Enar stood staring at Lily as she ran away from him, her necklace in a broken heap at his feet. Pain spread throughout his chest like a kick in the ribs, and he sucked down a lungful of air in a vain effort to soothe the ache. When he blinked, his vision wavered as if he looked through smoke. Rapid blinking followed by a swipe under his eyes solved the problem.

The priestesses and acolytes stared at him with confusion or pity before lowering their eyes and scurrying off, leaving him alone with the necklace and the sounds of chirping, happy birds. Blithering birds with their happy little songs. He picked up the necklace and fired it at the branch holding the closest trilling avian. Startled, the bird flew to another branch and continued to sing.

So much for silence.

He picked up the necklace, running his fingers over the round stones. He should run in after Lily, but she clearly didn't want him and he couldn't blame her. He'd lied to her, left her alone with his mother and allowed other Watchers to leer at her, all to show her off. All to prove he was as much a man as the next Watcher.

And what did he get for his pride?

The loss of his woman.

He knew he'd lose her if he took her back to his

village, but thought the loss worth the acceptance he'd see in the other Watchers' gazes and the pride he hoped to see in his father's eyes.

Now that he'd visited the land of been-there-done-that, he realized her loss wasn't worth it.

He lived with the shuns and taunts his entire life, along with his father's hate. Why hadn't he stayed with Thoren and Keara instead of taking Lily back to the Watcher's village where he knew he'd lose her—dare he say it—love?

No, he'd had to bring her home, to follow tradition, to assuage his pride.

He was a blithering idiot.

Once he got her back, and he would win her back if it was the last thing he did, they'd settle here, among the Draconi. Who apparently were his blood too.

And wasn't that a scary thought?

Which brought him back to the reasons he came to the Temple in the first place. His mother seemed to be a Draconi and a group of Watchers planned to kill their Draconi wards. In the grand scheme of things, both of those little niceties should rank higher than chasing a woman, but neither seemed as important as getting Lily back. Without her necklace on, he no longer owned her as a claim, which meant he needed to persuade her she belonged to him without using his persuasive magic.

How did one go about seducing a woman without using magic?

Goddess's toes, he'd hung around Thoren too long and was turning into a simpering male pining for his female. Oh, wait, maybe all that pining was because he had some Draconi blood in him.

Enar cursed.

He wanted Lily but needed to find Thoren. His friend would know what to do about all his dilemmas. Provided Thoren wasn't locked in his room with Keara. Why hadn't he thought of that before he came to the Temple grounds?

A disturbance shivered the air around him and Aryana appeared. Her green eyes narrowed, she took two steps toward him and slapped him across the face.

"What in the name of the Goddess was that for?" Enar rubbed his sore cheek. Who knew the female could wield a slap that hard?

"How dare you upset Lily! I can't even get a word out of her, she's sobbing so hard."

He rubbed at the ache that grew in his chest with her words. "So how do you know it's my fault?"

"Who else's fault would it be?"

She had him there. Not that he'd admit it. "I need to talk to Thoren."

"Thoren's busy with Keara. You'll be lucky to see either of them for a week. Who you need to speak with—"

He cut her tirade off in mid-sentence. His news being more important than her rant. "Some Watchers are talking about killing Draconi in order to stop guarding them and my mother has Draconi blood."

Ari paused, one finger hanging mid-point, her narrowed eyes growing wide, her mouth gaping. In two heartbeats, her mouth closed, her hand fell and she started blinking.

"What?"

"I said—"

"I heard what you said! I don't understand. Explain."

Enar told her everything he knew, which wasn't much. The longer he talked the more disturbed she looked, her face turned red, steam wisped out her ears, the corner of her lip pulled back into a snarl.

Beware the she-dragon.

"What? I can't believe they would do that! Are they crazy? I can't decide what part of that bothers me the most. They're both...By the Goddess." Ari put both hands to her temples and ran them backward over her head as she took a deep breath. "The first thing that needs to be done is to safeguard our people. We'll need to speak with the Council." Her tone of voice suggested eating rotten trash had more appeal. She shivered.

"I know. I'll see if any of the Watchers on the Council know what's going on." Specifically his father.

Ari nodded. "I suppose I'll need to go see the Council too. They might actually want my help. You have no idea how much I dislike talking to them."

"Why?" Good to know he wasn't the only one who didn't enjoy meeting with the Council.

"It's complicated."

Ari headed for the back gate of the Temple Courtyard, which opened to the path leading to the Council's Chamber. Had it only been four days earlier Enar walked this path? Seemed like a lifetime. Once he finished telling the Council about his mother and the rebellion, he could work on the more important issue of winning Lily back.

Somehow he'd figure out a way to convince Lily she belonged to him.

Or else learn to live with chest pains and a feeling of idiocy.

Aryana paused in front of the great doors to the

Council's chamber as if waiting for him to open them for her. Enar put both hands on the doors to push them open—nothing like a dramatic entry to get the males' attention—when he noticed the tenseness of her jaw.

"You really don't like them, do you?" Why did she dislike the Council so much?

"As I said, it's complicated. But here we are. Carry on." She waved a hand in the direction of the door and took a deep breath.

Might as well get it over with.

He threw the doors open and took a step into the circular chamber. It might have been a bit more dramatic if he'd let Aryana walk through first, but the crash of wood against stone managed to startle the group of males hunched over a table in the middle of the room. Equally startled, Enar stared at the males, who were playing cards. Cards?

What happened to the endless hours of plotting and scheming? Of sending spies out to search for Halflings?

Dismay froze his limbs until he saw his father's face. Viktor turned to look at him, straightening from where he leaned over Balthor, staring at the Draconi's cards. Viktor sneered and Enar felt his anger snap. How dare Viktor take an oath to guard the Draconi and their females and yet abuse one as his claim?

Why had he ever thought he'd find acceptance in his father's eyes?

The man was an ass's arse.

Enar lunged. Two strides and his fist slammed into his father's jaw, rocking the older male into Balthor. Viktor righted himself with a roar, one hand reaching for his dagger.

"Die, you son of a misbegotten whore!"

Enar jumped out of Viktor's reach, red clouding his vision. All those years wasted, wishing for his father to say one kind word to him. What a fool he'd been. His longing obscured him from noticing the evil consuming Viktor.

His father took a step in and stabbed up toward Enar's stomach. Enar hopped to the side and with a circular motion of his arm, pushed aside Viktor's thrust, his forearm colliding with his father's.

"Stop!" Alviss yelled and all motion ceased.

Enar stared at Viktor as his father snarled at him. The anger drained from him along with the red haze of his vision, leaving him filled with pity. Pity for the man who never cared to know him. Pity for Viktor's rage, his hate, his inability to love.

Why did the man dislike him so much?

Thump, step, step, thump. Enar cut his gaze to the sound, watching as Alviss shuffled into view, leaning on his cane, his feet dragging with his elderly steps.

"What is this about?" As usual, magic layered the old male's voice, sending a shiver down Enar's spine.

"This whore's son hit me! I was defending myself!"

"Maybe if you'd stop calling my mother a whore..."

"Enough!" Alviss glared at them both. "This is the Chamber of the Council, not a chamber of airing family grievances."

"This male is not my son." Viktor spat, the spittle landing on Enar's foot.

Enar felt his heart stop. A collective gasp rose from the Watchers at the words and their meaning. A meaning the Draconi clearly didn't understand.

Alviss huffed. "Viktor, you know that to be a lie. All with eyes can see he is your son. A twin couldn't look more like you. I do not understand the differences between you two, but I ask you not to air those differences in this chamber. Understand?"

Viktor stared at Alviss for a long minute while the rage cleared his features into a tight mask. He gave a curt nod. Alviss turned to Enar, who still reeled from Viktor's words. Not his son? Did the elderly Draconi realize what Viktor did when he spoke those words?

Probably not, but he soon would.

And Enar would face the consequences, but not now. Now he needed to tell what he knew.

Enar crossed his arms. "I learned something from my mother today that caused my reaction."

Alviss's eyebrows rose. "Oh? Because hitting another in these chambers is a pretty strong reaction for anything your mother could have told you."

"She has the Draconi mark and according to her, Viktor knew and claimed her anyway."

That tidbit of news managed to quiet Alviss.

For all of three seconds.

"What?" Alviss turned to Viktor, his eyebrows two questioning slashes.

Viktor paled and licked his lips. "He's lying. If I had noticed the mark I would have brought her to you. You know that."

A card fluttered off the table and landed on the floor in the silence. Enar kept his eyes locked on Viktor, watching his father's chest rise and fall, the snarl on his lips, the fleeting glimpse of shock and fear drift through the rage in his gaze.

"Let the woman speak for herself." Aryana's voice

echoed in the chamber and all eyes turned to her, as if noticing her for the first time.

"High Priestess. It's a pleasure to see you here." Alviss's lips curved, the expression going no further than his mouth.

Aryana's head dipped. Only because she had been his lover could Enar see the fine tremor that shook her. He doubted the others noticed. Her demure appearance, hands folded in front of her body, a hint of a smile on her lips, belied the strength and magic that ran within her. Along with a ribbon of fear and a cord of anger.

"It is nice to see you again, Alviss. Did you want to bring the woman in question to these chambers, or shall I?" She held Alviss's stare.

What was it between those two?

Alviss gestured, palm up, at Ari. She nodded and motioned for Enar to stand next to her. One hand grasped his wrist, a little too hard for his liking, fingers digging into his flesh. Green eyes bored into his and images of his mother popped into his mind as if sprung from hiding.

Aryana closed her eyes, and Enar felt her power beat against his skin where her fingers touched. A shimmer in the air congealed into a dusty mass that grew into a figure. The figure hunched over, hands shielding her ears, her mouth opened in a scream. The notes flew to the ceiling, hovering, gaining strength, before raining down upon them like hail in a storm, crashing into the marble floors, the echo dying into silence.

Her necklace dropped to the floor with a clatter, drawing flinches from the Watchers. Ayla straightened one slow inch at a time, her hands dropping to her sides, fright written on her features as clear as words in a book. Looking around the chamber at the males gathered, the blood left her face when she saw Viktor. Tremors moved her limbs and she took a step back, wrapping her arms around her waist. Enar yanked his wrist from Ari's grasp.

"Mother!" His legs ate the distance between them and he gathered her in his arms. Why had he never noticed how thin she was, how her shoulder blades stuck out in sharp planes against his skin? What kind of son was he? Her hands grasped his shirt as she fell into his embrace.

"Where am I?" Her gaze rose to his.

"The Council's Chamber on the grounds of the Draconi Temple."

"Draconi?"

Shivers convulsed her body as she dropped her head against his chest. A deep breath gasped into her lungs, followed by another and Enar smelled the stench of fear in her sweat.

"Don't worry. No one here wants to harm you." *Except for Viktor.* As if he would tell her that.

"The Draconi want to kill me," she whispered against his shirt.

"What?"

She drew in a shaky breath and pushed away from him. Looking him in the eyes, she placed a hand against his cheek, the edges of her mouth turning slightly upward in her pale face.

Before his lips could form words, her hand dropped as she looked over his shoulder. "I am ready."

"Good," Enar jumped as Alviss spoke from behind him.

It took a lot to startle a warrior like himself, but Alviss managed. And with only one word.

Pay attention, Enar.

Alviss held his hand out to Ayla. "Please give me your left hand."

Drawing in a shaky breath, Ayla placed her hand in Alviss's. With his opposite hand, Alviss touched the black mark on her forearm and shut his eyes. Ayla stiffened, her breath rushing between her teeth in a hiss.

After seeing Keara experience the same thing, Enar knew Alviss wasn't hurting his mother, but he felt a strange surge of protectiveness toward her. Not like the feeling he experienced with Lily where he'd kill any bastard who came near her, but close enough. It had been years since he felt that way toward Ayla, years since he watched his father beat her, unable to help.

All he received for his trouble was a busted nose. A broken wrist. Bruised ribs.

Viktor looked none too happy about Alviss's find-the-Draconi-blood-by-touching-the-mark spell. Or maybe the sour face was due to the bruise budding across his jaw.

Enar glared back at his father, meeting the older man's gleaming hatred and returning it with some of his own. In one instant, the man turned Enar's dream of acceptance into ash, banishing him from the Watcher's village.

For as long as Enar remembered, Viktor insinuated Enar was not his son, although today was the first time he said it. And once the shock faded, anger took its place. He'd hoped with Lily as his claim to gain his father's acceptance, but that goal remained impossible.

And after the revelations of today, did he really

want Viktor's acceptance? What kind of man took a female with Draconi blood and claimed her? And abused her? Even if she wasn't a Draconi, no man should abuse their claims the way Watchers did. Why didn't he understand that earlier?

He should be glad Viktor banished him, but a small part of him longed for his father's acceptance, acceptance that would never come.

Startled out of his thoughts by a movement, Enar turned to Alviss, seeing small whiffs of steam drift out the ancient Draconi's ears.

Alviss dropped Ayla's arm and grabbed her necklace off the floor. As if noticing for the first time it no longer hung around her neck, Ayla slapped a hand against her bare throat as Alviss dropped the strand of beads into her other palm, closing her fist around it.

"Thank you, Ayla. Please go with Aryana and she will tend to your needs."

Well, what do you know? Sound can come out of lips pursed together tighter than a rich man's money bag. Although Alviss should watch that throbbing vein in his forehead. Enar didn't blame Ayla for moving quickly to Aryana's side.

A quick glance at Viktor showed fury flashing through his eyes as he watched Ayla move to where Aryana stood. Amazing her necklace came off while Viktor still lived.

And Lily had kept his necklace, even though the clasp broke when he died. Which meant she liked him.

Right?

Yes, there was hope for him yet.

With a nod to Alviss, Ari grabbed Ayla's hand and transported them both out of the chamber.

With his mother taken care of, Enar turned to his other topic of business. "I have heard a group of Watchers are plotting to kill Draconi so they no longer have to guard them." His voice cut into the silence like etching on glass.

Gasps met his announcement. Enar looked at the Watchers, relieved to see all but one looking like they'd been slapped silly. Whether his father was in on the plotting or still upset about Ayla's revelation and losing her as his claim was hard to tell, but Viktor's gaze snapped to Enar. The fury and hate in those narrowed eyes almost caused Enar to take a step back.

One finger pointed at Enar and before anyone could formulate words to his announcement, Viktor took a step toward him.

"Liar! This male, who calls himself a Watcher, but who is not, has made up these lies! Do not believe him. All know Watchers guard Draconi. All know we are happy to do so. Do not believe this liar!"

He cursed. How many times in one day can a Watcher—for that was who he was no matter what his old man said—be stunned into silence? His entire life, he'd watched Viktor. Watched the man talk, walk, and fight. Watched him so much he knew what every nuance meant.

And Viktor was lying.

Obviously, not every Watcher was happy about guarding Draconi.

"Silence!" Alviss barked. "I don't want to hear another word out of you until I ask." Viktor seethed, but remained quiet.

As if he had a choice. Laced with magic, Alviss's command would remain in place until he spoke otherwise.

"Who knows about this?" Alviss turned to the Watchers, but they looked as shocked as the Draconi. Even Viktor acted shocked.

Should he point out Viktor's lies? Maybe not. Viktor might be lying when he said he was happy to guard Draconi, but that didn't mean he plotted with the others to kill them. For now, Enar would keep his mouth shut.

Alviss turned at an arthritic pace to face Enar. "How do you know about this if they don't?"

"I was told a group of Watchers planned to overthrow the Draconi's rule and be free to do what they wanted."

"And you learned this, how?"

"I ran into a lad who mentioned it and asked if I was of that mind-set."

"A lad?" One of the Watchers asked. "How do you know he spoke the truth?"

"Even if he didn't, shouldn't the threat be assessed?"

"True words," Alviss thumped around to look at the Council, his gaze fastening on one of the Watchers. "Perhaps you, Oren, should confirm this threat."

"As you wish." Oren nodded his head in acceptance.

"Now back to the other issue." Alviss leaned on his cane as he glared at Viktor. "Speak in your defense, Viktor, as to why you claimed and abused a Draconi female."

Viktor paled. "She didn't have the dragon-shaped mark on her forearm. Plenty of people have black, blobbed birthmarks. How was I supposed to know she was Draconi without the usual mark?"

"So you save your abuse for those you claim as your mate?"

Viktor snarled. "My claims are my business, not yours."

"Do you deny abusing them?"

"I refuse to answer that question. It has nothing to do with what you accuse me of."

"It has everything to do with it. No woman should be abused, especially by her mate."

"Thank you for the morality lecture."

Steam wisped around Alviss's head. "Don't backtalk me!"

Viktor swallowed the snarl rolling his lip. "Our women are clothed and fed and keep sequestered for their own security. I assure you, they are well."

"Ayla was not well. How do you explain that?"

"She fell and broke bones. Hardly my fault."

"All your fault. You think I didn't see what you did?"

Viktor pointed a finger at Alviss. "You lie! You could not see into her mind without her permission. She didn't give you permission."

"Think you my magic is as weak as my body?" The quiet, flat tone of Alviss's voice had Enar taking a step back. The air warped around him, heating until Enar thought his skin might blister.

"No offense," Oren offered, his words stopping the oncoming Draconi about to charcoal a Watcher session, "but Viktor has a point. Even those we question give permission for a mind search."

"Permission is a courtesy, not a condition. How could you not realize how he abused his claim?"

"Surely you cannot expect us to know what goes on between every Watcher and his claim?" Oren crossed his arms. "Do you know what goes on between every Draconi male and his mate? No? Then how can you expect the same from us?"

"He claimed a Draconi!"

"He did not know. She did not have the common mark. How could he have known?"

"Just because he didn't realize he was breaking the law, does not change the fact that he broke it. He should still be punished."

"Then banish him from this Council. Replace him with another."

The room grew silent as all waited for Alviss to speak.

"I wish for a stronger punishment. I say banish him from the land."

"That is not fair!" Viktor spat. "I should not have that kind of punishment when it was an honest mistake."

"True," Oren said. "Banishment is too severe. Banish him from these chambers. Forbid him from another claim, but do not banish him from the land."

Again, all waited for Alviss.

The elderly Draconi huffed. "Against my better judgment, I will do as you wish. Viktor, you are hereby banished from serving on the Council and will remain sequestered in your village, never allowed to replace Ayla with another claim. Do you still reject Enar as your son?"

Viktor spat and glared at Alviss.

"As you wish." Alviss turned to the Watchers. "Return him to his home and ensure he stays there. And know this Viktor, you try to get Ayla back and I will kill you. You deserve to die for your despicable treatment of her. Go, depart from my sight." He jerked his hand in a dismissive gesture.

Surrounded by Watchers, Viktor left the room, but not before he got in one final snarl at Enar.

Enar released the breath he'd been holding. He should want to see his father killed for abusing a Draconi female, or any female, but it was his father and he couldn't help feeling a sigh of relief the man wasn't sentenced to death. Although Enar still craved the chance to beat some sense into him. But even if he was given the chance, would the sense actually land in Viktor's head?

Doubtful.

And what about him? Losing Lily, being banished from his village, what would he do?

As if Alviss read his mind, the elderly Draconi spoke. "Enar. We have a seat open on the Council. As Thoren is now on the Council and you are his Watcher, you have first dibs for the seat. What say you?"

Shock froze his tongue. Him? On the Council? The one thing he despised? His world had taken a metaphorical trip to the land of the wild beasts, so why not join the Council? Add to all the oddness called life? If he took Alviss up on the offer, he would be able to stay here, with Lily. Provided she would still have him.

She would. He had to remain positive.

If he took the position, he could change things, starting with the way claims were treated. Then move on to stomping out the Watcher rebellion.

Not in his wildest imaginings would he have seen himself accepting this offer, deciding to sit on a Council he'd always hated.

The Fates were twisted bitches.

The whole thought of agreeing to the proposal, of embarking on a new life course...he'd rather face off against a rabid dragon.

In this case he would be facing six dragons, who although not rabid, still managed to scare his balls into his intestines.

Warriors did not allow hiding balls to keep them from doing things that needed done.

"I accept." Goddess help him.

Wrinkles convulsed Alviss's face as his lips turned. "Wonderful! Is there anything you'd like to see accomplished?"

Where should he begin?

For starters, once he left this chamber, he was getting his woman back. Not that he was going to mention that plan to the Council.

For now, he was going to see if anything could be done about the women in the Claims' House. Something he should have done many years ago, instead of hiding the abuse, enabling the abusers.

"I don't know if you can do anything about it, but Viktor's treatment of my mother is commonplace."

"What?" Balthor spoke, eyes wide.

"Watchers are not known for their kind treatment of their claims."

"Are you saying they abuse their women?" Alviss asked.

"Yessir. And the women can't leave either. Their necklaces keep them confined to the village."

"We need to do something. We cannot have abuse happening on our land." Steam trickled from Balthor's ears.

"Why did you never say anything?"

"I never realized anything could be done. I've never seen a necklace come off before a Watcher died."

"We still haven't caught that bloody rogue Draconi and until we do, this situation will have to remain open. But we will do something about it. We can't have that type of thing going on under our noses and let it lie there like rotten trash."

Enar nodded. "Thank you."

"Keep on the lookout for that Draconi. I want him captured. We have all our spies out looking for him, but he's escaping us. Would you like to join them?"

As Enar hesitated, Balthor spoke. "Let the male go home to his woman."

"Ah." A grin split Alviss's face. "I see. Go on now. But be on the lookout. We can't have a male like Fasolt on the loose."

"Will do. Thank you. For my mother."

Alviss waved a hand. "It wasn't enough, but it's done. Get on with you." He pointed to the door.

"Yessir." Enar nodded to the males and marched out the door. Grabbing the handles, he yanked the doors closed with a satisfying bang.

Now he could focus on Lily. Specifically on winning her back. If only he knew how to convince her he belonged to her. What did he say to erase the memories of her time in his village? To convince her she was his?

Hey, Lily, you're mine, necklace or not. Come here now.

That would go over like a dragon falling down a set of stairs.

He could do this. Despite Viktor's words, he was a Watcher, a warrior, and warriors didn't give up without a fight. She was his.

Each stride made to the Temple Courtyard reverberated with those words: *Lily is mine, Lily is mine.*

By the time he pushed open the back gate, the mantra stuck in his head. She was his.

And nothing would keep him from her.

Chapter 24

Lily paced around the foyer for the...what round was it now? Twenty, thirty? She'd lost count. After ascertaining she was physically unhurt, Aryana had marched out the door to confront Enar about making Lily cry. Several minutes later, twin beauties glided into the foyer, introduced themselves as Sofie and Vendela, took Lily to a room and gave her a change of clothing and a hankie for her eyes.

No surprise they didn't want her wearing the white transparent dress of a claim. Or ruining her borrowed dress with tears.

But they'd left her alone and alone was not a state she wished to be in. Too many thoughts. Too many wishes. Too many plots for Enar's destruction.

Her new white linen dress with green and gold trim cinched around her waist and fell in waves to her feet. Her usual outfits consisted of trousers and a tunic, and the feel of the material floating around her legs felt odd. And the room constricted her movement. And did she mention the being alone issue?

Since no one was around to stop her, she drifted down the hall until she came to the foyer and started pacing. Which was where she still remained. Pacing. It beat crying.

Twenty steps to the wall of windows. Why had she allowed love to overrule her aloofness decree? If only she'd stuck with the plan, she wouldn't be in this pacing predicament.

Ten strides to the chairs clustered around the lit fireplace. Why hadn't the High Priestess returned?

Thirty steps to the opposite side. Why was she still here? To be fair, she knew the answer to that one: where else would she go?

Most importantly, what did Aryana want her for? Was her dream where the High Priestess asked her to serve as the Temple Seer to come true?

Lily shook her head and resumed pacing. At least she had been taken in by people who appeared to want her. So the High Priestess probably had an ulterior motive for giving Lily a place to stay. So what? She'd been Enar's pawn too.

No longer. She belonged to no one but herself. From now on she made her own decisions.

Good idea. So why was she still pacing? Back to the fireplace, where the fire burned a cheerful crackling. Could a Draconi breathe a fire to life when they weren't in dragon form? Did their hands smoke like Ayla's? The next time she saw someone, she'd ask.

She did an about face and marched to the opposite wall. Where was everyone? Shouldn't priestesses be running around? Were they fawning over Enar? Again?

Her growl bounced off the wall in front of her and slapped her in the face. She might have entertained thoughts of Enar's destruction, but she'd be a goat's mother before she let another female flirt with him.

He was hers.

Wait a minute. What was she thinking? He wasn't hers. After his lies and deceptions, did she still want him?

It shocked her to realize the answer to that question was a resounding yes.

Evening sunlight drifted through the open window bathing the foyer with the smell of cut grass and the sound of birdsong. Even the stone walls breathed peace.

The foyer might bring peace, but Lily couldn't bring herself to stop pacing long enough to see if her spirit could attain the condition.

"Lily?"

Lily turned, her skirt flaring around her ankles. "Keara?"

"Lily!" With a squeal, Keara launched herself at Lily, grasping her in a bone-crushing hug. "I thought I'd never see you again. What are you doing here?"

"Enar and I went our separate ways and I came back here. Why are you not with Thoren?"

Keara held Lily at arm's length, her eyes narrowed. "Thoren went to get Jamie. We're adopting him today."

"Congratulations. I think."

"He's not so bad. What happened with Enar? Come sit and tell me."

Once Lily started talking, she couldn't stop, the words tumbling from her mouth like a flood. Keara held her hand the entire time, the little squeezes a silent show of support.

"So here I am. I'm hoping Aryana meant what she said about teaching me to be their new Seer."

"Oh, Lily, I—"

Pop! Whatever Keara planned on saying vanished at the appearance of two figures.

Lily's mouth fell open. What was Ayla doing here? And why did Aryana have smoke steaming from her ears, her face a message of vengeful anger? Lily stared at Enar's mother as the woman looked around the high-ceilinged room with wide eyes and trembling lips. Color drained from Ayla's already pale face and she swayed, stumbling into Aryana.

Aryana grabbed the Ayla around the waist, while Lily and Keara surged toward the two. Ayla might be bitter—and who could blame her—but Lily knew she needed a friend at the moment, someone she didn't fear. It wasn't until she drew closer to the older woman, that Lily realized what was different in Ayla's appearance.

She didn't wear her necklace.

Lily smiled and threw her arms around Enar's mother, taking some of her weight. "You're free!"

"Lily? What are you doing here?" Ayla returned the hug, hanging on like Lily was a rope in a stormy sea.

"Who is this?" Keara asked.

"This is Enar's mother, Ayla," Lily answered.

"I need to get her to the infirmary." Aryana spoke through gritted teeth. Despite her clenched jaw, her voice swirled like a wind storm, bouncing off the stone walls, slamming with vehemence into the air. "I transported us here so she could see the Temple. This room was designed to bring peace."

Lily didn't need to read minds to see Aryana needed the peace offered by the foyer. Anger rolled off her like a tangible fist beating into Lily's bones.

"Keara, keep Lily with you. And tell Thoren I need to speak with him." Aryana grasped Ayla's hand. "Follow me and we'll see to your arm."

"Is there something I can do to help?" Keara asked.

"You're needed for Jamie's adoption ceremony. I'll be back."

She strode down the hall, leading Ayla, the two disappearing from sight, the cloud of rage dispersing.

"You are welcome to stay with Thoren and me, you know."

"I know. It's just...I wish things could be different between Enar and me."

"Maybe you should give him a chance to explain himself."

"What's to explain?"

"Maybe he wanted to protect you from reality. You never know with men. They come up with some wild thoughts and then tell us we're not logical." Keara shook her head.

Lily sniffed. Keara's words rang true, but Enar still needed to do a lot of explaining. And apologizing.

"Maybe."

"Why don't you come to Jamie's adoption ceremony? It's a small gathering, just family."

"All right."

Lily followed Keara to the same chapel her friend was mated in several days ago. She met Thoren's large family, his mother, three sisters, one brother and a nephew. Discovered Annaliese was Keara's aunt and that she had left Ayla in the care of one of the other healing priestesses. Thoren's father, Balthor, and Keara's grandfather—who received the designation as the oldest person Lily had ever seen—popped into the room.

"Sorry, work held us up."

As soon as they sat, Aryana began the ceremony. Lily dabbed at her eyes, which started to leak again. Stupid things. She'd never cried so much in her life as she had in the last hour. Too late now to go back and protect her heart. Even if she had the choice, would she go back and change things? Go back and ensure she never fell in love with Enar?

It surprised her the answer was no. When she first met Enar, she knew loving him was her fate. Why else would she want to protect her heart, to never become like her parents, disillusioned by a love gone sour? As Aryana droned on about adoption and families, Lily mulled over her feelings. She should be paying attention to the words, but all she could think of was her life since meeting Enar.

Life. By rescuing her, by saving her from death, he'd rewarded her with life. And love. Not to mention talented fingers in the bedroll. But if she'd only allowed him to touch her at night, she wouldn't have experienced the ups and downs of life, of loving another. Protecting her heart wasn't the answer. Learning to live with the one she loved was.

But how did she go about doing that when he lied to her about his people? About his mother, his father? She refused to return to the Claims' House. Wasn't happening. Refused to wear his necklace. Refused to be lied to. He might not want her on her terms.

In which case she needed to provide for herself, learning to use her Sight instead of fleeing from it. No time like the present to get started on her new life.

If she had her mind made up, why were her eyes still watering?

Must be all the incense in the room. Pining away was not on her to-do list.

The ceremony ended before Lily finished dabbing her eyes. Quick and succinct. Or maybe it had been drawn out and wordy. Her thoughts consumed her to the point where reality disappeared.

What a way to show support for her friend by tuning out the whole ceremony.

"Lily?" Aryana touched her arm, Keara's worried face peering from behind her shoulder.

"I'm sorry. Lost in thought."

"It's all right. Why don't we get you to your room?"

No, no, no. Not alone time in her room with nothing but her thoughts. "Why don't you show me how to become a Seer?" She might as well get started on her new life. Plus keeping busy would give her time to figure out what to say to Enar the next time she saw him.

Convincing him to want her topped her to-do list.

Aryana exchanged a look with Keara. "All right. You can come with me and I'll explain to you the role of a Seer."

"Thank you." She swiped her cheeks with her now damp hankie. Why did her stupid eyes continue to leak? She was not pining. Was. Not. Pining.

Keara gave her a hug. "It will be all right. I'll come find you later."

Lily squeezed Keara's waist. "I'll be fine. Don't worry about me."

Keara gave her cheek a peck. "Enjoy your time with Ari. I won't worry about you much." She grinned and Lily answered the smile.

Aryana walked out of the room and Lily followed, stepping into her new life.

****

Enar strode down the corridor to the chapel where Sofie or Vendela—he could never tell the twins apart—

told him Lily would be. Apparently Thoren was adopting Jamie.

May the Goddess bless his friend. The male needed all the help he could get with that boy.

Just like he needed all the celestial assistance he could get to win Lily back. Speaking of Lily.

His woman walked behind Aryana, her eyes staring in a determined manner at the back of the High Priestess's head.

"Lily. May I have a word with you?"

"You may not. She is now an acolyte and is going to training class." Aryana crossed her arms and gave him a glare that rivaled one of his fiercest.

"I don't mind speaking with him."

His heart gave a leap at Lily's words. So what if she spoke them through gritted teeth? One step down, many more to go.

Ari whirled. "You don't have to if you don't want to."

"You have no idea how much I want to."

"Very well. When you are finished, someone will show you to your room. There are things I need to attend to if you do not wish to begin training tonight."

"Thank you." Lily inclined her head.

Ari marched up to Enar, eyes narrowed in a glare that would make a lesser male's balls shrivel. "You make her cry again and I will personally burn you until you are nothing more than a large blister," she hissed.

Enar gulped and forced his feet to remain still instead of darting back several steps. "I don't plan on it."

"Good. Keep it that way. I'll see you later, Lily." With those words, she vanished.

White lines bracketed Lily's lips as her hands twisted a piece of cloth. Was that a hankie? His chest ached to see her red-rimmed eyes, the blotches of color sprinkling her face. The knowledge his actions caused her tears. The only good thing coming from this was he finally realized the cause of his chest pains. Thoughts of losing Lily. What kind of a male was he to not realize that earlier?

He took a deep breath. To apologize. To say words he rarely, if ever, used. Since when had he apologized for anything? *Oh, sorry about lopping your head off, my mistake.* As if that would ever happen. But he needed to say the words, no matter how strange they felt in his mouth.

"I'm sorry, Lily. You were right. I should have told you what to expect."

"So why didn't you?" Her fists slapped against her waist.

He shoved a hand through his hair and stared at the smooth stone wall. "I didn't want you to hate me."

"And you thought I wouldn't get mad when you hid things from me?"

Well, yes. He had. But judging by the look on her face, admitting his lapse into idiocy wouldn't be the smartest thing to do. He shrugged.

"You should have told me the truth. Instead of leaving me at the Claims' House. Instead of not telling me about your mother or the treatment of the claims."

"I know."

"Then why did you?"

He swallowed and checked out the smudge of dirt on his boot. The hardest part of telling the truth was admitting once the words escaped his lips, the knowledge they contained became reality. But she deserved to know. And he needed to set the thoughts free.

"Because of my father. He didn't like me. My whole life, he hinted around I wasn't his son, which is a lie. I look like his twin. And a Watcher will not lie with another Watcher's claim while the owner of the claim still lives. That's why I took you to sign you in instead of going by myself."

"So someone would kill you and take me?"

"Don't be ridiculous. They can't kill me. No, I took you there..." Enar took a deep breath and stared at the wall. So calm and motionless. Unlike what he felt now. Telling the truth was harder than he expected. "I took you there to show you off. To prove to the others that I was my father's son. And to maybe gain approval from my father. But it didn't work. I scared you. And my father disowned me anyway tonight. I'm not allowed to live in the Watcher village."

One hand touched her lips as her eyes widened. "Oh, Enar. That's horrible. A man shouldn't do that to his son."

"I'm surprised he didn't do it earlier."

"What did he have against you?"

"I don't know, but I think it had something to do with my mother. I definitely know now how he feels, which is better than thinking he might feel differently at a later time. And you know what the worst part is?" She shook her head. "I messed up a good thing for something that would never happen. It's not him I want, Lily, it's you. I can't live without you."

She shut her eyes and took a deep breath. "I thought I loved you."

Karilyn Bentley

His heart did a quick hop at her words and he opened his mouth to tell her how he felt, but she held up a hand to silence him.

"I thought...but then you withheld from me things I needed to hear, needed to know. You turned distant. You left me!" Her fists balled at her sides, her eyes sparking lights that would make a Draconi proud.

"I'm sorry. I should have told you...no, I shouldn't have even taken you. I should have kept you here."

"You should have told me what to expect."

"I know."

"Do you plan on pulling something like that with me again?"

"Woman, if you take me back, I will not hide things from you again. I promise." He took a step closer to her, releasing a breath he didn't realize he held when she didn't move. The skin of her cheek felt warm as he cupped her face. Her eyes glistened as she tilted her head to meet his gaze.

He lowered his lips to hers, watching to make sure she didn't pull away, didn't reject him. Instead, her arms grasped his nape, pulling him closer, her lips pressing against his. He deepened the kiss, diving into the depths of her sweet mouth, branding her his.

His to love. His to cherish. His to keep from harm.

Right as he tightened his arms around her, melding her body to his, she pushed against his shoulders. With a groan, he released her.

"I'm still mad at you."

"I like the way you kiss when you're mad."

Lily glared at him and appeared to fight a grin. "I'm not wearing the necklace."

"I can think of other things to do with it." He

318

waggled his brows.

"Oh, can you now?"

"I can. I'm good at coming up with alternative ways to use things."

"Hmm. We'll have to see about that."

"Now?" Maybe he shouldn't sound so excited about the prospect.

With a wink, she walked past him, her steps carrying her to the foyer. Like a dragon on the scent of gold, he followed. Leading him to a cluster of chairs around the fireplace, she sat down, motioning for him to sit next to her.

All right. Not exactly what he had in mind, but it beat her foot in his arse kicking him out the door. Point for him.

"If I'm no longer your claim, what do you want from me?"

"Woman, what kind of question is that? I want you. All of you. Forever."

"Are you saying you love me?"

"I better be." He took a deep breath, willing to get in touch with his softer side, his sapped-out Draconi side. Words he never thought he'd say tumbled out of his mouth. "Lily, I love you." Not nearly as scary as he feared to speak those words.

"Oh, Enar. You don't know how much I've wanted you to say that."

"I love you." He tried out the words again. Much easier the second time around.

"I love you too. But what will we do? If you aren't allowed in your village. Not that I'd ever return there."

"I took a position on the Council."

One fine, white brow tried meeting her hairline. "I

thought you hated the Council."

"My father is no longer on it and it allows me to try to change things. Plus, I can make sure Thoren stays out of trouble. And you can let the priestesses turn you into a Seer. Provided that's what you want to do."

"I might as well learn to control my visions. I don't know if I'll be what the priestesses hope for, but I can't go on seeing things happen and not being able to help the person in trouble."

He touched her hand, one finger stroking her silky skin. "If you will have me, we can stay here." More of the breath holding followed by the incessant reminders to inhale.

She looked at their hands and flipped hers over, grasping his palm. Such a small hand in his large one, such trust that he would do right by her. Trust he would not break this time.

"Of course I'll have you. I love you. You've saved my life at least three times. Without you, I never would have been in the position to learn how to become a Seer. I never would have come to Draconia. I never would have learned love. But you must promise never to hold things back from me. To treat me as your partner and not lie to me. I'm not going to let that happen again, understand?"

"Woman, I swear on my sword I will never withhold the truth from you again." He frowned. "You don't plan on asking me if that dress makes your arse look over-large, do you? Because it never will, you know."

She laughed, her face transforming into lines of happiness.

"May I kiss you?"

"Since when do you need to ask?"

Gentle at first, he gave in to his body's demands, ravishing her lips, running his hands over her body, pulling her into his lap. Inhaling her scent, hearing her soft sighs, drove him over the edge. She belonged to him, she was his, now and forever and this time he would not let his pride get in the way of love.

A word about the author...

By day, Karilyn works in the research department of an oncology clinic. By night, she tells the stories of her imaginary friends. Karilyn and her most wonderful, ever patient husband share their home in the great state of Texas with two partially psycho dogs and a handful of colorful fish.